DEVIL'S DANCE

A Novel by

RICHARD R. KARLEN

Ironbound Press, Scotch Plains, New Jersey

1998

DEVIL'S DANCE

Published by Ironbound Press, 55 Highlander Drive,
Scotch Plains, N.J. 07076

Publisher's Note
This is a work of fiction. Names, characters, places and incidents either are the product of the author's imagination or are used fictitiously, and any resemblance to actual persons, living or dead, events, or locales is entirely coincidental.

Library of Congress Catalogue Number
97-093997

ISBN: 0-9660831-0-5

ACKNOWLEDGEMENTS

This book is dedicated to my wife Hiroko. Without her encouragement and love, it never could have been written.

I wish to thank my friends Musa Mayer, Gaby Koppleman, and Peter Friedman for their continual support. I also wish to thank them for correcting the misplaced punctuation marks.

Next in line for 'thank yous' are my team of medical advisors, my brother, Dr. William Karlen, and my good friends, Dr. Edward Rachlin, Dr. Michael Sananman, and Ikuko Hinckley. Their medical expertise has been invaluable.

And finally there are the children, Debbie, Andy, Naomi, Michael, Ricky, and the grandchildren, Alex, Kim, Jeffrey, Michael Jr., and Annabella. They are the writer's legacy, his ultimate reason for being willing to coop himself in front of a word processor for hundreds of hours on end. It is for them, more than for anyone else that the writer works in the perhaps vain hope that he may strike a note of truth here and there, which they will remember.

August 18, 1998.

DEVIL'S DANCE

*"If I chance to talk a little wild, forgive me;
I had it from my father."*

William Shakespeare
"Henry VIII"

DEVIL'S DANCE

CHAPTER ONE

The Accident

1980

Though I have been a practicing internist for fifteen years, the middle-of-the night phone call still has a way of jarring me into a preternatural fear of death,one that goes back to childhood when Grandma had her heart attack,and Dad,his galoshes unbuttoned, ran out of the house into the grey winter night. Harry and I, awakened by the commotion, sat with Mom in the kitchen drinking hot cocoa, until about an hour later when Dad called from the hospital, and Mom covered her face with her hands and started to cry.

I am awakened at the first ring. While reaching for the phone, I check the fluorescent dial on the clock radio. Three a.m. When I discover it is my sister-in-law, Sandy, calling from the Muhlenberg ER, I sit up at the edge of the bed. Sandy's usual calm, lucid manner of speaking borders on the hysterical, and I am barely able to understand her.

"Calm down or I'm hanging up on you," I say to Sandy. In a million years I would never hang up on my sister-in-law.

"Don't you understand? Harry's been in an accident."

"Is he alive?" Always the first question I ask.

"Of course he's alive. Very much alive."

Not dead! Relief is instant. If you survive the initial trauma from an automobile accident, barring brain damage or a spinal injury, your chances for a full recovery are dramatically improved.

I awaken Doris, who over the years has conditioned herself to sleep peacefully through these nocturnal invasions of our life. "It's Sandy," I whisper "Harry's been in an accident." I switch on the night-light. "Hold on, Sandy," I say into the phone.

Doris props herself up against the thick walnut backboard. "Oh, my God! Oh, my God!" Doris likes to express serious feelings with repetitive expletives, a minor annoyance one learns to live with after twenty years.

"How badly has he been hurt?" I ask Sandy.

"I don't know exactly."

"Is he conscious?"

"Yes."

"Fractures?"

"I don't think so."

I put my hand over the phone. "Harry is alive and conscious." Doris's *Oh, my God's* immediately turn into a series of *Thank Gods!*

Hospital rounds are at six-forty-five. Office hours start at eight. With luck I'll finish the day by seven. After supper I deal with Medicare, Medicaid and private insurance forms. I have religiously kept up this schedule since I have been in practice. Going to the hospital at three in the morning, however, is a part of the job you never quite get used to.

Harry likes to tell me that I work too hard for the wrong reasons, that I don't know how to enjoy my life. *"The bow cannot always stand bent, nor can human frailty subsist without some lawful recreation."* Now and then Harry, the English professor and author of four novels, and one book of poetry, will quote you from the classics to remind you how illiterate you are. He recited this particular quotation two years ago at a cousin's wedding in a rare moment of brotherly concern. At the time he was half-drunk. Still, when Harry

2

spoke, I always listened, a habit I had acquired early in childhood.

"Have you any idea of the extent of Harry's injuries?" I ask Sandy.

"The doctor said something about a possible shoulder separation."

"Is that it?"

"As far as I know."

"And yourself?"

"Me?" Her voice registers surprise. "I'm perfect, Roger. Just perfect."

"I'm an internist, Sandy. I know as much about shoulders as you do." An exaggeration. Nevertheless, you would have guessed that Sandy, a high school biology teacher, would have known a thing or two about the human body, and realized that I am the wrong man to consult for this type of injury. "Did the ER doctor call in the Orthopedic resident?"

"You don't understand--" A recorded voice interrupts demanding an additional five cents for the next three minutes. "I can't explain it over the phone." When the recording begins to repeat itself, Sandy cries: "Please come down, Roger! You've got to help me!" Then she hangs up. Just like that. For want of a nickel Ma Bell can do terrible things to a normally rational person.

In the bathroom I splash cold water on my face. I look into the mirror, step back as far as I can, suck in my gut. To get rid of my pot Doris wants me to ride stationary bicycles and run on mechanized walkers at Jack LaLanne's on Route 22 in Springfield. She has already joined with her dumpy sister, Irene. Twice a week they work out for thirty minutes, then go to the Scotswood Diner and eat cheesecake, drink coffee, and brag about their children.

I return to the bed and sit at the edge where I

begin to play with my socks.

"Why are you dawdling when your brother's in an emergency room?" Doris asks.

"Relax. It doesn't sound very serious."

"They don't put people in emergency rooms for nothing."

"It happens. A heart attack turns out to be indigestion. A fracture becomes a sprain. Hypochondriacs spend their lives in emergency rooms. Have you forgotten that my brother Harry is a little crazy?"

"But Sandy isn't. She wouldn't have called you unless she thought it was important. Now get going, Roger."

Just once, Dear Lord, make Doris go rushing out into the night, while old Dr. Kildare returns to his soft, sweet bed where he can enjoy five more uninterrupted hours of blissful sleep.

I find my shoes under the dresser, then go to the closet. "Where's my gray pants?" I ask, while rummaging about.

"Look!"

"Who messed up my closet?"

"You are being unnecessarily hostile."

Twenty years ago Doris had been a psych major at college, which accounts for words peppering her vocabulary, such as "neurotic," "anxious," and especially, "hostile." Surprisingly, she rolls out of bed, and in seconds finds the pants I have been looking for, then underhands them at me like a soft ball pitcher. The pants are on the wrinkled side, and I make a face.

"I'll get out the iron," she says back in bed.

The last time Doris ironed my pants was in her dreams. I straighten out the creases the best I can. "I wish you'd be a little more congenial toward my brother," I say. "It's because of you that we never

4

seem to get together anymore."

"That's not true. The real reason is that he's not interested in seeing you, except, of course, if he needs you professionally. Like now."

Doris is not an unkind person. Her anger toward Harry has some real basis. More than once over the years I have heard Harry ridicule an opinion she had thoughtfully expressed. Doris, never one to share a joke at her own expense, doesn't care or try to understand that Harry's sense of humor is more often than not good-natured.

"What you don't realize is that Harry and I play games with each other," I say. "Harry needs to boss me around, and I let him do it because it makes him happy."

"Why is it so important to make Harry happy? He doesn't care if he makes you happy."

This is a discussion we've had more than once over the years. Before it becomes an argument, one I always lose, I finish dressing and disappear into the bathroom to brush my teeth and comb my hair. "I'll call you from the hospital," I say on my way out of the room.

"Don't bother." She rolls over. In a muffled voice, her mouth pressed against her pillow, she says, "Call me, call me."

All I hear is a sick whine when I turn on the ignition to start my Mercedes. A thirty-five thousand-dollar car with nine thousand miles and a battery as dead as the night at three-twenty in the morning. I open the other garage door. Doris's Range Rover purrs neatly, and I think, as one who grew up watching old World War II movies, that in an emergency Americans are better off counting on the English for help than the Germans.

Driving into the physician's parking lot, I realize that I have left my magnetized card key in the Mercedes and am forced to back up and park in the guest parking lot. I do not appreciate the extra hundred yards walk back to the ER, especially when I observe Sandy pacing about in front of the entrance, alternately checking her wristwatch and searching the street.

Sandy is a tall, graceful woman in her early forties. Her face is a bit on the bony side for my taste, though I suppose most men would find her sculptured look attractive. She is wearing one of those colored gypsy type dresses that drape down almost to the ankles. Her long straight brown hair falls loosely over her shoulders. She uses no makeup to brighten her pale, clear skin. It is Harry who likes her to keep that Sixties's hippie look.

Sandy's greeting lacks the usual perfunctory kiss that has become our habit after twenty-two years of being related by marriage. "What took you so long?" she barks, then grabs my arm and pulls me into the waiting room.

Except the receptionist and a middle-aged black man sleeping peacefully in a corner, the large room is deserted, unusual for an urban area where street violence is routine. On a wall mounted TV, a Jimmy Stewart, Marlene Dietrich film is playing: "Destry Rides Again," which next to "Shane" is my all-time favorite cowboy flick. In a contralto that sounds as if it has been soaked in vinegar, Dietrich is serenading a room full of drunken cowboys. Her eyes flash seductively toward Stewart, who is leaning against the bar jawing on a wad of tobacco bigger than his mouth.

The receptionist, a young Oriental woman, is

sitting at a desk partitioned by glass from the waiting room. Lined up behind her are filing cabinets and a copying machine. She keeps glancing up over her computer toward the TV, but seems bored with the old black and white movie. The room, with its dropped ceiling and fluorescent lighting, its scrubbed cream colored walls and frayed wall to wall carpeting, is pretty much the same as any number of emerency waiting rooms I have passed through over the years.

Sandy whispers angrily, "I'm going to leave him, Roger. I can't take it anymore."

Harsh words from my normally placid, sweet-tempered sister-in-law. One of the few constants in my life is that Harry and Sandy would be together for eternity.

"Why don't you tell me what's going on?"

"Harry is playing around," she blurts out angrily.

"I don't believe it." Harry is eccentric, but he would never cheat on Sandy.

"He is fucking every little girl he can lay his hands on, and this is the result."

Sandy never curses. "Have you been drinking?" She offers me one of her wry little grins, which over the years invariably have had the effect of stopping me dead in my tracks. "I think you're a little excited right now," I say. "Where's Harry?"

"Inside." She points toward the swinging doors that lead into the ER. "The doctor said something about making sure he was okay before letting him go. It was a good thing he was wearing his helmet or they'd have been picking his brains out of the gutter."

"His helmet?"

"You didn't know about the Yamaha?" She appears astonished at my ignorance.

"Harry plays the piano with a helmet on?"

7

"Yamaha also makes motorcycles, Roger. He bought his 600 over a month ago. A couple nights a week, he puts on his jet black leather jacket and his jet black helmet with Thor's red thunderbolts painted on its sides, and rides off into the night like one of Hell's Angels. Sometimes he doesn't come home until early morning."

"Harry rides around all night on a motorcycle?" In his youth Harry liked to brawl. He always drove cars too fast. But motorcycles and young girls?

"He claimed he hit an oil slick and the bike went out of control. It was a miracle he didn't break every bone in his body," she says. Then as an afterthought she adds, "But the girl riding with him wasn't so lucky."

"He had a girl with him? Who?"

"One of his students, I think." For a moment I am afraid that she might burst into tears, but she perks up and says, "The girl's been hurt badly."

"Was Harry drinking?"

"I don't know. More likely drugs."

"What kind of drugs?" Not impossible. In the Sixties Harry experimented with LSD and marijuana. His first novel was about communal living and drugs. After Alan was born, he and Sandy left New Mexico to live in New Jersey, and Harry began to teach English at a junior college in Union County. Harry cut his hair and shaved his beard, practiced being respectable, but he was always edgy, which was reflected in his second novel, the tale of a suburban real estate broker who wanted life to be more than PTA meetings and backyard cookouts. He began to use cocaine, and wound up stealing bicycles and old tires from his neighbors' garages to help support his habit.

"One moment he's sullen and brooding, the next a maniac," Sandy says. "Big mood swings." She takes a deep breath and gives me her pinched lips look, the hurt, confused one. "Last week he accused me of having an affair with the gym teacher at the high school. According to Harry, we have been practicing gymnastics in my office after hours."

"Gymnastics in an office?"

"Roger, what's the matter with you? You're a grown man, for crying out loud."

She becomes misty-eyed and I want to console her, but I am distracted by gunshots and look toward the TV. Jimmy Stewart, a smoking six-gun in hand, is shooting it out with Brian Donlevy. I love the old westerns: no moral dilemmas, no shades of gray, goodness always triumphant over evil.

I take one of Sandy's hands and pat it lightly. "It'll be okay," I say, just as Donlevy takes a bullet in the gut and goes crashing to the floor on his way to hell.

I find Harry stripped to his underwear, resting on an examining table in a booth partitioned by six foot walls and a curtain covering the entrance. When he sees me, he props himself up, swinging his legs around and over the edge of the table. "Hey, little brother. Come to rescue me?"

"You look like you were in a coal mine explosion."

He has a small bruise on his right elbow and a cut above one eye. A lacerated right thigh has been sutured but not bandaged. Dirt is smeared on his forehead and cheeks; his thick, black hair is wildly unkempt; he hasn't shaven in days.

"Nice to see you, kid."

"Are you okay?" I inch in closer and try to get a whiff of his breath.

"Never felt better in my life."

"Why didn't you let them take x-rays?"

"What for?" He flails his arms and kicks his legs about. "Nothing broken." Then he winces in pain and touches his right shoulder.

The ER doctor has informed me that other than soft tissue injuries to his thigh and elbow, Harry appears to have suffered nothing more serious than a minor shoulder separation and a slight concussion. Since Harry refuses to be X-rayed or give urine or blood samples, the doctor couldn't be positive that he might not have internal injuries.

"Do you mind if I examine you?" Something about his expression puzzles me. His eyes are unable to focus on me, as if his ocular muscles do not function normally.

"How's Mitzi?" he asks.

"Mitzi, I take it, is the name of the girl who was riding with you?"

"Every time I ask about her, I get doubletalk from one of the geniuses around here."

"The admitting nurse told me that she's upstairs in intensive care." A strange lingering half grin on his face quickly dissipates.

"When can I see her?" he asks.

"I don't know."

"Can't you do something? You're a big shot in this hospital." The old habit: Harry trying to boss me around.

"You just don't go barging into ICU."

"You can do it."

"They're probably running all sorts of tests on her. She could have a sub-dural hematoma, a fractured skull."

Harry's facial muscles knot grotesquely. His upper lip begins to quiver, as he seems to be experiencing an involuntary facial muscle spasm. He tries to talk, but is unable get the first word out, like a chronic stutterer.

"Take it easy, Harry."

He nods and breathes deeply. His struggle to speak is painful to watch. "I-I-I must see her, Roger," he says at last. "Please." Harry never begs. He has this pride that is cast in iron. You don't break it, you don't bend it. Me. I'm always apologizing for something. I apologize out of habit. I go out of my way to find things to apologize for.

"I'll find out what I can as soon as possible," I say. He looks baffled, then closes his eyes for a second. When he reopens them, he appears more alert, more normal.

"I'd like to examine you," I say.

"The other doctor already did."

"It'll only take a few more minutes."

"Go ahead, if it'll make you happy."

"A few questions, first."

"The third degree. I love it."

"How fast were you going when you fell off the motorcycle?"

"Mach one. I wasn't watching the speedometer, Rog. I was having fun."

"Sandy said something about an oil slick."

At the mention of Sandy's name he becomes aroused. "What does she know? Was she there?"

"Were you drinking?"

He makes a peculiar grimace where he lifts one side of his mouth and seems to smile sardonically. "A few beers." He pulls himself up a little higher.

"How hard did you hit your head?"

He begins to sing: *"He flies through the air with the greatest of ease--"*

"For Christ's sake, Harry, have a heart. It's the middle of the night."

"We landed on somebody's recently sodded lawn. Soft and cushy. Lucky, wouldn't you say?"

Not so lucky for Mitzi, I am tempted to remind him. Baiting Harry never works for me. I always wind up feeling worse. "Did you lose consciousness?" I ask.

"Birdies were singing, but not for long." His mood changes and he becomes sullen, angry. Finally he says, "Did Sandy tell you I was drinking?"

"Not exactly."

"The woman is psycho."

My inclination is to take my sister-in-law's side, but I hear Doris telling me that it is none of my business. "Sit up straight, and don't move," I order.

I walk behind him and pull up his tee shirt. The skin covering his lean, muscular back is unbruised except in the area around his right shoulder joint where there is a slight laceration and swelling. I reach around him and with a gentle bear hug compress his rib cage. I percuss his lungs, listen to his heart. One can never be absolutely certain about an internal injury. Six months ago I examined a patient whose only symptom was an occasional shortness of breath. He turned out to have a ruptured aortic valve from horsing around with his grandchildren.

"Lie down," I command.

"Am I going to live, doc?"

I palpate his abdomen, check his spleen and liver. In motorcycle accidents anything is possible. "Sit up again."

"Up, down. How much is this costing me?"

I bend his neck, poke at his extremities. With my ophthalmoscope I look into his eyes, switch points and examine his ears, nose, ask him to stick out his tongue. He is only able to protrude a small portion of the tongue outside his mouth. "Stick it out," I tell him.

"That's as far as it goes, Dad." Again I observe that peculiar smirk of us.

"Hold out your arms." The right hand seems to jump around, an odd little dancing movement. "How long have you had those tremors?" Not exactly a tremor, but I don't know what else to call it.

Harry quickly withdraws his arms, resting them against the table. "Never noticed," he says.

"Stand up and walk back and forth."

I detect a slightly widened gait. Parkinson's comes to mind, and I remember Dad once mentioning that he had an aunt who had the disease late in life.

"Why do you look at your feet when you walk?" I ask.

"'Cause I got beautiful feet."

"Sit down again. A few more questions, if you don't mind."

"Does the bill go up?"

"Have you been feeling okay lately?"

"Like a million bucks."

"No headaches, funny pains--"

"Nothing."

"--irregular bowel movements, blood in your urine."

"What do my bowel movements have to do with flying off a bike?"

"Do you find yourself blinking excessively, grinding your teeth when you're angry?"

Harry leans to one side and rests on an elbow. He nods his head up and down, then side to side. Yes, no, yes, no. He wants to annoy me, a childhood habit he would sometimes employ against me in retaliation for my incessant teasing. Several years ago I examined a sixteen-year old girl, who had this inverted way of shuffling when she walked, her hands shaking the way Harry's right hand did. I referred her to the neurologist, who diagnosed her condition as a generalized dystonia, a rare condition occurring in Jews of Northern European extract. Parkinson's, dystonia, what would I be thinking of next? If I had flown off a motorcycle at fifty miles an hour and had landed on my head, my hands might be shaking, too.

"Is that it, Doc?" Harry asks.

"What about cocaine?"

"What about it?" He looks at me with a blank stare, then begins to laugh as if I have just delivered the punch line to a really funny story. After he calms himself, he says, "Why don't you ask Sandy what she's been using lately?"

"You can't keep cocaine a secret for long."

"Once in a blue moon I smoke a little pot. It's nothing. You ought to try it yourself. It might shake some of the bullshit out of you."

"Jesus, Harry, you could lose your job."

"What world do you live in, Roger? Every day half the faculty is high on something." Harry stands up. "I'd like to get out of here. Where are my clothes?"

"You can't leave yet. They still have to bandage your wound, and run a few more tests on you."

"You guys never quit, do you?"

"You could walk out of here feeling okay, and drop dead on your way home."

"Terrific, then Sandy could sue the hospital. She'd be able to buy a new car, furs, jewelry, lace panties, build a gym in the basement."

He sits again on the examining table. For all his bravado, he looks repentant, his eyes, half-closed, an expression, morbidly grim. His lean, powerful body slumps down on the table as if his spinal column can no longer support the weight of his skeleton. "I wanted to give Mitzi my helmet, but it was too big for her," he says.

"How did you meet her?"

"She was one of my students." He doesn't bother turning his head to look at me, preferring to stare at the ceiling. The Harry I had known all my life always looked you straight in the eye, demanding that you pay careful attention to what he was saying. "Several months ago she came to my office and complained about the low grades I was giving her on her papers. She was already on probation. If she flunked English she'd have to go home. She said she'd become a hustler first. The girl wrote sentences like a camel, but you had to admire her spirit. Now and then I'd bump into her at the University Tavern and we'd have a few beers together, which is what happened last night. Later, she asked me if I wouldn't mind giving her a lift back to her dormitory."

"After all, you didn't want her walking the streets."

Harry laughs. "There are some things that never change. You're still a pussy, Roger."

"What about this nocturnal life of yours?" I repress my anger the way I always have when Harry would insult me.

Harry's eyes swing upward. *"'Over the mountains\Of the Moon, \Down the Valley of the Shadow, \Ride, boldly ride,'\The shade replied--\If you seek for Eldorado!'"*

"How about Alan?" I ask.

"What about him?"

"How do you think he's going to feel when he finds out about Mitzi?"

"I come home in the evening and only the dog greets me. Alan is in his room doing his homework, or playing his violin. He's doing his life. He doesn't need me to wipe his nose anymore."

"You know that's a lot of baloney. And Sandy?"

"Sandy is putting mileage on the car and running down our bank account. I'm not complaining. Just don't make a big deal out of how much my family needs me."

I want to tell Harry that he is going through a mid-life crisis, that he is probably going to wind up losing his job and his family. But he'd only laugh and call my opinion mid-life bullshit. I pick up my physician's bag and start to leave. I turn and say, "I'll try to find out about Mitzi. After they finish you up at the ER, go home. I'll call you first thing in the morning."

He looks at me again with that unnatural grimace of his. Maybe he's disappointed that I don't seem interested in quarreling with him.

I push aside the curtain and leave the examining room. At the front desk, I call upstairs to the ICU and ask about Mitzi. She's unconscious, but stable.

In the waiting room I find Sandy slumped in her chair, half-asleep, a strange faraway look on her face. I sit next to her and she immediately straightens up.

"So?" she asks.

"I couldn't find very much the matter with him."

"What about the girl?"

"She's alive."

I am suddenly very weary and want only to return to bed and grab a few precious hours of sleep before I have to start my day anew. I stand up. "I'll call you tomorrow," I say.

"Where are you going?"

"Home."

She arises from her chair. Standing next to me, her mouth is almost on the same level as mine. She drapes an arm on my shoulder and stares at me with large, expressive eyes that could charm a grizzly. She is waiting for me to give her answers about Harry. I like her hand on my shoulder, but I need to go home, get back into bed, try to make something out of what's left of the night. "No sense hanging around here," I say apologetically.

"You're running out on me, you bastard."

"Harry's your husband, Sandy. He's only my brother." I leave her to brood over Harry and walk to the physician's parking lot before I remember that I have left my car in the visitor's lot in the rear of the hospital. I pass by a parked motorcycle and envision Harry and Mitzi crashing into the curb, hurtling through the night as if propelled from a circus canon.

Driving home, it begins to rain heavily and I shift into four wheel drive. I like the feel of the gears kicking in and the tires grabbing hold, and think how great a comfort it is to be able to drive a solid car in such inclement weather without fear of winding up in an emergency room, or the graveyard.

CHAPTER TWO

Mitzi

Mitzi Whalen regains consciousness the morning following the motorcycle accident. The next day she is moved from ICU to Orthopedics. I look in on her before morning rounds. It is an awkward situation, but I've never learned how to say "No" to Harry.

Her chart indicates that she has fractured her left elbow and bruised several ribs. She's a lucky girl. Multiple fractures, internal bleeding, grievous head injuries: those are the rule in your average motorcycle accident.

Mrs. Whalen, Mitzi's mother, is sitting on a chair at the foot of the bed when I enter the hospital room. Both she and Mitzi think I am just another attending resident, and I don't bother correcting the mistake. Mitzi is propped up, her left arm in a plaster cast. After speaking with the head nurse on the floor, I learn that within the next few days, the surgeon will be operating on the elbow. After setting the fracture he'll unite the broken ends with a surgical pin. Joint fractures can be a problem, but barring the unexpected, Mitzi should recover full movement of the arm within three or four months.

"How're you feeling today?" I ask Mitzi, moving to the side of the bed.

She gives me the once over, a sly little glance that demands that I identify myself and state my business. "I've got a headache and my ribs hurt," she says categorically.

There's a nasty abrasion on her narrow forehead, and a band-aide that covers the bridge of a blunted, thin nose that looks as if it may have been altered for cosmetic reasons. Her color is ashen, her lips are slightly swollen and blue. Her eyes are her best feature: clear and intelligent. There are splotches of freckles on her cheeks and if her chin were a little stronger she'd be pretty. Off hand I'd have to rate her looks as a bit on the mousy side, and I wonder what Harry sees in this ordinary looking adolescent.

"How's your arm?"

"That hurts too, but not as much as my head or ribs."

"After I leave, I'll ask the nurse to bring you something to help the pain."

"Does that include getting rid of her?" With her good right hand she pokes her thumb like a hitchhiker in the direction of her mother.

Mrs. Whalen laughs nonchalantly. "What a comic you are, Mitzi. Just a great sense of humor." She then addresses me. "Do you have kids, Doc?"

"Two girls."

"Are they as hilarious as Mitzi?"

I have dropped into the eye of a hurricane. I shift about uneasily, and consider exiting in a hurry.

"All day she sits and stares," Mitzi says to me. "Like I wanted to wind up in a hospital. According to her, I did it just to annoy her."

Mrs. Whalen stands up and stretches. She is a short woman of medium build and about my age. Her face is fuller than Mitzi's, but also a bit on the mousy side. She tries to make herself look attractive with dark eye shadow and thick pink lipstick. Her hair is cut short and bleached blonde, coiffured into a sort of mini-tidal wave. She looks as if she could use a good night's sleep.

"I'm going to take a little walk," she says. "She's all yours, doc." She is wearing spiked heels and a tight black skirt, and walks with a nice shifting about of round, womanly hips.

Her mother gone, the glum expression on Mitzi's face dissolves instantly. Why is Mitzi so piqued at her mother? Doris and I have made our own two girls the foci of our lives. If one of them were lying in bed in pain like Mitzi, wouldn't we be at her side night and day, no different from Mitzi's mother? Would we be receiving the same "thank yous" that Mitzi now offers her mother?

"Will you do me a favor?" Mitzi asks me. Her tone becomes confidential, almost a whisper. With her mother out of the room, she has become a different person, more ebullient, more alive.

"If I can."

"I want you to get in touch with someone. Tell him I want to see him. Right away! "

"Who are we talking about?"

"Harry Stone. He's an English professor over at State University. Call the Dean's office. They'll give you his number."

"Why don't you ask your mother?"

"Are you kidding? He's the one I was riding with on the motorcycle. She wants to have him arrested for attempted murder."

"Why don't you have your phone activated? Then you could call up this Harry Stone yourself." Actually not a good idea. If Harry isn't in his office, his secretary might give Mitzi his home phone. If Sandy picked up, Harry's domestic problems, already in a disastrous state, may well exacerbate. I had stopped by their house yesterday to check on Harry. He was unaccountably cheerful. The same could not be said for Sandy, who refused to talk to me, lumping Harry and me together into a brotherly package of falsehood and deception.

"I tried. But mother refuses to pay for a phone,"

Mitzi says petulantly, "and I have no money. It's her way of punishing me." Judging by my own two girls, a teenager without a phone is like a shipwrecked traveler marooned on a desert island.

"There's a pay phone in the hallway next to the elevator."

"I told you, I have no money. Anyway, she watches me day and night. I'm a prisoner."

"All right," I say "I'll call him for you. But you mustn't tell your mother."

Her face lights up. I guess she never expected me to agree. "Hey, that's cool, Doc. I really appreciate it."

How nice to be cool. I sit at the edge of the bed and wonder if I'm overstepping my boundaries with this girl. She leans back and begins to pull on the fingers of the hand sticking out of the cast.

"Doesn't that hurt?" I ask.

"I don't have any feeling."

"You've had a bad accident, but it's just a matter of time before you'll be able to use your arm again."

"What about this operation they're talking about?"

"It's no big deal. You'll be just fine."

"Yeah, you can say that. It's my arm you'll be cutting up."

"I'm an internist, Mitzi, not a surgeon. I examine people and decide what's the matter with them. The doctor who's going to operate on your arm was in earlier today."

"I thought you were the guy." She is genuinely disappointed. I am starting to like her better.

"Nope."

"Are they going to put me to sleep?"

"You won't feel a thing."

"It's not dangerous or anything, is it?"

"I wouldn't worry. You're young, and you're not in

bad shape considering how close you came to leaving this world permanently."

She becomes silent. Something is wrong. "What's the big problem?" I ask.

She shrinks under the sheets. "If I tell you, will you promise not to tell my mother?"

"Whatever you say is just between us."

"How do I know if I can trust you?"

"If I tell anybody anything you've told me, and don't have your permission, you can sue me. It's the law."

"Is that a fact?" The possibility of suing a doctor perks her up more than I would have expected.

I lay my hand on my heart. "So help me God," I say with the solemnity of a witness standing in a juror's box swearing to tell the truth.

"I'm pregnant."

The unexpected--right between the eyes. "Are you sure?"

"I've missed a period and I never miss a period."

"Do you have any other symptoms?"

"Like what?"

"Morning sickness--nausea, vomiting, headaches, anything."

"I was feeling pretty good until I fell off Harry's bike."

"You might be mistaken. You can miss a period for a lot of reasons other than being pregnant."

"I'm pregnant, Mister Doctor, I just know it."

"Why didn't you tell the resident when he was taking your history? My God, Mitzi, don't you realize how important it is for the doctors to know that?"

"This morning I woke up with a head like it had just run into a brick wall and everyone starts in with the third degree. I just didn't feel like talking. Anyway it's none of their business."

"It's a miracle that you didn't abort from the accident." I shake my head in amazement. "Am I to understand that you haven't told your parents either?"

With considerable effort Mitzi pushes herself up against the back of the bed and runs her good right arm across her chest in a gesture of adolescent defiance.

"Are you kidding? When they find out that Harry's the father, Jesus--" She blows a thin stream of air through her pale lips.

"Harry Stone is the father!" The unexpected has become a family nightmare. I take a deep breath and clear my throat, try to maintain a professional posture. "Have you at least told him?" I ask.

"I was going too, soon as I got the chance. Now this happened. That's why I need to talk to him. I need to tell him before you guys spill the beans to my parents." She grows pensive, purses her slightly swollen lips. "Tell me, Doc, if you were Harry, what do you think you'd do?"

"A tough question, Mitzi. I guess it would all depend." Not much of an answer. *If I were Harry?* There were times in my life when Harry was all I ever wanted to be. She is asking the wrong person for advice.

"The problem is--Harry's an important person." Tears well up in the corners of her pale, brown eyes. "And who am I?--a big nothing, that's who."

"Mitzi, you're simply going to have to tell your parents. They may surprise you."

"The only surprise would be if they don't shoot me."

I see no point in disputing what is so evident to her. Nevertheless, I press on for what appears to be her only sensible course of action. "You must tell them," I say.

"And if I don't, then you're going to, aren't you?"

"No, I won't. Didn't you listen to me before? I can't repeat to anyone what you tell me unless you say it's okay."

"Right. Or else I can sue you--like in a hundred million light years." She moves her head from side to side. She is ready to burst into tears. "You know they're going to want me to have an abortion," she says.

"That's your decision."

I misjudge her. Mitzi is not a crier and wipes her eyes before the tears have a chance to flow. Her voice drops as she apes her mother. "'You're just a kid. What about college? You've got no job. You're not married. Babies are a lot of trouble.'" She waves me away with her good right hand. "I mean it's so obvious the bullshit they're going to fling at me."

"Babies *are* a lot of trouble," I say.

"I don't care." She suddenly becomes very agitated, abandoning all discretion. "I want my baby! *Don't let them kill my baby!*"

I am startled by all this emotion. Kids today are so indifferent to questions about life and death. You lecture them about the evils of smoking, for example, and they'll tell you that everybody's got to die of something. I would have guessed that you could have easily talked Mitzi into an abortion. "Mitzi, no one can make you have an abortion without your consent," I say.

"They could put me to sleep and do it."

"They won't do that."

"I don't trust any of you guys."

"You can trust me."

"Why? What's so special about you?" She purses her lips and stares at me unpleasantly. Then she slips her good arm under her sheet and gives me a funny, little nod, which, coincidentally, is close to the same gesture that my older daughter gives me when I tell her to clean up her room. "You know, age has nothing to do with love," she says.

"I never really thought about it." I really haven't, and if I have any opinions on the subject I will be sure to keep them to myself. Avoiding controversy is not only a part of my nature, but an absolute necessity in the practice of good medicine.

"Did you know that Charlie Chaplin was three times as old as Oona O'Neill when he married her? Everybody said it would never work, but they had nine kids and a great life."

Oona O'Neil and Charlie Chaplin? She is putting herself and Harry into fancy company. "Tomorrow morning you've got to tell the doctor who comes to examine you that you're pregnant," I say. "He'll want to run a few blood tests to make sure."

"More tests. That's stupid. I told you--I'm pregnant. No one has to tell me what I know positively."

"Doctors have their little routines they feel obliged to follow. Being pregnant may complicate your arm surgery."

She becomes more attentive. "How come?"

"Normally they'd give you general anesthesia--put you to sleep. But that may present some risk to your pregnancy."

"I don't want anyone taking chances with my baby," she says aggressively. "You tell them that."

"They can give you an injection."

"An injection. You mean a needle? I don't want any needles."

"They'll sedate you first. You won't even know what's happening. Tomorrow you'll talk it over with the doctor who's going to operate on you, then you can decide."

25

"Not before I talk to Harry."

"I'm advising you to first talk it over with your parents."

"You don't listen, Doc. My parents are going to want me to have an abortion."

"How do you know that? What's your religion?"

"Catholic."

"Aren't Catholics opposed to abortion? Your parents may even be willing to help you take care of the baby."

"Are you kidding? My mother works two shifts at a diner, and my father wakes up every morning with a hangover."

She talks of her father's drinking so matter-of-factly that I wonder if she might not be making it up. Kids like Mitzi love to feel sorry for themselves. It gives them an excuse for their anti-social behavior.

"This Harry Stone--you're sure he's the father?" I am stepping out of line, but feel compelled to ask the question.

"One hundred and five percent."

You don't argue with one hundred and five percent. "I have an important question to ask you," I say.

"No more questions unless you promise to call Harry for me."

"I already said I'd do it." I pretend to reflect on the information she had given me earlier in the conversation. "Harry Stone. State University. Dean's office."

"English Department," she reminds me.

"Right." I make a phony notation on my prescription pad. "Now it's your turn. The night of the accident--had you been drinking or using drugs?"

"I had a beer."

"How about Harry?"

"He had a few."

"Did you use cocaine?"

"*I don't do cocaine!*" She hesitates, then, anticipating my next question, adds, "And neither does Harry." She is very positive, and I want to believe her, but you couldn't be sure that she wouldn't lie to protect Harry.

Suddenly, she winces and rubs her side with her good hand. You live to be a hundred and see the worst, still you never get used to other people's pain.

"I'll be leaving soon. I'll get the nurse to give you a pill."

"I'm okay. Don't go yet. Please." She looks at me curiously, then smiles as if she has just discovered something amusing. "Funny thing," she says, "but you remind me of Harry."

"Can you keep a secret?"

"Maybe."

"This one *you've* got to promise on."

"If I don't, will you be able to sue me?"

"I could get in trouble if you don't promise."

She holds up two fingers. "Scouts' honor."

"My name is Dr. Roger Stone. I'm Harry's brother."

"Roger, the Dodger!" She smiles through her pain. She has a nice smile, even white teeth, a small dimple on her right cheek, little crinkles around her eyes. She was probably the cutest child in kindergarten. "I should have guessed. Harry told me about his genius brother."

"Harry said I was a genius?" She begins to laugh. "What's so funny?" I ask.

"You won't get mad."

"I never get mad."

"He also said that you were a pussy."

"And what exactly is a *'pussy'*?"

Without hesitation, she defines me perfectly, "Someone who always does exactly what he's supposed to do."

"That's me all right."

"Don't you ever get the urge to be rotten?" She has hit a raw nerve, but I remain unruffled. "You can get tired of always being right, Uncle Rog?" she adds playfully.

'Uncle Rog.' Mitzi has already moved into the family. I wonder how Sandy will react to that. "Harry asked me to look in on you," I say. "That's really why I'm here."

"You also wanted to check me out. Right?"

"What do you think?"

"I think you're checking me out. Will you be one of my doctors?"

"I don't think so."

"I don't want any other doctor but you," she says.

"That's not possible. There's the surgeon, the anesthesiologist, the resident, and they'll probably be calling in an obstetrician."

"You're the only one I trust."

"I'll keep an eye out, but it can't be official."

"Don't you want to get paid?"

"No."

"A doctor who doesn't care about money. Now I'm not so sure I trust you." She smiles again. I love that dimple.

"We'll keep it to ourselves who I am. Later I'll tell your parents. Remember, you promised not to tell them about me."

"Christ, Uncle Rog, I gave you my scout's honor."

She winces again, then grabs hold of her heavily taped left rib cage. She tries to slump backwards, but the upright position of the bed makes it impossible. I stand up and lower the bed, then help her settle under the covers. She looks at me gratefully.

"Will you speak to my parents and make them understand that it wasn't Harry's fault?" she asks.

"Do you think they would listen to me? Get some rest. I'll stop in tomorrow morning." I back away from the bed.

"Tell Harry about my being pregnant?"

"I thought you wanted to tell him yourself?" I wonder if I sound a little desperate.

"Suppose he doesn't give a damn. Suppose he says he isn't the father and I should go to hell."

I want to tell her that Harry would never do such a thing. But the Harry I observed in the ER was not the Harry I had known all my life. This Harry is bizarre, unpredictable.

Mitzi tries to smile again, though it is clearly a terrific effort. "I wish you really were my uncle," she says.

I walk back over to her and impulsively bend down and kiss her on the cheek. She surprises me and throws her good right arm around my neck and hugs me.

In the hallway I meet up with Mitzi's mother. She is standing by the water cooler, slightly bent, looking subdued.

"These past two days have been a nightmare," she says, straightening up. "You can see how tough she is. She thinks this is all a big game . . . Did she tell you about Harry?"

"No," I say without thinking. If Mitzi later tells her mother that she had talked to me about Harry, it would be a bad lie. But to revoke it now seemed worse.

"Harry is Harry Stone, Mitzi's English professor. He's the one she was riding with. It was his motorcycle. What do you think of those French Fries?"

I reach for a drink from the cooler. Mrs. Whalen presses on, "Did you ever hear of him? I never did until Mitzi showed me one of his books a couple of months ago. I'm not much for reading, but since Mitzi made such a big deal out of this man, I gave it a shot. I tell you Doc, absolute trash. Nothing but sex and violence and four letter words. The ending made about as much sense as Einstein's Theory of Relativity. Mitzi thinks Harry Stone is some sort of God, but I think he's psycho."

My impulse is to defend Harry's writings, but at this juncture a discussion with Mrs. Whalen on what is good literature seems inappropriate. You have to feel a little sorry for this middle-aged waitress. She works two shifts a day to support a daughter, who has nothing but disdain for her, and a husband, who wakes up every morning with a hangover.

"Mitzi will be all right," I say. "Her head injury isn't as serious as we first thought, which is the best news. Her ribs will heal, and in a few months her arm will be as good as new."

Mrs. Whalen starts to cry. Without warning, she buries her head against my chest. "I thought she was going to die," she wails. "I watched her lying there unconscious, her skin so white, almost like she was dead already. I kept telling myself that it can't happen. *She can't die.*"

I pat her shoulders. She steps back at my touch and forces a grin. "I'm so embarrassed. Please forgive me, doctor."

"There's nothing to forgive." The poor woman's cheeks are streaked by mascara. The whites of her eyes are pink mists.

"You're very kind. Thank you for looking in on Mitzi. What a hospital. You don't even ask, and they send you the best."

I excuse myself and go to the nurses' station where I order Percocet for Mitzi. As I am riding down in the elevator I consider Mrs. Whalen's reaction if she knew who I was. In a moment of anger, Mitzi could break her promise to me and tell her. I could hear her mother's enraged response. "We're going to sue you, the nurses, the doctors, this whole hospital." Hospital management never appreciates that sort of complaint.

Later I'll call Harry and tell him about my seeing Mitzi. I wonder how he'll react when he finds out that Mitzi is pregnant? Why should I be concerned, I ask myself? None of this is any of my business. The next time I see Mitzi I will tell her that I'll no longer be able to take care of her. I will be a little more honest in expressing my feelings about the way she has lived her life, and the way she is treating her mother. I am reminded of a scene in *The Maltese Falcon* when Sydney Greenstreet advises Humphrey Bogart that one should never forget who he is, and where his best interests lie. Ah, yes, how very true!

CHAPTER THREE

Harry's In Jail

I am sitting at my desk filling out insurance forms when Doris returns home with the girls from swim practice. My study is ten steps off the common hallway leading in from the outside, but my daughters elect to by-pass my open door and go directly upstairs to their bedrooms. I call out a big "Hello," but receive no reply. Be grateful, I tell myself, at least they're not riding around on motorcycles in the middle of the night.

Doris comes into the room and automatically asks if I have enjoyed dinner. Weekdays, I eat by myself, since swim practice is from six-thirty to eight. Microwave leftovers are okay, except when the rice is clumpy, and the chicken tastes as if it has been parched on a desert rock rather than roasted in an oven. But Doris seems tired and preoccupied, and I tell her that everything was delicious. Then, moving on to the next step of our nightly ritual, I ask her to offer up her list of the day's calamities.

As usual, she starts off with small potatoes: the maid didn't show up; one of our neighbors complained that our dandelions are spreading across her lawn like the plague. The worst is always last--there's big trouble brewing in my brother's household.

She stares at me for what seems like an eternity, making sure I'm giving her my undivided attention before she will divulge information only she knows. I must move to the edge of my chair before she will begin. "Sandy and Harry had a fight yesterday, and Alan called Naomi to ask if he could live with us for awhile. He can't take the fighting. When I talked to

Sandy, she poured her heart out to me." Doris waits for a reaction from me. She loves it when people pour out their hearts to her. Once again she's a social worker involved with misery and unhappiness.

"What did she have to say?" A question I know I have to ask before she will proceed.

"I won't bore you with the details. Last night after dinner Harry became violent and struck her."

I don't believe it. In twenty-two years of marriage, I have never once witnessed or heard that Harry had ever lifted a hand against Sandy.

This morning I tried to reach Harry at his office to inform him of Mitzi's condition. Harry had never showed up for his classes. He had never even bothered to phone in. I called Sandy at the high school. My sweet-tempered, well-mannered sister-in-law told me to mind my own business, then hung up without a "goodbye."

"Your whole life you've placed your brother on a pedestal," Doris says. "Now you know what sort of a person he really is."

"I refuse to believe Harry actually hit her."

"You think I would make it up?"

"Maybe he was defending himself."

"Did you know that there was a girl riding with him on his motorcycle when he had his accident? He swore to Sandy that he would never see her again. Last night after supper, your brother announced that he was going out. When Sandy blocked the doorway, he knocked her out of his way." She crosses her arms, dares me to refute these sensational revelations.

"Wherever he went, it wasn't to see the girl."

"How do you know?"

"They operated on her today. Except for her parents, nobody's allowed to visit." Doris views me skeptically. It's time to confess. "I've been over to see her a few times."

"Why did you keep this from me?" I am in for it.

"I thought I had mentioned it." I tell myself to stick to the facts like a newspaper reporter. "The girl had a concussion, bruised ribs, a broken arm. Harry asked me to look in on her." It is the wrong time to bring up the subject of Mitzi's pregnancy.

Doris commands me into the kitchen. Dishes have to be washed, but our conversation has just begun. Obediently, I follow her.

"You want fresh coffee?" she asks. *The calm before the storm.*

"No, thanks." I sit down at the table and wait for the next round of questions.

She serves me the coffee anyway. I wave her off when she begins to pour milk into the coffee, but she ignores that too. Then she sits opposite me with her own cup. "Is she pretty?" Slowly, tantalizingly, she stirs the one lump of sugar she has plopped into the cup.

"Who?"

"Mata Hari! The girl, that's who."

"Fair. . . Not so hot."

"How old is she?" When I don't reply immediately, she becomes impatient. "Eighteen, nineteen, twenty? You read her chart, didn't you?"

"Nineteen."

"Nineteen. Now that wasn't so hard to say, was it?" Sexist battle lines are being drawn. "So she's not so hot," she repeats. "Harry doesn't think she's not so hot, does he?" She calmly sips her coffee. "Does she have a name?" Doris's habit of making you feel that you are on the witness stand when she converses with you is a character trait acquired from her father, a combatant trial lawyer, who likes to ask a question in reply to a question.

"Her name is Mitzi Whalen."

"Irish?"

"Could be. I didn't ask."

"Harry's in trouble with this girl, isn't he?" When I fail to respond fast enough, she blurts out, "Harry's your brother, and Harry's in trouble, and you went to see the trouble because that's your nature, Roger. You've got this big heart and I love you for it, but isn't there a little minor violation of ethics in your not telling Mitzi Whalen's parents who you are? Let me ask you something, Roger? Do you think Harry would give a damn if you were in trouble? Do you think he would stick his neck out for you?"

"He would. A thousand times he would."

"You're talking out of your skull. Harry's an egomaniac. He uses people as conveniences for his own needs, his own desires, you included." She lapses into silence, nervously fidgeting with her cup handle. She is far from through. She is in fact, if I know my woman, just beginning to warm up. "Sandy thinks Harry's a drug addict," she says at last.

"I don't think so."

"You don't think so. May I be allowed to ask exactly why you don't think so?"

"I admit that his behavior was strange when I examined him at the hospital."

Doris throws back her head, her eyes glowing with certainty, and emits a giant "Aha!", revealing three hundred dollars of recent bonding on her front teeth.

"He wouldn't allow anyone to do any tests on him. No blood, not even a urine. Of course, one should never jump to conclusions following a head injury, even a minor one. He seemed okay until he began to stutter. Harry never stuttered. When I asked him to stick out his tongue, he couldn't do it. And he's got this involuntary facial twitch. Something's the matter with him all right, but I don't know what it is."

"I'll bet he's using cocaine."

"You bet! What do you know about cocaine?" Actually, good social workers probably know a lot more about addiction than internists practicing in the suburbs. Most junkies wind up in clinics and rehabs after a couple of nights in a detox. You never see them until they have other medical problems. "You can have a personality change without necessarily being on drugs. After years of marriage people fall out of love. It happens all the time."

"Does that include beating up your wife?"

It isn't an argument I'm going to win, but I don't feel like throwing in the towel quite yet. "By the way, Harry told me a few things about Sandy." Doris raises her eyebrows. I've caught her off guard. "What would you say if I told you that she is having an affair with the gym teacher at her school?" Once the words are out of my mouth, I can hardly believe I've actually said them.

"Harry's a liar. He'll say anything to make it appear that he's done nothing wrong."

"How do you know it isn't true?"

"Sandy would never cheat on Harry."

Doris coming to Sandy's defense? That I never would have expected. After Mom and Dad had moved to Florida five years ago, Doris and Sandy had managed to take turns making holiday dinners without complaint, and on occasion help each other out in family matters. However, I would not exactly call them the best of friends. Doris spends a fortune on clothes to hide the bulges, while Sandy looks good in torn jeans and dirty sneakers. Doris never made it a secret that she thought Sandy liked to put on airs, especially when men were around.

"And suppose she is having an affair?" I say.

"You're twisting things, Roger. We're talking about Harry, not Sandy."

"I like to know all the facts before I start condemning people." Who am I kidding? Fact one: Mitzi. Fact two: Harry may have left Sandy and Alan. Fact three: Harry has impregnated fact one. "Harry will come to his senses. Give him a little time."

The telephone rings. Saved by the bell. Doris answers. She pales, then hands me the phone. "Harry's in jail--in Westfield," she says to me, looking as if someone has slapped her face.

"Five hundred bucks will bail me out," Harry says right off the bat.

"I have a pile of insurance forms I have to fill out, and then I'm going to take a shower." I am about to pitch the receiver against the wall when an inner voice tells me to stay calm. "In the meantime why don't you hang yourself." I say to the inner voice as well as to Harry.

"Great idea," he says. "But I think I'll wait until after you've taken your shower." The line goes dead.

"Let him rot," I say to Doris after hanging up.

"You're not going to get your brother out of jail?" What is she getting so excited about? Five minutes ago she was ready to castrate Harry.

"I'm taking a shower first," I say with determination.

"What's the matter with you, Roger? Put on your jacket, and do the right thing."

As if I don't, always.

At the Westfield police station, a husky policeman with a skull shaven as clean as Yule Brunner's unlocks a steel door, then leads me down a short corridor past two empty cells. Harry is sitting in the third, his feet on the top of the supporting bar of the army cot, his hands folded under his head. He is whistling *Home on the Range*.

The officer opens the cell door and tosses a pair of shoes towards the cot. "Your brother paid the bail," he says. "You're free, professor. Go home and behave yourself."

Harry is wearing a loosely fitting red cotton sports shirt crumpled like tissue paper. His brown slacks, torn at one knee and shredded at both ankles, looks as if the fabric had been attacked by rats. Grime is smeared across his forehead and blood is caked at the corners of his nostrils. He looks worse now than he did after the motorcycle accident. If he passed you on the street, you'd run after him and offer him a quarter.

"Let's get out of here," I say.

Casually he puts on his shoes, then stands up and stretches his long, muscular body as if he has just been awakened from a drugged sleep. The policeman escorts us back to the front desk where he returns to Harry his wallet, a book of matches, three keys strung on a paper clip, and a piece of lined paper with some writing scribbled on it, then hands him a clipboard and a ballpoint pen. "Sign here." He points to the spot where he wants Harry to sign, as if he is assisting a child to find his place in a first grade reader.

"Thanks a lot, baldy." Harry lifts his eyes like El Greco's St. Jerome searching the heavens. *"'From troublous sights and sounds set free;/In such a twilight hour of breath,/Shall one retrace his life, or see/Through shadows, the true face of death?'"* He signs the form and returns the clipboard, neatly pocketing the pen. "Time for us to find a better life," he says to me.

Outside of the station house I remind him that if he fails to show up in court for his hearing, I lose my five hundred bucks, and he goes back to jail.

"I'm off to Alaska to make my fortune, Willy. I'll mail you a check." He does a few, quick, jumping jacks. "Rog, how about you treating me to a hamburger before I wither away."

We drive out of Westfield, where the only restaurants open at this hour would have refused to seat Harry, and head towards Newark on Route 22. I wait patiently for him to explain what had happened. But all I get is *Home on the Range*. I pull the car onto the shoulder and stop. "Who beat you up? How did you get arrested?" I refuse to restart the car until he gives me a few answers.

"There was a minor disagreement between me and the protectors of our great society." He clears his throat and spits out of the window a huge wad of phlegm that splatters obscenely on a telephone pole. "Bullseye!"

"Disagreement? Jail? Who in our family has ever been arrested?"

"*'What other dungeon is so dark as one's own heart! What jailer so inexorable as one's self!'*"

"I bailed you out, which is more than you deserved. I ought to make you walk home."

"Please, Rog, take pity on your old, beleaguered sib. Over dinner I will pour out my soul to you. Right now I'm too weak to offer much more than spittle."

I pull into a trucker's diner and order coffee and a Danish, while Harry polishes off half a roast chicken, mashed potatoes, lima beans, a chef salad, and a double portion of hot apple pie, ala mode. Every time I ask him a question, he waves me off and stuffs another forkful of food in his mouth. When he is finished, he burps, pats his gut, and says, "Whatta say we go for a few brews? We'll pontificate all night."

Harry knows a tavern a mile down the highway that I had never noticed before, though I must have passed it scores of times on my way into Newark.

Jimmy's Bar and Grill is like any other tavern with its gloomy subterranean atmosphere, made more alive only by pictures of boxers and movie stars on the walls. A few drinkers hang around the bar. The booths are all empty. An older couple is playing darts in the back. Just as the woman is about to throw a dart, the man gooses her, and they both roar with laughter. We sit ourselves in one of the booths and Harry calls out to the bartender to bring two cans of Heineken beer.

I pour the beer from my can into a glass, while Harry drinks straight from his, thick white foam dribbling down his chin, which he casually wipes away with the back of his hand.

"How's your shoulder?" I ask.

He rotates his arm. "Perfect."

"How about your head?"

"My head?" He slaps the side of his temple as if he is trying to knock water out of his ear. "Still attached." He looks around the bar--I don't know whom he expects to recognize--then points to my glass of beer. "Drink up, Rog." He lifts his can. "*Ale, man, ale's the stuff to drink/For fellows whom it hurts to think.*"

I drink half a glass. The beer doesn't sit well with the coffee and the Danish, and I feel slightly nauseous.

"Where've you been?" I ask.

"In jail."

"Before jail."

"Here and there. Doing a bit of soul searching. It isn't every day your wife throws you out of your house."

"Sandy told Doris that leaving was your idea."

"Sandy is a liar."

"She also said that you had hit her."

"A little shove. Self-defense, Rog. One shouldn't jump to conclusions. The woman was about to poke out my eyes with a fork."

Whether or not he is telling the truth, you couldn't help but feel sorry for him, so beat up and forlorn. Feeling sorry for Harry is a new experience for me. It has now happened twice within the last week. "Go home and make it up with her." Giving Harry advice is also something new for me. No one ever tells Harry what to do, especially Roger, the pussy.

He leers at me with that strange grimace of his. An involuntary muscle twitch? Nerves? One of the symptoms of tardive dyskinesia, a condition induced by long term use of phenothiazine, a drug used in the treatment of schizophrenia, is involuntary muscle movement. I make a mental note to call a neurologist friend.

"So how did you wind up in jail?" I ask.

"In cuffs." He raises his right hand. "I swear to tell the truth, the whole truth, and nothing but the truth. I have been framed. This afternoon, Your Honor, I received a ticket for driving down a one way street the wrong way. Someone had turned the sign around." He finishes off his beer, then the rest of mine, then shouts across the room to the bartender to bring two more cans. He gives me another one of his phony little grins, then begins to stare at a movie poster of CASABLANCA: Humphrey Bogart in trench-coat and hat, a gun in his hand, the face of Ingrid Bergman, shining, radiant with love for Bogart, in the

41

background Greenstreet, Lorre, Rains, and Henreid. Perhaps Harry is seeing himself as Bogart, tough guy, idealist, romantic. For the moment the poster appears to have totally engaged Harry's attention, short-circuiting his thought processes.

"Who beat you up?" I ask trying to get him back into focus.

He continues to stare at the poster, a vacant, hollow look, then without warning he recaptures his trend of thought and goes on: "As a civic duty I upended that One Way sign, and was in the act of disposing it into the lake at Tamaques Park when two off-duty cops happened to pass by. I thought they were muggers and felt obliged to defend myself."

"You hit a policeman?"

"It was an altercation that should never have occurred, an unfortunate misunderstanding." Harry calls to the bartender to bring another round. "Hey, Rog, maybe you know some crackerjack barrister who can strike a deal with the local power structure?"

"The police beat you up?"

"I think I'll go into training. Joe Wolcott was past forty when he won the heavyweight championship from Ezzard Charles."

I stare at this bruised, slightly battered older brother of mine, and am reminded of when we were kids and he rescued me from Stanley Horowitz, who was about to put out my lights for teasing him. "Do you remember when you kicked Stanley Horowitz's butt for me?"

He is bewildered. He cannot remember Stanley, who lived next door to us in Newark for almost ten years until his father won the Irish sweepstakes, and bought a one family in Maplewood.

"You hauled me into the house like a sack of coal, all the time shouting at Stanley that nobody fooled with your kid brother without special permission."

Harry shrugged. "So I kicked his butt, you say. Yes, I remember vaguely. He was an oafish bully. Liked to pick on girls and little fellows."

Actually Harry never paid much attention to me when we were kids growing up. I was a nuisance he tolerated. When he beat up Stanley Horowitz to protect me, I think we were both surprised.

"Does your nose hurt?" He has a minor septal deviation, the result of a brawl twenty years ago defending a drunk against another tough guy. The nose is slightly swollen.

He places an index finger on the tip and gently presses the soft tissue. "Intact, I think."

"You're lucky you didn't wind up back in the emergency room."

"Ah, yes, then Sandy could have rushed over to the hospital and once again been the dutiful wife."

"Sandy loves you, Harry. What's the matter with you?"

"You are an anomaly, Rog. Nobody really believes anymore that monogamy should rule the roost for a lifetime." The bartender arrives with two freshly opened cans of beer. Harry lifts one."To Virtue," he proclaims. This time he doesn't bother trying to wipe the foam that drools off his lower lip.

"And Alan?" I ask.

"When kids are little, you rock them on your knee and read them bedtime stories. They question you about the wonders of the Universe and you kiss them goodnight. But all that ends, Rog. They grow up. By the time they're seventeen they need you about as much as they need a dose of the clap. Alan will be what he'll be, even if I put on a dress, or sodomize the Pope."

"You don't care what happens to Alan. You don't

care what happens to Sandy. What do you care about, Harry?"

"The whole human race, brother. I guess it just doesn't show."

"And Mitzi?"

"Mitzi?" Another one of his blank looks.

"She was operated on today."

"Operated?"

"They set her elbow. Pinned it with stainless steel."

He perks up "Damn! Give me a dime. I must call her immediately."

"She doesn't have a phone."

"Let's go see her. Tonight."

"Her parents will have you arrested if you go near the hospital."

"What do I give a damn about her parents. She could die. I 've a right to see her."

"She's not going to die."

"Yeah, not to worry. Mitzi's tough as nails. The world needs more like her. Why don't we let kids run things, a little innocence to make things right? Are you going to drink your beer?"

I push my filled glass towards him. He knocks it over as he reaches for it, and a wicked stream of yellow liquid spirals its way insidiously towards the edge of the table. I stop the flow with a paper napkin, but some of the beer has already dripped onto his lap. Angrily, he calls the bartender and demands a refill.

"Mitzi asked me to tell you something," I say.

"She's one terrific kid. Too bad she can't write a decent sentence."

"This terrific kid is pregnant. She says you're the father." His eyes light up, the first honest display of emotion he has shown since I bailed him out of jail.

"Let's hope its a girl," he cries joyously.

"That's all you've got to say?"

"Girls like to bake nice things, brownies, cookies, apple pies. Don't you agree?" Harry settles back in his chair. He seems to collapse like a balloon that is slowly losing air. "How are your girls, Rog? I hope by now you've got them on the pill."

"You don't care that Mitzi is pregnant and you're the father?"

The waiter arrives with the next round of beers. I grab one of the opened cans and pour the beer into a glass and carefully hand it to Harry. "It tastes better when it goes into your stomach instead of your lap," I say.

He looks at me steadfastly. "My head is full of thoughts, Rog, but most of them make no sense." His grimace begins to fade. He appears more normal. "The motorcycle made sense, but that's been wrecked."

"You need help, Harry. Maybe you ought to see a doctor."

"You're a doctor."

"I'm the wrong doctor."

"I don't need a doctor. What I need is a new life, a new start. I need to get away."His expression brightens. "I think I'll become an airline pilot."

"You just can't become a pilot." Why do I speak to him as if he is a rational human being?

"Why not? A few navigational courses. Get into the right program. Within a year, I'd be flying jets. Then I'd not only be able to see Planet Earth, but I'd be able to fuck all those cute stewardesses. What do you think?" Harry finishes off his beer and again reaches for mine.

"I've got to get going." He is disappointed, and I am tempted to stay with him a little longer, but he is too crazy. "Let me drive you home."

He shakes his head. "Lend me a hundred bucks. I'll pay you back tomorrow."

He accepts the two fifties without thanks, stuffing them in his pocket as if they are dirty Kleenex. Then without warning, he leans forward and messes up my hair with his sticky fingers. "Nobody fools with my kid brother," he says. "Drop me off at the Rainbow Motel. It's just down the highway."

"Please come back to my house tonight? You can sleep in the guest room."

"Yeah, but at the motel I can watch dirty movies."

Doris is rooted in front of the TV, and I slip into the study and sit down at my desk. I begin to fill out medicare forms, but all I can think of is Harry standing before me looking like a street drunk. I wonder if there might not have been something more I should have said to him tonight that would have convinced him to return to his home, or at least come back here with me. He could easily wind up drinking away my hundred bucks and sleeping on someone's front lawn. You shouldn't have left him, I tell myself. He's your brother, and he's dying.

CHAPTER FOUR

The Return of the Lone Ranger

Today I receive a letter scribbled in pencil. The envelope is postmarked from Newark. No return address.

"Life is a jest; and all things show it./I thought so once; but now I know it./" The letter is signed *"The Lone Ranger."*

After three months, Harry has come back to New Jersey.

Office hours over, I walk to my car in the parking lot behind our building thinking about my last patient, a thirty-two year old woman, who complained of a numbness in her gums. She is convinced that she has cancer of the jaw. Two months ago, she self-diagnosed a large freckle on her forearm as a malignant melanoma. Six months ago she decided she had a brain tumor that was causing her headaches. Since becoming married three years ago, she has been to my office more times than I can remember with similar complaints. Her husband, a Portuguese building contractor, asked me today if I couldn't give her a pill and make her better. When I gave him the name of a psychiatrist, he grabbed his wife by the arm, and together they stormed out of my office. Patients like Maria Rodrigues make you want to give up the practice of medicine and learn to play the kettle drums.

My nephew Alan is sitting on the bumper of my car reading a book. He glances up and greets me with a neat, little "Hi," as if it is the most natural thing in the world for him to be hanging around my office at six in the evening.

"How did you get over here?" I ask him, startled by his presence, still thinking about Maria Rodrigues.

"Got my driver's license last week." He points to Sandy's Celica parked several cars from mine. For your standard teen-ager getting one's driver's license is a serious milestone, but Alan, unfailingly modest as always, is almost apologetic, telling me that he had to take the test three times before he finally passed it.

"I flunked the test twice, myself." Actually I had only flunked once.

He nods gravely, then says, "Mom doesn't know I'm here. I told her I was going over to the library."

Alan never lies. He is this perfect kid who has never given his parents a moment of real grief. Harry's recent behavior has so confused his family that my sister-in-law, a decent, polite woman, hangs up on you without saying 'goodbye', and my super-honor-roll nephew now lies to his mother.

"If I told her I was going to see you, she'd ask me a lot of questions which I wouldn't have felt like answering," Alan explains.

Except for the chiseled facial bones, and the small cleft in his chin, which belongs to Sandy, my nephew has inherited my brother's dark, brooding looks. He is a quiet introspective adolescent, who expresses himself best when he is playing his violin. A concert master in the high school orchestra, he auditioned and was chosen last summer to play in the Young People's Symphony at Chautauqua Institute, a sixty-five-piece orchestra that accepts only the best from around the world.

"How're you doing?" I ask.

"Okay, I guess."

His expression remains unwaveringly somber and I want to kid him a little, try to cheer him up, but I'm not very good at that sort of thing. Harry, on the other hand would have asked him something like "How's your love life?" or "Keeping it in your pants these days?" or some other dumb question that might have elicited a smile out of him.

"Are you going back to Chautauqua this year?" I ask, while waiting for him to tell me what's on his mind.

"I doubt it." He shrugs. "Actually I was thinking of quitting the violin." I react with a surreptitious, little smirk, which he is quick to pick up on. "Nobody ever asked me what I wanted. Maybe I never wanted to play the violin."

"Nobody ever asked you if you wanted to read either."

"Yeah, well maybe I didn't like it all that much. Maybe I'm sick and tired of all the practicing."

"Nobody ever forced you to practice."

"You play in orchestras, you have to practice."

"What else would you rather do?"

"Why can't I just do nothing? Lots of people do nothing and manage to live their lives without everybody on their backs all the time."

Be patient, I tell myself. His father has deserted him, his mother is depressed. Every day you hear and read about families falling apart, but when it happens to you, to your family, it doesn't help to know that there are others just as miserable as you.

"Did you tell your mother about your decision to quit the violin?"

"Not yet."

"Do you think giving up the thing you like best might have something to do with your father?"

"He wouldn't care that much. He's always telling

me that you've got to do whatever feels right to you."
He moves off the car and stands up. "That's what he's
doing, isn't he?" In the past two years he has grown
half a foot, and is now several inches taller than both
Harry and myself. Like many teen-agers who grow
too fast, he tends to slouch while standing, and walks
with long, ungainly strides.

"I think that you're angry with your father, and
quitting the violin is a good way to get back at him."

"I'm not angry with him. He can do any damn
thing he pleases. We can live perfectly well without
him."

"Is that your opinion, or your mother's?"

"Mine. Mom thinks that any day Dad will miraculously appear, and everything will be just the way it
always was. In meantime she walks around the house
talking to herself. She's becoming very weird."

"How can I help?"

"Talk to Dad. See what's going on with him.
Personally I don't give a damn what he's planning to
do. She's the one I'm worried about. After you talk to
him, then talk to her."

"I don't know where he's living."

He pulls a letter out of his pocket. "This came
yesterday." Another messy little note scribbled in
pencil: *"How's the world treating you, kid? Be seeing
you one of these days."* Great prose for a novelist that
a celebrated critic had once compared to Bernard
Malamud. Unlike the letter he had sent me, Harry
wrote an address at the bottom of the page on this
one.

"Why don't you talk to him yourself?" I ask.

"I'm too busy."

"To see your father?"

"I've got a job delivering pizza after school."

"You just got your driver's license and you've

become a delivery boy?"

"We need the money."

"Your parents have money."

"Dad cleaned out our entire savings account the day after he left. It looks like he had it all planned."

Harry stole bread from his son's mouth? *Never.* Harry could humiliate you, embarrass you, drive you into a wild rage, but over the years he had lent out more money to friends in trouble than he could afford, most of which was never returned.

"Your mother has to get herself a lawyer."

"She doesn't want to divorce him. I told you, she thinks he'll be coming home any day now."

"And you're going to pay the mortgage by delivering pizza?"

"We're economizing. We'll work it out. He can rot in hell."

"I thought you weren't mad at him."

"I'm not. I don't give a damn what happens to him."

We are on a merry-go-round. I stuff Harry's letter in my suitcoat pocket. "I have to go to the hospital. Afterwards I'll try to hunt him down. Any messages you want me to deliver for you?"

"Nothing." He backs up a few steps. "I guess you could tell him that I got my license. He was the one who taught me how to drive."

He spins around and heads for his car. It occurs to me that I have just broken a world's record in time spent talking to my nephew. I watch him as he drives through the parking lot toward the street. He uses his directional signals, even though there isn't anyone behind him. Once at the corner he waits patiently before sliding into traffic, and I think of how Harry would burn rubber when he first began to drive. Not to worry, I tell myself, it may take a while, but Alan will be okay with or without his father.

Harry and Mitzi live in a converted attic of an old frame house in the Ironbound section of Newark. The fourth floor apartment is a large room with a sloped ceiling, and a tiny bathroom barely large enough to accommodate a toilet, a sink, and an old iron bathtub. An electric hot plate sits on a folding, bridge table held upright by three legs and a pile of books. A fan hanging from the ceiling directly over the double bed circulates the stale, stagnant air. When you inhale deeply, you can smell an odd, mildewed type of odor.

"This is where you live," I say to Harry, who is sitting on a cushion leaning against the wall writing in a loose leaf notebook.

I am still puffing from the climb up the four flights, and look for a place to sit. Books are piled up haphazardly all over the floor. Two major piles of clothes are on either side of the bed, and I suspect one is clean and the other waiting to be washed. There is no bureau. Mitzi and Harry are living out of suitcases, which are opened and stashed against the walls. I sit at the edge of the bed.

Harry acknowledges my presence with a little effeminate wave of his fingers, but Mitzi is all smiles and hellos and jumps up to greet me with a nice kiss on the cheek.

"How did you find us?" Mitzi asks. "We're hiding out."

I tell her about my meeting with Alan, his wanting me to come to visit his father. Then I ask, "Who are you hiding from?"

"Her old man," Harry says. "John 'ole blood and guts' Whalen."

"He wrote us a threatening letter."   Mitzi is
surprisingly lighthearted. "Harry's scared to death." I
guess after three months of living with Harry, you
either kill yourself or become as crazy as he is.

"We're on the lam, Rog, the man's dangerous,"
Harry says. "Read him the letter, Mitzi."

Obediently, Mitzi reaches down and pulls out a
torn piece of lined paper from one of the opened
suitcases. She clears her throat as if she is preparing
to read an essay on Tolstoy before a roomful of
scholars, then recites in a clear, precise voice:

"Dear Harry Stone,
You are the scum of the earth. You have poisoned my
daughter's mind against her parents. God will strike
you down one day. If he doesn't, I will.
John Whalen"

Harry puts down his notebook and raises his
ballpoint pen like a dagger. He cries: "'Avenge O
Lord, thy slaughter'd saints,'" then presses the tip of the
pen against his chest. "I am done for, Horatio. Fare
thee well, old pal." He slumps forward, and emits a
giant fart.

Mitzi doubles up in laughter. Nothing like having
someone to appreciate your sense of humor. After
she uprights herself I notice how she is beginning to
bulge in the middle, her jeans unbuttoned at the
waist, allowing a glimpse of pink flesh emerging
above black panties.

She folds the letter into a paper airplane and sails
it toward me. The letter nose-dives at my feet. I pick
it up and give it the once over. Scrawled in pencil,
the letter is only slightly more legible than Harry's
letter to Alan. These two deranged fathers should
write not to their children, but to each other. It could

be a *literary potlatch*. The first one that could make out the other's handwriting would win the battle. The loser would have to write a thousand times on a blackboard: "I am a moron."

"How did he find you?" I ask Harry.

"He called up the University. Some dummy called in a forwarding address." He yanks a thumb toward Mitzi.

Mitzi chooses to ignore Harry's remark. "Daddy's always making threats to people," she says. "A couple of years ago he wrote a letter to President Carter demanding that he send in the Marines to rescue the hostages in Iran. If the President of the United States doesn't know how to act like a man, what does he need balls for. A couple weeks later two F.B.I. agents rang our doorbell and warned Daddy that he'd better stick his foot in his mouth if he knew what was good for him."

"Suppose he comes down here looking for you."

"Actually Harry called Daddy up last week. He thought he could kill him with kindness."

Harry chuckles idiotically. "I was merely being civilized. I wanted him to understand that to know me is to love me. I even offered to buy him a beer. My God, before you know it the man's going to be a grandfather, and I'll be calling him *Dad*."

"Harry really tried," Mitzi interjects.

"He said he'd rather have a beer with a Great White shark, then threatened to prune my dick and pin it on the bulletin board outside my classroom."

Harry waits a moment then starts to laugh, a rib splitting, gut wrenching laughter that doesn't subside until the muscles on the right side of his face begin to twitch violently. He grabs his cheek, digging his fingers into his skin as he attempts to stop the involuntary muscle spasms. After a few seconds the attack subsides and he stares at me with a cheerless, melancholy expression.

I go over to his side and pat him on the back. "Are you okay?" He pulls away from me with a pained expression. Upset, I walk over to the far side of the room where I look through an undersized attic window. The adjacent building is about fifteen feet away, nothing but rotting wood shingles. Below is an alley strewn with garbage and junk scattered around the base of a large maple tree that has miraculously survived in this subterranean environment of darkness and concrete. Branches from the tree block whatever natural light comes through the window, and the only real illumination in the room is from a sixty-watt bulb that hangs precariously on a wire directly over the bed.

"Do you enjoy living here?" I ask Harry.

"I love it," he says.

"I can't believe you resigned from the University."

"They called me in, Rog. Gestapo tactics. The Dean and two of his henchmen took turns questioning me. 'Mitzi could have been impregnated by God himself," I pointed out to those nitwits. 'By golly, fellows, you believed it once, why can't you believe it again? '"

"You have tenure. They can't fire you without a proper hearing."

"True. But why must I spend the rest of my life trying to teach the difference between a colon and a semicolon to a bunch of morons. If you don't count the Asians, the average student I.Q. is less than the speed limit on the Turnpike."

"You're going to just pack it in after fifteen years of hard work?"

"I am at the present time engaged in a giant, cleansing action, Rog. I am flushing all the bullshit down the toilet--family, university, garbage collectors, bus conductors, telephone operators, insurance salesmen, dentists, tax collectors, garage mechanics, grocery clerks, pipe cleaners, orange pickers,dermatologists, ophthalmologists, and especially shoe salesmen."

"Don't forget lawyers and priests," Mitzi says.

"I am especially going to expurgate them."

"Harry's a great expurgator," Mitzi says proudly. "He's writing a novel about expurgation."

I note that his typewriter is still in its case lying under a huge pile of papers. "Other than *expurgation*, does it have a plot?" I ask.

Harry's expression turns leaden, as if all this jocularity has exhausted him. "It's about lies--"

He begins to stutter and Mitzi interrupts. "The lies we tell ourselves every day to make our lives more tolerable" She seems to have taken on the role of translator, as if Harry is speaking in a foreign language.

"Th-that's not what my book is about." Harry's temper flares. "Don't you remember anything?"

"We talk about a lot of things, Harry. I can't begin to remember everything we talk about, for crying out loud."

Inexplicably, he becomes cheerier. "Writing a book is like raising a child." He raises himself up, becomes more alert, suddenly a lecturer addressing a classroom of students. "In its infancy the book is innocent, immature, at best hopeful of a future. It begins to grow as the author unravels naked truths buried inside his head for a lifetime. If the book is worth a damn, the writer is more surprised than the reader by its revelations." He begins to write again in his notebook. He no longer appears interested in the conversation.

Mitzi claps her hands, then asks me: "You like a nice cup of tea, Uncle Rog?"

"That would be terrific."

While the water is boiling, Mitzi pushes aside a bundle of clothes under the window sill, and lays down a cushion in the empty space. "Flop down on that," she says. "You'll be more comfortable."

Once on the floor I stretch my legs and lean back against the wall. Mitzi hands me a cup of tea along with several packets of sugar bearing a Wendy's label. She sits next to me, her butt innocently pressing against my thigh. Then she offers me a chocolate chip cookie.

"They're from the A & P. I'd make them myself if we had a stove."

"Can't you afford to move to a better place?" Alan had told me that Harry had cleaned out their joint savings account. Given the way Harry and Mitzi are living you have to wonder if there is any truth in the accusation.

"Harry says we have to economize until he finishes his book. But don't worry. I've got some money saved. We'll be just fine."

"How's your arm?" I ask.

"Good as new. They put a pin in it. If it bothers me, they said they can take it out later on."

"Wait until after you've had your baby . . . then decide."

"Yeah, that's what I think I'll do."

"What about school? Are you attending classes?"

"I transferred to the Newark campus, but Harry thinks I'm wasting my time."

Harry looks up. "My sweet potato is too fucking dumb to realize it," he says, then goes back to his scribbling.

Mitzi smiles. "After expurgation, Harry's favorite

topic of conversation is *how fucking dumb I am.*"

"What's the matter with you, Harry?" I say. "Why do you insult Mitzi for nothing?"

"Don't pay any attention to him, Uncle Rog. He needs to talk to keep his big mouth exercised."

I sip the tea. "Very good."

"Orange pekoe. All natural. No caffeine. Would you like to take some home? Maybe Aunt Doris would like to have some. Don't worry, I've got lots more."

Aunt Doris? If I tell Doris that she is now Mitzi's aunt, she will have to take an extra dose of Mylanta before going to bed tonight. "Thanks. I'm sure she'd love some."

Mitzi looks at her wristwatch. "My God, it's almost eight. No wonder I'm so hungry. I'm going to run down to Burger King and pick up something. You like anything, Uncle Rog?"

"No, thanks."

She rises with a small degree of difficulty, and I wonder what kind of prenatal care she has been receiving. Hamburgers, French fries, soft drinks--the sensational diet of today's youth. I make a mental note to bring over vitamins and Brewer's yeast on my next visit.

"Bring me a whopper," says Harry. "Hold the mayo, and ask for extra pickles."

At the door she turns and says to me. "I'll only be a little while. Please wait."

"I have to get going, but I'll come again soon."

Harry shouts as she is closing the door. "Don't forget the pickles!"

I sip my tea and listen for Mitzi's footsteps on the staircase. The front door slams shut. Harry continues writing on his pad, paying no attention to me. I think of Alan asking me to act as an intermediary between his parents. What Alan doesn't realize is that given Harry's state of mind, he and his mother are better off living by themselves.

I am about to leave when Harry looks up and says, "I was in court yesterday. My case was plea bargained to reckless driving. Later the prosecutor handed me one of my novels and asked me to autograph it."

"It sounds like you got away with murder."

"Not murder, assault. I'm considering crossing off judges and prosecutors from my expurgation list."

"What about my five hundred bucks?"

"You're not worried about a measly five hundred, are you?"

"Who said I was worried?"

"Money worries you more than anything."

"I've got plenty of money, Harry. You're the one who's out of a job."

"When I finish my novel, I've been thinking about going back to teaching."

"Is it true that you cleaned out your joint bank account?"

"Who told you that?"

"Alan."

"Alan tells you what Sandy has told him. And Sandy is a liar. The amount of money in our account wasn't worth taking."

"You had no money?"

"You think teachers are doctors. Teachers make less than garbage men."

"I don't believe you, Harry. How do you expect them to live?"

"Let them sell the house and move into an apartment. Lots of people live in apartments. Look, I'm living in an apartment."

"You're living in an attic."

"*'Beauty crieth in an attic and no man regardeth.'*"

What's the use, I tell myself? "There's something else. Mitzi should be seeing a doctor regularly. She's got to eat properly, exercise, take vitamins and food supplements."

"She get's plenty of exercise walking to Burger King and eating Whoppers."

"What about yourself? You've lost ten pounds."

He pinches his midsection. "Maybe five. So what?"

"Hold out your hands."

"What for?"

"I want to see if they shake."

"I don't feel like holding out my hands."

"I think you're getting Parkinson's Disease. Now hold them out."

His hands are steady as a rock, no shaking, no hint of a tremor. "Happy."

"How are you sleeping?"

"Like a baby. How do you sleep, Rog?"

"I want you to call up my office and make an appointment to come over."

"Why? I feel terrific."

"I don't care that you feel terrific, Harry. Just come over and let me examine you."

"This is Sandy's idea, isn't it? Because I don't want to live with her anymore, there's got to be something the matter with me."

"Sandy thinks you're coming home any day now. I'm the one who thinks you're sick."

"Nerves, Rog. It's all nerves. I've lost my job. I'm broke. I'm living with a sappy teen-ager."

"It can't hurt to let me run a few tests on you."

"Sometimes it's better to let things be, little brother."

"Let me help you, Harry."

He stands up and stretches his arms, then actually manages a few fast jumping jacks before stumbling over himself. He winds up unhurt in a pile of clothes. "Getting out of shape," he says. "Too much lying around in this hole in the wall. I need to work out, but the only place around here is a playground full of teen-age delinquents."

He begins to dress. He seems to have no problem putting on his clothes until he tries to tie his shoe laces. After a few seconds he gives up. He's breathing hard.

I bend down and help him. He gives me an odd look, but lets me do it for him. "Maybe you need glasses," I say.

"You think that's it?"

"Presbyopia, Harry, you're getting middle-aged."

"Sounds religious. I will have nothing to do with it." He straightens up, brushes back his hair with the palm of his hand. "Let's go find Mitzi," he says. "Why don't you have a whopper with us? It'll put hair on your chest."

"I already have hair on my chest. Another time."

Downstairs, in front of the tenement, I say to him, "Alan wanted you to know that he passed his driver's test."

"It's about time."

"He'd like to come down to visit you."

"I don't think that would be such a good idea."

"Call him up and arrange to meet him. He needs to talk to you."

He gives me the once over, a sort of quizzical, one-eyed look that reminded me of when we were kids and he wanted me to lie to our parents for him. "Maybe," he finally says.

We separate, walking in opposite directions. I notice that he seems to be developing a peculiar limp, and muscular dystrophy comes to mind. But I immediately reject the notion. When he was doing his jumping jacks, he could have twisted his knee slightly, a simpler, more logical explanation for his limp.

As I drive home I think about many things--Mitzi and her father's letter, Mitzi's pregnancy, Harry's novel, what I'm going to tell Alan, but mostly I think about Harry limping down the street, and my bending down to tie his shoe laces as if he were a four-year-old child.

CHAPTER FIVE

Izzy

Mom has a lymphoma. Dad's voice over the phone, always vibrant with optimism, is a whisper. I prod him for details. "Advanced," he says. "There's a mass in the liver the size of a tennis ball. The best we can hope for is two months."

I make reservations for a late afternoon flight to Fort Lauderdale. Doris and Sandy will be flying down the next morning. Alan volunteers to move into my house to chauffeur his cousins around while we are in Florida. The children will visit their grandmother after she has returned home from the hospital. I pack a bag and leave.

On my way to the airport, I drive into Newark to find Harry.

Mitzi is squatting on a cushion strumming a guitar and singing with her mother *My Darlin' Clementine* in voices that sound as if they are practicing for a hog calling competition. I haven't spoken to either Harry or Mitzi in a month and am surprised to discover that Mary Lou Whalen has become a regular visitor to Mitzi's attic, after Harry had taken to disappearing for days on end.

"He just ups and goes," Mitzi tells me matter-of-factly. "Couple days later he'll pop right back, always broke and looking like he's been sleeping on dirty tires." Unlike Sandy, she appears willing to accept Harry's vagaries without complaint.

"Where's he now?"

"Couldn't say."

Mary Lou Whalen butts in. "You've got to feel sorry for the man. He's in a lot of pain and doesn't want to be pitied."

"What kind of pain?" I recall my last conversation with Mary Lou at the hospital and am amazed that she is all that understanding and sympathetic toward Harry.

"He's got the devil inside him that's just sucking the life out of him," she says.

Mary Lou's analysis of what ails Harry, while hardly scientific, has a certain plausibility that disturbs me. That Harry is degenerating both physically and psychologically is becoming evident to those who know him best.

"Why don't you go home and live with your parents?" I say to Mitzi. "At least until you have your baby." Good advice, but I can see from the way she stubbornly shakes her head that I am talking to a deaf person.

"I've been begging her for weeks to do just that," Mary Lou says. "Is this any way to live?"

"Harry needs me. I've got to be here when he comes back." Mitzi is adamant. You've got to admire her loyalty, if not her intelligence.

"What can you do with such a stubborn person?" Mary Lou throws up her arms in disgust.

I scribble a note on the back of a prescription: "Mom is dying. Call Florida."

"Give this to him," I say to Mitzi. "I've got to go."

Mitzi reads aloud what I've written, and begins to cry. Since she has never met my mother, you have to wonder about all this emotion. She begins to strum her guitar and sing *The Old Rugged Cross* with a new voice, one that is cracked and slightly off key. Her mother immediately begins to harmonize. Before I am asked to become part of the choir, I head for the exit.

Mary Lou stops singing and accompanies me to the doorway. "God bless you," she says. "Mitzi's told me how kind you've been. I never met your mother, but I'm sure she's the best."

"Thank you. I wish I could make Mitzi understand that she should go home with you."

Mary Lou nods appreciatively. Dressed in cutoff jeans and a sweatshirt, and without makeup, she looks more like Mitzi's older sister than her mother. I suddenly find myself liking her. I'll bet she's a great waitress, serving customers with a smile, even if the food she is serving makes you want to throw up.

I would like to ask her about her husband, John, *the great avenger*, and how he feels about her spending so much of her time with his daughter in Newark, but my mother is in the hospital with a lymphoma, and I've got a plane to catch.

The plane arrives late and I decide to stop in at the condo before going over to the hospital. Nobody is home and I let myself in with my own key. I call Mom's hospital room and am a little shocked when she picks up. Her voice is normal and for a second I wonder if this is all some sort of crazy mistake. She tells me that Dad has already left, and Harry and I should come visit her in the morning. She's too tired to talk any more tonight. She'll make sure she's still alive in the morning. She hangs up on me before I have a chance to tell her that Harry isn't coming.

I raid the refrigerator, then flop down on the couch with a medical journal. After a while I toss the journal aside and pick up a dental journal off the coffee table. Dad has been retired for more than five years, and I'm surprised that he continues to read about what's going on in his profession.

After awhile I doze off, the opened journal sprawled over my chest, when Dad walks in carrying a grocery bag. He puts down the bag and hugs me, a rare display of physical affection. Awkwardly, I hug him back.

In the kitchen he begins to unload the groceries. I sit at the kitchen table and study him as he slowly goes about his business. He is very careful, very orderly in the way he puts the different cereals on the shelf, making sure that the labels can be read easily. Then he lines up the different juices in the refrigerator according to size and color, the way he lines up his socks in his bureau drawer. Over the years I have observed Mom ridicule this part of Dad's character, but it seems to me that you can't be a good dentist unless you're a compulsively neat and meticulous person.

Dad has aged considerably since Doris and I were down to visit four months ago. The tropical sun has dried out his skin. He has lost weight and become slightly bent. In his prime he was a bull of a man, short and compact, forearms like Popeye, a trunk that resembled a fireplug. On his next birthday, he will be seventy-five. He is going to be upset when his friends no longer tell him he looks like sixty.

Finished with his task, he sits opposite me. "Are you hungry?" he asks.

"I grabbed a yogurt and a banana."

"A cup of coffee?"

"I'm okay."

"We'll toast English muffins for breakfast tomorrow. There's cream cheese and lox. We can have coffee at the hospital."

"What time should we go over to see Mom?"

"They're giving her radiation at eight. She'll be

back in her room by ten. I told them no chemo. Just help her with her pain." Then he adds with a slow nod, "It's all over."

"Why didn't you call me sooner?" I ask.

"I didn't know she was sick. She's been in pain for months and never once complained. You know your mother."

Two years ago Mom tripped while walking down stairs and fractured three ribs. She waited three weeks before she agreed to be x-rayed. I think this toughness has something to do with her leaving her parents and sisters in Poland before the war and never seeing them again. She is a quiet, reserved woman, and when she isn't cooking or cleaning spends most of her time reading historical novels. In those made up stories of the past she seems to find a world that suits her better than the one she lives in.

"For months she didn't sleep well. Most of the pain was in her right shoulder and hip. She would talk about how her mother had suffered from the same arthritic pain, and she wasn't going to give in to it the way she had. I finally got her to go to the doctor. They ran a few blood tests. Then they did a bone scan and a liver biopsy. After tomorrow's radiation, I'm bringing her home. I will not let her die in a hospital or a nursing home."

"Doris and Sandy are flying down tomorrow. I have to pick them up at two."

"Where's Harry?"

On the plane I tried not to think about this moment when I would have to explain to my father why Harry wasn't with me. Kids lie to their parents routinely to avoid punishment. When I would lie to my father, it was like trying to ride my bicycle on two flat tires. He would look into my eyes, as if they were mirrors into my brain, and know immediately what a no-good, worthless person I was. What I never could understand was how Harry always managed to get away with the most monstrous fabrications.

"Harry's not living at home," I finally say. "He and Sandy have split up. I went over to his apartment but the woman he's living with doesn't know where he is." It's the wrong time to be so damn honest, but like I said, I don't know how to lie to him.

"Harry left Sandy. I can't believe it." He is confused, and gives me a desperate sort of look. "What's going on, Roger?" he asks.

"I can't exactly explain it. Harry has become another person. Maybe it's just a temporary thing. Some sort of breakdown."

He lapses into a prolonged, unnerving silence. "Your mother warned me that one day this might happen, but I refused to believe it," he finally says, very solemnly.

"What are you talking about?"

"Tomorrow at the hospital, ask your mother. This is her business."

Something about Treblinka? A dark secret from the past? We knew from a cousin that Mom's family-- mother, father, two sisters--all had died there. The Holocaust hung over her like a malevolent cloud, but it wasn't a subject ever discussed in our house. "Make sense, Dad."

"I told you--tomorrow. Speak to your mother."

"Mom is in the hospital, dying," I say almost in anger. "I can't wait for tomorrow."

He wipes his forehead with his handkerchief. I've never seen him so agitated, so unsure of himself.

"Get me a drink of water, Roger. Then I will tell you the story of your life."

In the refrigerator I find a bottle of water, pour him a glass, then return to the living room. What can he possibly tell me that would be worse than knowing that your mother is dying of a lymphoma and your brother has become a lunatic?

"We have lied to you and Harry for a lifetime." I edge closer to the table. A mosquito lands on my arm. I swat it, and it bleeds. The little beggar has taken a chunk out of me. "The fact is--" He stops himself, stares at me with an embarrassed expression. "The fact is--I married your mother while she was pregnant with you. Harry was still in diapers. Your real father was already dead."

"My *real father*? Who are you—Houdini?"

"I'm your adopted father, your step-father. Your father's name was Israel Horowitz. Mom met him while she was on vacation in New York. She never went back to Poland. That was in 1936." He looks at me oddly. Do I believe him? Then he adds for good measure: "Two years after they were married Israel committed suicide."

"This is a bad joke?" Who could make up such a lie?

"No joke."

But why couldn't they tell us? And how did they manage to keep such a secret from us all these years? Dads' parents had both died years ago when Harry and I were children. Still, he had a sister in Chicago, whom we would see now and then on holidays. There were old friends who must have known. I imagine it's just not the sort of thing you talk about to children. You figure they know so what's there to say. After a while everybody takes it for granted that this is the way it is, and all is eventually forgotten.

"He hung himself," Dad says solemnly. He hunches forward and breathes deeply. I hear crackling sounds from inside his lungs, like tissue paper being crushed. Is he going to be sick?

"Are you okay?"

"Yes, yes, I'm fine." He straightens up, color slowly returning to his Florida tanned cheeks and forehead. "Actually, I can't tell you what a relief it is to finally tell you the truth. For years I worried that you would hate me if you ever found out."

This father, who now tells me he is my stepfather, taught me how to tie my shoe laces, to comb my hair, to shave, to play chess, to keep a box score at a baseball game. When I was eight, a neighbor's dog bit me on the leg. With his good, strong hands he washed the wound, sterilized it, dressed it, then didn't sleep for a week worrying I was going to get rabies, though he made the neighbor's vet put it in writing that the dog had been inoculated. How old was I when I clung to him as he carried me down hospital steps after recovering from pneumonia? Who taught me the importance of being a good doctor, one who truly cares about his patients? If you want a course on fathering, get Sam Stone to teach it.

"So you're not our natural father. What's that got to do with Harry?"

"You've heard from me all I intend to say. The rest is her job."

Her job? Deathbed work? Something to take your mind off dying? I want to press on, but I know this man too well. Once he's made up his mind about something, that's it. I am resigned to wait. Okay, Mom, tomorrow you will tell me about this Israel Horowitz, who Dad claims is my *real* father, and then we will put him back into the closet where he belongs. And Harry? Like father, like son? Is that what all this is leading up to? Which is why Dad, after a lifetime of silence, felt compelled to tell me the truth about our origins. Has Harry inherited from his father some genetic flaw that produces depression or schizophrenia, which would account for his bizarre behavior? I refuse to believe it. I need proof. Mom's deathbed work.

"You want to watch TV?" Dad asks.

"Sure. Why not."

We move onto the couch in the den, and watch the last twenty minutes of "Midnight Cowboy." Ratzo is dying in Buck's arms as the bus speeds down Interstate 95 into Florida, one of your great movie endings that always manages to put a lump in my throat no matter how many times I've seen it. I glance over toward my father. He is sound asleep, his head slumped on his chest, snoring lightly. I awaken him and help him to his bed, and he dozes off almost as soon as his head hits the pillow. I remove his shoes, then return to the TV in time to catch the final credits and that great theme music.

"He shouldn't have told you," Mom says. "It's none of your business."

She is propped up in one of those electrified hospital beds that moves up and down by pressing a button. She looks better than I had expected. Her cheeks are full, slightly puffy, and it doesn't appear as if she's lost much weight. But that could be deceptive since she is on Prednisone, which can bloat the patient and give her an appearance of health. The other bed in the room is empty. Dad is downstairs in the cafeteria buying fresh coffee.

"We had a right to know," I say.

"Nonsense. Do you tell your children everything? Parents are always deciding what's best for their children. It's part of the business of parenting." Calm down, I tell myself, she is your mother and she is dying. "How could it have possibly benefited you and

Harry to know that you had a father who committed suicide? Do you think you could have had a better father than the one who raised you?"

"Did you never intend to tell us?"

She waves me off as if I'm a horsefly buzzing around her. "You know you look exactly like him," she says.

"Who?"

"Israel, of course. Who do you think we're talking about, Man o'War?"

"Is that why you've always favored Harry?" Why am I giving myself a dose of guilt that I might regret for the rest of my life? She throws me a crooked look, her mouth all bent, one eyelid raised higher than the other. "Are you deranged? I've always treated my sons equally. You surprise me, Roger. I never realized you harbored such resentments."

"Always the dutiful son. Right?"

"Right. Not like Harry who was in trouble all the time, either fighting in the schoolyard, or talking back to the teachers. You could never tell him anything, so defiant and obstinate. But you, Roger, you never caused us one moment of grief. We were so proud of you when you graduated medical school."

"So you could brag to your friends." Another insidious, nasty crack, which I will regret someday. "I want to know about this man that I'm supposed to look like."

"He's been dead for more than forty years. I can hardly remember him myself."

"I don't believe you."

"All right. I'll tell you about Izzy, if you'll just stop being so angry. Please try and remember that I'm the one with the cancer. . . Sit me up better. I can't talk this way."

So Israel Horowitz has become "Izzy." I feel a certain excitement, an emotion beyond curiosity, knowing that she is going to relate to me events she has kept to herself for a lifetime.

I crank up her bed a little higher. Once comfortable, she folds her hands and places them in her lap. She has a faraway dreamy look. "In 1936 I was visiting New York with a small group of young women from the University in Warsaw. We were at Times Square searching for the subway to go downtown. Since my English was supposed to be the best, I was elected to ask for directions, and Izzy was the first person I went up to. He laughed at my accent. When he realized how offended I was, he not only apologized but led us to the subway and rode with us to Greenwich Village. Later, he took the four of us to lunch, then to the Statue of Liberty. The next day he was waiting for me in the lobby of the hotel. The man had a lot of nerve. He wanted me to ditch my friends and spend the day with him."

"But you did it, didn't you?"

She grins, an impish little smile, and I see the young innocent girl beneath all the wrinkles and the pallor. A smile like that would knock any man cold. "First he took me to the Yankee Stadium. Who was this Lou Gehrig? What kind of crazy game were they playing? For dinner we went to Luchow's, then to the Paramount to hear Rudy Valley sing through a megaphone. The next day he made me walk with him along the East River and watch the tugboats. For hours he rattled on about his legal practice, his clients, his love of the law. How that man loved to hear himself talk."

"He was a lawyer?"

"Of course. A very educated person. You think you inherited your brains from a street cleaner." Nothing is ever what it seems. Her face becomes brighter and brighter as she talks about Izzy Horowitz. "Clarence Darrow was his hero. If it wasn't for Clarence Darrow, he told me, our schools would still be teaching us that the earth was created in six days and evolution was a crackpot idea made up by the Jews and the Communists. To tell you the truth I didn't know what he was talking about, but you had to admire the intensity of his feelings."

Who was this man who could make her remember every word he spoke forty-five years ago?

"The tour took a bus to Washington. As I walked up the steps of the Lincoln Memorial, I recall saying to myself 'If only Izzy could be here with me.' When we returned to New York, I called him at his office to say goodbye. He begged me to see him one more time before I left for Poland the next day. We ate hot dogs and walked across the Manhattan Bridge. We were halfway to Brooklyn when he started to climb over the railing. He looked back at me and stretched out his hands toward me, like some sort of saint. 'If you don't marry me, I'm jumping,'" he cried. She smiles again, this time it is her womanly smile, a big, wide-mouthed joyous one, seldom employed, held in reserve for her most fanciful flights of thought. "He would have done it, you know." She stops talking abruptly, waiting, I think, for the memories to settle into place before continuing. The thinness of her face makes the lines in her desiccated skin cut extra deep.

When she begins to speak again, she is more determined, less self-conscious. "Izzy was crazy about Harry. At the Museum of Natural History he hoisted Harry onto his shoulders and marched with him everywhere. 'Look, look, Harry, see that huge dinosaur. Millions of years ago dinosaurs, not men, ruled the earth.' He'd say that a child's education starts the day he is born. He filled our apartment with books and records. I'd be cooking supper while Izzy would be reading *The Tale of Two Cities* to Harry. In the background you could hear Beethoven's *Appasionato* on the victrola. Harry would be sound asleep in Izzy's arms, but Izzy would still be reading, while conducting with an index finger."

Again she stops. She reaches out to cover one of my hands that is resting on the side bar. I like the feel of her hand. "Yes, you look like him, Roger, but you're different. You're less impulsive. More sensible. You're more like your Dad." She withdraws her hand, leaving my own acutely naked. "Blood isn't everything," she says. "Izzy never remembered his own father. He died when Izzy was three. I think Izzy wanted to be the perfect father, but since he never really had one, he had to figure it out for himself."

"How did his father die?"

She pulls the sheet higher around her neck as if she is trying to protect herself from a sudden chill and says, "One day he said goodbye to his family and took a walk in the woods and shot himself in the head."

Father, grandfather. What else? What other dark secrets has she kept from us for a lifetime? "Why did Israel Horowitz kill himself?" I pronounce the name of my biological father, thinking as I do that I will never again be quite the same person.

"This is very painful, Roger, but you insist upon knowing all, so I'm going to tell you. But you must promise never to talk about this with me again."

"I promise."

"Without warning, his mind began to deteriorate. He flew into rages over nothing. One day he accused me of sleeping with his best friend. He started coming home late at night. There'd be lipstick on his shirt collar. He'd smell of cheap perfume. One night he didn't come home at all." Her voice begins to fade as if the telling about Izzy Horowitz is sapping what little strength she has left in her ailing body.

"Why didn't you leave him?"

"And go where? My family was in Europe. Hitler was screaming night and day that he was going to kill the Jews. How would I have lived? Who needed a pregnant woman with a toddler? We didn't have welfare systems like we do today. I was afraid. The worst part was that I still loved him. He had been my prince in shining armor. My whole life had seemed like less than nothing before I had met Izzy. Then he started having headaches. He'd forget names of people he had known for years. I tried to get him to see a doctor. He said I was the one who needed the doctor." Like Harry she is *expurgating* demons that have plagued her for years; mother and son cleansing their souls simultaneously, as if their thoughts were on the same frequency. "One day in court he began to quarrel with the judge, and called him an obscenity. He was held in contempt and sentenced to a weekend in jail unless he apologized. Izzy refused. He insisted on going to go to jail so that he could see first hand, 'the inequities and injustices of our judicial system.' The next day he hung himself from an overhang using his suspenders." A lifetime of toughness pours out of her in giant tears of sorrow. She is still half-crying when she speaks again. "He didn't have to do that, did he, Roger? A few days in jail isn't forever. How could he do that to Harry and me?"

"He was sick, Mom. He didn't know what he was doing."

She straightens herself up abruptly and wipes her face with a corner of the sheet. "Yes, he was sick," she says angrily. "The disease was in his blood. It was the same sickness that made his father kill himself."

I experience a moment of real weakness, a skipped heartbeat, I would guess. Mary Lou's diagnosis of Harry flashes before me--*He's got the devil inside him.*

"Roger, I can't talk anymore. Roll down the bed. I want to rest."

By the time Dad comes upstairs with the coffee, she is sound asleep. Her face is a death mask. You could feel the life being drained out of her, little by little. A part of my world is disintegrating, and I look to my father, but he is lost in his own reveries, and cannot help me. I am alone.

CHAPTER SIX

Uncle Joseph

The inscription on my father's gravestone reads:

ISRAEL HOROWITZ   1907-1938
FATHER, HUSBAND, SON.
"HE LOVED THE LAW."

I sit on a small stone bench near the grave and think about this man whom I am supposed to resemble. He died in prison, a victim of the very *Law* that was the cornerstone of his life. A few days in jail aren't forever, my mother had said to me. But within hours those concrete walls and iron bars must have closed in on Israel like giant pincers, choking the life out of him, driving him into a frenzy of self-destructiveness.

A Boeing 727 takes off from La Guardia, its afterburners drowning out the sounds of the cars speeding along the Long Island Expressway. The plane quickly rises above Chayes Stadium, the U.S. Open Tennis Center, and the Hebron Cemetery, where my father is buried. It would appear that I have been within walking distance of my father's grave on many occasions over the years.

Just last summer a patient gave me two tickets to the U.S. Open. Harry and I hadn't spent a day together without our families since college, and, for the hell of it, I invited him to go with me. It was a splendid day. The weather was shirtsleeve pleasant. We talked about our children, our wives, our work, strolled from court to court watching the matches, while eating hot dogs and drinking Cokes. We had said it all to each other by the time we drove back to Jersey, and were content to listen in silence to classical music on WNCN.

More than anyone else I wish Harry was here now, sitting next to me, sharing the loss of a father we never knew.

I think of all the years of grief my mother suffered after Israel hung himself. If he could have envisaged the bitterness and misery that his death would cause to this quiet, decent woman, who still loved him forty years later, would he still have done it? To be remembered by your children as some sort of psycho is a bitter legacy to leave behind.

Mom has given Israel a *human persona*. I wonder if the chronic depression she has suffered all her life has been as much due to his death as to the loss of her family at Treblinka.

I am angry that I have been cheated out of not knowing this man who enjoyed reading the classics to his son while at the same time conducting a Beethoven sonata. I stare at his gravestone and see a man, a replica of myself, stepping from the grave and hoisting Harry onto his shoulders, carrying him through a great museum, lecturing to him on the woners of the Universe. I see Mom, youthful, energetic, full of smiles, walking next to him. Perhaps at one point, Israel might have stopped and affectionately patted her enlarged abdomen. Did he love me, his unborn child? Yes, of course, he did. So why did he do it?

Directly behind Israel's grave are two other plots. Their inscriptions read: **MORDECAI HOROWITZ 1875-1910**, and **RUTH HOROWITZ 1878-1966**. My grandparents. Ruth was eighty-eight years old. Nothing the matter with her. We would never know how long Mordecai might have lived if he had not chosen to take a walk in the woods and blow out his brains at the age of thirty-five. Did Israel, who was three at the time, remember him? What did his mother, Ruth, tell him about his father? Perhaps she had kept it a secret from him for years just as Mom had kept Israel a secret from Harry and I.

Next to the Horowitz plots are three other graves. **RACHEL GOLDSTEIN 1912-1968, DANIEL GOLDSTEIN 1934-1979, JONATHAN GOLDSTEIN 1936-1970.** An aunt? Cousins? Had an entire family been plagued by premature death? Cancer, diabetes, muscular dystrophy, hemophilia, spina bifida, pyloric stenosis, Tay-Sachs, cystic fibrosis? Are the Goldsteins related to the Horowitzes other than by the proximity of their graves?

At the airport Dad had handed me a piece of paper with a name and an address on it. "He's the one who can tell you everything," he said.

I had waited a week after returning from Florida to call Joseph Horowitz, Israel's brother, at his home in Bayshore, Long Island. It was Joseph who had told me the whereabouts of the cemetery. "We must talk face to face," he had said, then invited me to lunch with him. I drove from the cemetery to keep my appointment, to talk to the man who could tell me everything.

Joseph Horowitz is a big boned man with an unruly mop of wavy hair, almost totally white, and a solid jaw covered with a thick, white beard that contrasts sharply with his even, deep tan. I imagine Harry at seventy, twenty pounds heavier, bearded, slightly bent, not quite Joseph, but the resemblance is unmistakeable.

He greets me with a strong handshake, then

engulfs my hand in both of his and squeezes it. The handshake would have been more than enough, but as we walk into the restaurant, he slips an arm around my shoulder and hugs me. I am embarrassed by this display of affection from a man I have never met before, but pretend that it is normal and natural rather than risk hurting his feelings.

"You don't know how long I've waited for this day," he says exuberantly.

The restaurant overlooks the Great South Bay. From our table I can see a ferry starting out toward Fire Island, the rippling effect from its wake causing anchored sailboats to gently rock on the smooth gray water. In the distance motorboats and sailboats speckle the sea. I was never much for cruising around aimlessly, but I think right now I wouldn't mind being in one of those boats, enjoying the sense of freedom one must experience in the middle of all that vast expanse, rather than sitting here with a man who is part of a past so dark that my parents refused to speak to him, or even mention his name, for a lifetime.

"Esther's son! I can hardly believe it. How many years since I've held you in my arms?" Joseph laughs good-naturedly. "You were always crying and belly-aching. I had to stand on my head to get a smile out of you."

"That was Harry," I correct him. "I wasn't even born when my father killed himself."

"Wrong," he says emphatically. "I spent a great deal of time with your mother after you were born."

"But she never mentioned you." Another unexpected revelation.

"Nevertheless, I was there." He has a triumphant look on his face, the nature of which I don't understand. Then he says, "Over the phone you told me you were a doctor. I can't tell you how proud that makes me. And you have two girls. What are their ages?" His dark eyes flash. I suddenly realize that it was Harry, not me, who looked like Israel, that Mom had lied to me. But why? "Seventeen and fifteen," I say.

"I'll bet they're beautiful, intelligent girls. I'd give anything to see them. And Harry is a distinguished English professor."

"He's written five novels." Though I will be forever jealous of my brother, I never fail to brag about his literary accomplishments when given half a chance.

"I've read them all. Harry sees the world as chaotic and nonsensical. Yet he loves his characters, loves their weaknesses as well as their virtues. He is above all a Humanist. In that sense he reminds me of his father. Israel was always ready to jump in to defend some miserable beggar. I, on the other hand, though sympathetic to the downtrodden, prefer to get paid for my services." He scans the menu, makes up his mind, then tosses it aside. "By the way, I read from one of the book jackets that Harry has a son."

"Alan."

"And what kind of a boy is Alan?"

"Intelligent."

"Ah, yes." He grins. His front teeth are yellowed by age, but strong and healthy. "I'm not surprised. I can still remember when Harry was two how he would sit on the front stoop and stare into space while he sucked his thumb. He never spoke, never showed much reaction to what was going on around him. Everyone thought he was mentally retarded. Then one day without warning, he began to speak, not in words or even phrases as most children do when they first learn language, but in whole sentences. He knew everything. We were all flabbergasted. He was like a computer that had suddenly turned itself on." Again he smiles. You can hear the pride in his voice as he talks about Harry. Is it possible that he has been talking about Harry this way for the past forty years? "I have no family, you know." He grows hesitant, a little nervous, I think. "Esther, your mother, was the only woman I ever really cared about. Does that surprise you? But as it turned out, marriage wasn't in the cards for me. And I did other things: built a solid law practice, traveled the world. I've lived in places like Jerusalem and Tokyo. Spent a month in Bangkok. Traveled the coast of Alaska. Voyaged to Antarctica. I even tried a little mountain climbing in Nepal. Not too successfully, I must confess. Couldn't take the altitude." He grins self-consciously. "By not allowing myself to become too involved with women, I've managed to have a few splendid relationships. You know, Roger, when there are no strings attached, you can be yourself one hundred percent of the time, a luxury, I imagine, not always available to people when they're tied to each other contractually." Joseph has lived the life that Harry had always dreamt about. Personally I don't envy Joseph. I have always enjoyed the solid feeling that comes with the planting of roots, then watching them take hold. Pleasures that endure--marriage, family, a profession--are the ones that matter most for a *dependable* fellow like me. "I can't tell you how relieved I am to discover how healthy you and Harry are. You're not knowing about our family was probably a blessing. Israel, my sister Rachel, myself--not a day went by during which we didn't think about what might be in store of us. Esther did the right thing shielding her sons from their father's family."

Rachel Goldstein, one of the names on the

gravestones next to my father's--my worst fears have surfaced. "Rachel Goldstein was my aunt?" I ask.

"Yes, of course." He appears baffled that I didn't realize that fact. "And Daniel and Jonathan were her sons. Your first cousins. They were also lawyers, you know. Both worked in my firm until they became ill."

"And how did they die?" I ask with trepidation.

"Daniel ran his car off a bridge in Connecticut." Before I could ask about my other cousin, he adds, "Jonathan choked to death while eating."

Father, grandfather, cousins: nightmarish deaths. "And Rachel?" I ask.

"She died of a heart attack after being sick for almost fifteen years." The recounting of these deaths has plunged Joseph into a black silence. At last he says, "That's not uncommon with HD."

"HD?" What happened to manic-depressive psychosis, paranoid schizophrenia?

"Huntington's Disease." He must have observed the astonished look on my face, for he quickly adds, "Perhaps, you're familiar with its more common name, Huntington's Chorea."

In the fifteen years I have been in the practice of internal medicine, I have never treated a patient with Huntington's Disease. I know virtually nothing about it, except that it runs in families and is extremely rare. While in medical school, I recall Dr. O'Reilly, a staff neurologist, lecturing to us on diseases of the basal ganglia.In his brief discussion of Huntington's Chorea, he had showed us slides of emaciated, demented patients, before going on to the more common diseases of that part of the brain, such as Parkinson's.

"Are you all right?" Joseph asks.

"I didn't know."

"Didn't Esther explain it to you? What about the dentist?" I shake my head. He stares at me uncomprehendingly. Without choice, he has been elected the person asked to divulge our family history. He is a little taken aback by this unexpected responsibility, but you can see that he is more than up to the task. He plunges right in. "Your grandfather, Mordecai, brought it here from England." He speaks with the assurance of a scholar who knows his subject. "He had two sons, Israel and myself, and a daughter, your aunt Rachel, before he shot himself. He also had a brother, Samuel, who emigrated to Chicago. Samuel lived in such terror of the disease that he finally went insane and died at the Cook County Hospital at age seventy-two. Both his daughters were normal and so were their children.

Not so lucky was my brother Israel, my sister, Rachel, and her two sons." He signals the waiter to bring us several glasses of wine.

"How is it transmitted?"

"If one parent has got it, it's fifty-fifty."

"Autosomal dominant. I should have remember-ed."

"All the men in the family were under thirty-five when they first showed signs. Like myself, it would appear that you and Harry are out of the woods."

"Yet you never considered marrying once you were past forty. Why? There was still time to have had a family."

He strokes his beard. I have touched a raw nerve. "It had nothing to do with HD. Your mother turned me down and that was the end for me. Some men can't accept that sort of rejection more than once in a lifetime."

"You *blame* my mother?"

"Never." He rises to her defense. His voice is strong, determined. "She was the most wonderful, bravest woman I've ever known."

"But she didn't love you." More dark secrets. *Mom and Joseph.*

"She might have. I'm not sure." He stares out across the bay. "I'd like to tell you a story, one I have kept to myself for a lifetime."

Too much already, I feel like shouting. I didn't want to know about that personal, private part of my mother's life, no more than I ever wanted to peek through the keyhole of my parent's bedroom door as a child. But short of being rude there was no stopping Joseph. He plunged right in:

"After Israel died, Esther moved to New Jersey, to Newark. Rents were cheaper, but I think the real reason was that she wanted to create a distance between herself and the prison on Riker's Island where Israel had hanged himself. Harry wasn't quite three, you were still in diapers. In those days I was driving a red Hudson, and on weekends I would often go out to Newark to visit her. Sometimes we'd drive to the park with you and Harry, go boating and pic-nicking, maybe later take in a movie if we could find a babysitter. On one occasion, after you and Harry went to bed, we were listening to the radio for news about the impending Nazi invasion of Poland. She became terrified. What would happen to the Jews if the Nazis conquered Poland? She'd never be able to return to Europe to see her parents. 'It'll be okay,' I said, 'I'll take care of you.' At the time Esther was working at a factory in Newark where they manufac-tured light bulbs. She worked sixty hours a week for forty cents an hour. She gave five dollars a week to the woman upstairs to watch the children. After rent, food, clothing, diapers, medicine, coal, and all the other necessities one needed just to get by on, there was never anything left over. When Harry developed an ear infection, she didn't have enough money to pay the doctor's fee and the cost of the medicine. Only then did she accept ten dollars from me, though I had offered her a hundred.

"She started to cry. Impulsively, I asked her to marry me. She was so startled that she immediately stopped crying and wiped her eyes. She rejected me without the slightest hesitation. 'You're Israel's brother,' she declared, as if that said it all. 'But I'm fine,' I insisted. 'That's today,' she said. 'What happens tomorrow when you go crazy?' I fought back like a man who saw his life about to go down the drain. 'It won't happen to me. Look, I'm already thirty-five years old. I'm okay.' But there was no changing her mind. 'Think what might happen between us even if you never became sick. I'd be watching you like a hawk. If you came home late, or lost your temper, no matter for what good reason, I'd see it as the beginning. Eventually, I'd drive you crazy. It won't be long before you started to hate me.' She had a mindset and there was absolutely no changing it. In the end I gave up the battle. A few months later she met the dentist."

"There's something I haven't told you, Uncle Joseph." Calling Joseph 'Uncle' is unexpectedly easy. He had loved me as an uncle when I was a child. He loves me even now. "Mom is in a hospital in Boca Raton . She has a lymphoma. The doctors are talking about another month or two."

It is his turn to be stunned. "Do you think I could see her?" he asks dejectedly.

"What would you say to her?"

"How are you? How are you feeling?" Tears well in the corners of his eyes. "It would be a goodbye from an old friend. How can it hurt?"

"I'll call my father and ask him if he thinks it'll be okay."

"I would appreciate that very much, Roger." We

are distracted by the blast of the horn of the ferry coming in from Fire Island. Then he says, "I have a summer home on the Island. Perhaps, you and Harry and your families would like to spend a few days with me sometime. There's plenty of room."

"Sounds nice, but there's something else I must tell you." I hesitate, then decide that I am obliged to finish what I have started. "I believe Harry has HD."

His response is immediate and direct. "How is that possible? I refuse to accept that!" he says adamantly

"Six months ago Harry left his wife to live with one of his students."

"You don't have HD just because you leave your wife! Lots of men leave their wives to live with younger women." He has become excited, almost outraged. He isn't prepared to grieve over another Horowitz. "He's past forty, too old. You can't be sure. It could be anything."

"Is it possible that it might have started a couple of years ago and no one realized it?" I ask.

"Anything's possible. But I'm sure you're mistaken."

"There've been physical changes as well. His facial muscles seem to grimace involuntarily. Occasionally, he stutters. I examined him recently and discovered that he can't stick out his tongue all the way. I suspected some kind of neurological disorder, but Huntington's Chorea never occurred to me."

"We've got to be sure! We must put him in the hands of experts."

"I wanted to send him to a neurologist, but he refused. His wife thinks he's on drugs."

"Drugs!" The idea has an immediate appeal. He is suddenly elated. "Maybe she's right. From what I understand it's quite the fashion these days." Then, without warning, his mood shifts. He becomes morose. He is a lawyer, and lawyers, if nothing else, are realists. "You just never think it's going to be you," he says. "I begged Israel not to marry. He wouldn't listen. Harry was such a beautiful, adorable child, so they wanted another." He slams his fist on the table. "Damn that man! My sister Rachel also refused to listen to me. What was the result--both her sons dead? Today, her husband Aaron lives in a nursing home, a depressed, melancholy person, no less a victim of HD than if he had actually contracted the disease himself." Once again he gazes out across the bay, an obtuse, distant look. "I did my best to talk them out of marriage, but people in love refuse to consider the odds."

"Would I have been better off if I had never been born? I like being alive."

"Reasonable sentiments, which I have more often than not shared. I suppose one might argue that everyone dies, it's just a matter of when, and if your life is shortened, it doesn't mean that it had no value. Nevertheless, I cannot help but think how cursed is our family, all the more so when you consider that if we hadn't been afflicted by that damnable gene, we would be a family of scholars and professionals. We would be enjoying the fruits of our intelligence, procreating a line of talented offspring capable of making real contributions for the betterment of humanity." Suddenly he assumes an introspective pose, his broad forehead knotted in deep thought, his thin lips pursed. Finally, he resumes speaking: "First of all, you can't be sure he's got it, and even if he does he could live another ten, fifteen years." Once again I have a vision of Dr. O'Reilly's slides of HD patients. Tormented faces, emaciated bodies. Joseph must have seen the worst in his lifetime, still he is remarkably resilient. He goes on, buoyed by a renewed confidence, " And you know, they're doing a lot of research on genes these days."

Fanciful talk. Genetic research is in its infancy. It's a million to one shot to isolate a specific gene, no less try to analyze it and understand how it is defective. Even then it wouldn't end there. There would still be the near insurmountable problem of correcting the defect and coming up with a way to alter the human genetic code.

"Once he knows the truth, Harry may also want to kill himself," I say, my darkest thoughts surfacing.

"Keep him alive, Roger. This family cannot afford any more suicides. I still remember how affected my mother was after my father shot himself. For years she refused to leave the house. After Israel committed suicide, twenty-eight years later, she was barely sane enough to realize what had happened. I never told her about Rachel. By then her mind was totally gone. If Harry kills himself, you'll understand what I'm talking about." Joseph reaches across the table and places a large, sinewy hand on my wrist. "You're going to live to be a hundred, Roger. And so are your children."

You're God, Uncle Joseph. You're giving me guarantees. *Where are you, Harry?* Right now more than anyone else I would want him to be next to me, to put a comforting arm around his kid brother and quote to him a little Keats, or Burns, or Shakespeare. Who else could make me smile and with his unbounded optimism make me believe that there is always a chance? But that Harry no longer exists. That Harry would never be more than memory, and that is the saddest thought of all.

CHAPTER SEVEN

Sandy

Doris is with the girls at swim practice. I pass up the cold cuts in the refrig and decide to wait until she comes home. Perhaps, I think, we might go out for a bite, something we haven't done in a while. Not going out has mostly been my fault, since lately I have become a tough guy to live with, always irritable, generally unpleasant. Doris, with her usual psycho-analytical way of viewing misbehavior, has decided that I am identifying with my brother Harry, that unconsciously I wish to abandon my family and run around with young women. I suppose you can't blame her for wondering about me, since she knows nothing about my meeting with Joseph Horowitz two weeks ago. I cannot explain my reticence to tell her about that meeting, and who Israel Horowitz is. It is like the horror of what is happening to Harry and myself and our families has for the moment blunted me into a deathly silence. Still my mother *is* dying, and it wouldn't kill her to be a bit more sympathetic.

I go into the den and switch on the answering machine. A broker from Merrill Lynch wants to talk about tax-free bonds. The other message is from Sandy. "Roger, call me immediately." Her tone is more demanding than usual.

Unsolicited brokers are high on my own *expurgation* list, and I am not in the mood to speak to my sister-in-law, who calls me every other day, blaming me for everything that is wrong in her life, just because I'm Harry's brother. I'm expected to listen without comment. On those few occasions when I try to offer constructive advice on how *one must get on*

91

with one's life when one's mate has abandoned one, she shoots me down as *insensitive.*

I flop on the sofa in front of the TV, and using the remote zip from station to station with machine gun rapidity, which has the effect of driving Doris berserk. I find nothing on to distract me from myself.

I dial my father in Florida. He is the one person who might understand why I'm so edgy. The line is busy. I wait a few minutes than try again. Still busy. I know his friends have been calling him day and night to cheer him up since he brought Mom home last week. I change my mind, stop dialing his number. Does he need my voice of gloom at this time in his life?

The phone still in my hand, I call Sandy. Might as well get it over with, I decide.

"It's about time you returned my call," she says.

"I only got home a few minutes ago. What's so important that I had to call you 'immediately?''

"You don't care about your nephew?" she snaps at me.

"Of course I care about him."

"Then you might be interested to know that yesterday he went out with his friends and didn't come home until three in the morning." There is a significant pause before she finishes off what is apparently too painful for her to say without first taking a deep breath. "He could hardly stand up."

"He had a few beers. He's seventeen, for crying out loud."

"I want you to speak with him, Roger. He's out of control."

"Put him on," I say, though I am actually disinclined to butt in. Alan is obviously in some sort of confused state of mind. But he's too sensible a boy to let his feelings get the best of him for long.

"You're too late. An hour ago we had a shouting match, and he stomped out." Predictably, she adds, "Just like his father."

"I'll speak to him tomorrow, I promise."

She softens. "Please, Roger? I'm at the end of my rope. Maybe he'll listen to you. You're the guy in the family who holds things together."

"Not lately."

She picks up on my sour mood. "Are you okay. You don't sound like yourself."

"Doris suggested the other day that I ought to take a pill."

"Doesn't she understand all the pressure on you? You've got a brother who's flipped out and a mother who's dying." *How insightful.* I am suddenly feeling more generous toward my beleaguered sister-in-law. "I was thinking of sending Alan over to see his father. Maybe he can knock some sense into him."

"Harry's not around, Sandy. He's discovering America." Since returning from Florida I have been to Harry's apartment twice. Still among the missing. Last week Mitzi received a postcard from Redlake, Minnesota. Harry's handwriting was so illegible that it was near impossible to decipher. I was able to pick out two phrases--"fishing for bass" and "climbing totem poles." I tell these things to Sandy, who listens without interruption.

"It's what he's always wanted to do. Go completely crazy." When she talks about Harry these days, she is usually more fatalistic than angry.

Impulsively I ask her, "Have you had dinner yet?"

"I'm not much for eating alone."

"I was thinking of going out for a bite. Maybe you'd like to join me? We could commiserate together."

Her voice notably brightens. "Like a date?

93

Where?"

"How about the Pines on Route 22?"

"Shall I dress?"

"If you like."

"I'll meet you in thirty minutes. Don't be late."

I take a fast shower, shave for the second time today, brush my teeth and comb my hair. I wear a tan gabardine suit that Doris bought me a month ago for a *bar mitzvah*, an off-white Oxford shirt and a beige silk tie. Before leaving I write a note to Doris informing her that I have gone out to dinner with Sandy and will be home by midnight. I am in the garage, when I turn around, go back into the kitchen, and tear up the note.

The Celica arrives in front of the restaurant a moment after a parking attendant has driven away my Mercedes. I never noticed before Sandy's special way of sliding out of the front seat of a car, her long legs swinging in one graceful arc onto the driveway. She is wearing a low cut, green chiffon cocktail dress; a strand of cultured pearls rings her slender, elegant neck. She stands tall, statuesque, on emerald green high-heeled pumps, as she hands the keys to the parking attendant with precise instructions on how to shift her car. "You must be gentle," she says. "My baby does not respond to a rough hand." Then she sees me and smiles happily, as if I am special. This sister-in-law of mine, the same one who thirty minutes ago over the telephone sounded as if she were ready to jump off the Brooklyn Bridge, now quickly walks across the driveway to greet me with a moist, little kiss on my mouth.

I slip the Maitre D' a ten-dollar bill. *Schmearing* a Maitre D' is a new experience for me, though I have observed my partner Jack *schmear* Maitre Ds' whenever we'd go out for dinner with our wives. Doris considers the practice to be vulgar, but I rather enjoy the way a Maitre D' can palm a bank note with the deftness of a magician, then guide you to your table, clearing a path for you like a sweeper in a curling match. For ten bucks you become for a few moments a kingly presence.

Sandy and I settle down in a secluded corner and observe the Maitre D' finish off his performance by igniting the candle on the table with a deft flick of his cigarette lighter. The candlelight glimmers across Sandy's face showing off the fine, chiseled symmetry of her facial bones. She smiles at me, and I could feel her presence right down to my toes.

Before he departs, the Maitre D' snaps his fingers and a bar waiter appears miraculously and asks us if we'd care for cocktails before dinner.

"A martini, extra dry." says Sandy. "Make it a double. How 'bout you, Rog?"

"The same." Martinis are a risk since I seldom order anything stronger than a beer or a glass of wine. Doris claims that I have a *compulsive need* to always be in full possession of my faculties, part of my inferiority complex, which is why I refuse to drink hard liquor. She is probably correct, though I don't know why she is so *compulsive* in her need to point this out to me just about every time we dine out with friends.

"I was thinking Alan and I might fly down soon to see your mother," Sandy says.

"Doris and I and the girls are going in a couple of weeks. Why don't you come with us?"

She gives me a little affirmative nod, then, without warning, bangs the table with both fists. "Harry's leaving has thrown Alan's whole life upside down. I could kill that man."

She makes no effort to wipe tears that quickly blotch her vision and wet her cheeks. I lean toward her and clean her face with my handkerchief. We are inches from each other. She looks at me strangely, says nothing, no thank yous, no don't bothers. I pull back self-consciously.

The drinks arrive. Sandy takes several short sips, then polishes off the cocktail in one long gulp. I follow suit. The taste is disagreeable, but I hardly notice. What I notice is how the alcohol rushes to my head in a matter of seconds.

"Have you tried talking to Alan?" I ask. "I mean really sitting down and talking to him. Telling him how you feel? Asking him how he feels?"

"I think he blames me for what's happened. Is that fair? His father runs off with a nineteen-year-old girl. What am I supposed to do? I was nineteen once, but now I'm forty-two. I can't help that. No one can stay nineteen forever."

"You're more beautiful now than when you were nineteen," I say.

"A lot you know. After nineteen it's all downhill."

"I don't think so. I'll bet that when you were nineteen you had bad skin and a dumb expression on your face."

"That was when I was fourteen." She grins, a sheepish little smile that displays a lineup of white teeth that could be used for a toothpaste ad. "Roger, do you really think I'm pretty?" she asks.

"You're gorgeous."

She leans toward me and slides a hand against my check, then lightly slaps it. "Harry doesn't think I'm so gorgeous."

"He does."

"How do you know?"

"Harry's not that crazy."

"Alan is like his father. He's got his same impulsive nature. Always wanting more, never satisfied. You'd think it'd be enough to score fifteen hundred on your SAT's and play the violin like Heifitz. What is it with people like Harry and Alan? All that talent and brains, yet they're always miserable. You've got it under control, Rog. That's what I've always admired about you. You know exactly who you are, and you don't pretend to be anyone else."

Without realizing it, the waiter has cleared away our glasses and brought two more drinks. Sandy immediately begins to sip hers. I stare vacantly at mine while trying to understand what she is talking about.

"I admit I'm dependable," I finally say. Doris, when she is trying to be kind and not telling me how *compulsive* I am, calls me *Dr. Dependable. Dr. Dependable* will be my epitaph, indelibly etched on my gravestone, the unavoidable consequence of a lifetime of always doing the right thing.

We drink the second martinis faster than we had drunk the first ones. Before I can stop her, Sandy orders a third round. Her gloomy expression has brightened considerably. There is a clever sparkle in her eyes.

"The next man I go to bed with will have to buy me diamonds," Sandy announces dramatically.

"Diamonds?" Was this the same woman I had known in the sixties, the one who always seemed to be *Marching on Washington* protesting *Poverty, War,* and *Social injustice*?

"Diamonds. And cars. Big, beautiful cars. I love convertibles." She throws back her head and laughs, then leans forward and whispers confidentially, "What I really want, Rog, is to be able to buy a new car just once before the transmission in my old one falls apart." She pouts, her perfectly curved, pink lips puffing up and blowing a minuscule stream of air right between my eyes. Then she says, "I ask you, is that so unreasonable?"

"Perfectly reasonable."

"What kind of car does Doris drive?"

"A Range Rover."

"Sounds like a horse. How much you pay for it?"

"Thirty thousand." She whistles loudly. "It's got four wheel drive," I add with bravado.

"Don't all cars have four wheels?"

"This one can go through snow and ice without getting stuck."

"A car that can drive through snow and ice without getting stuck. Better than a horse. More like a Sherman tank. No wonder it costs so much. I'll bet that cars that drive like tanks and cost as much as a house never go clunk and stop working."

"They give you your money back if they don't work."

"Isn't that nice? And I'll bet Doris never had to wait all afternoon for a tow truck because her Sherman Rover went clunk, while some stupid cop kept bothering her for some stupid papers she was supposed to be carrying, or else he was going to arrest her like she was some pervert who had just axed her family. Of course not. You know why? Are you listening to me, Rog? Do you know why?"

"I'd love to know why more than anything else in the world."

"Then I'm going to tell you. You see, Rog, Doris is married to this sweet, rich doctor who buys her cars with four wheels that never get stuck in the snow and ice, and never get so old that they go clunk and stop working. That's why."

"I gotta go to the bathroom, Sandy."

The dry martinis are spinning my head in different directions at the same time, and finding the men's room requires repeated instructions from several waiters. After relieving my bladder I splash water on my face to rouse myself, but manage only to soak my collar.

A fresh martini awaits me. Sandy is sitting sideways, her legs crossed, modeling knees and ankles that are exquisitely bare. She shoots me a scrumptious smile, as I reseat myself and pick up my drink.

Then she lifts her own and proposes a toast: "To automobiles that have four wheels." She tilts her head at a forty-five-degree angle and winks at me slyly.

Almost on cue, a middle-aged piano player wearing a tuxedo that hangs on him as if he has shoulders made out of steel rods, enters from the other side of the room. He begins to dash off romantic Gershwin ballads, "*Love Walked In*," "*Embraceable You,*" "*Our Love is Here to Stay.*" He hums as he plays, his eyes half-closed. He appears hypnotized by his own music, though he must play the same songs every night. Is that part of his act, or does this wasted piano player live only in a past invoked by Gershwin tunes? Sandy, too, closes her eyes and begins to sing. "*In time, the Rockies may crumble/ Gibraltar may tumble/ They're only made of clay/But, our love is here to stay/.*"

She and the piano player, two romantic peas in a pod. Is she with Harry in her reminisces, or some teen-age boy whom she loved in high school? It doesn't matter. What matters is that she is sitting at a table with me, looking into my eyes as if I am the most important person in her life.

I raise my glass. "Another toast," I say over her warbling.

"Another toast," she repeats, then picks up her glass.

I cannot think of whom to toast. Finally I say, "To the piano player," and down my martini in one long gulp.

"Play it again, Sam," she says and follows suit.

"Maybe we ought to eat before I pass out."

"Why don't we dance first?"

"But there's no one else dancing."

"Scared to dance with me, Rog?" Before I know it, she is standing behind me and leaning on my shoulders. She whispers in my ear, "Let's do it."

I am glassy-eyed but game. She flops in my arms and somehow we manage to do a neat college one step without treading over each other's feet. We finish off the number with a classy dip, in which I bend Sandy's remarkably agile body almost in half. After we straighten up, Sandy wraps her arms around my neck and clings to me so tightly that I can hardly breath. When the piano starts up again, she begins to slowly, tantalizingly, undulate her hips and groin against mine swaying ever so gently to the rhythms of the music. She sings in my ear: *"I'm biding my time/ For that's the type of gal I am/"* I probably would have been arrested for trying to undress her right on the dance floor, if the Maitre D' didn't come running toward us, waving his hands like a referee signaling that the fight is over.

"Excuse me, doctor," he says in a hushed, very discreet voice. "This isn't a dancing area. At ten we open up the Venetian lounge for dancing and after-dinner drinks."

The miracle is that we don't stumble head on over another patron as we reconnoiter the way back to our table. Sandy is annoyed with the Maitre D'. "He should be demoted to bus boy." She winks at me.

"You're slick, Rog."

"Harry's the dancer in our family."

"Harry's got club feet."

"My brother Harry's a great dancer," I protest. "He's as smooth as Fred Astaire. He's as smooth as Ginger Rogers."

"Harry's a charmer. You think you love him, but he's not real. He's a gas bag. Take it from me, Rog, you're the real McCoy. You're no gas bag."

The waiter appears. Sandy orders jumbo shrimps as an appetizer and the filet mignon-lobster combination for an entrée. I order the Chicken Cordon Bleu because it is the first entree on the menu and I can't be bothered reading the rest.

"Sour cream with the potato?" asks the waiter.

I check to make sure Doris isn't around to remind me of my harmless, little potbelly, then order the sour cream. "For Christ's sake, Doris, who the hell can eat a baked potato without sour cream," I say.

"I beg your pardon," says the waiter.

"Why are you talking to Doris?" asks Sandy. Then she says to the waiter, "It's okay. He's talkin' to his wife." He shrugs and departs for the kitchen.

"Doris wants me to eat the potato without sour cream."

"That's like eating French fries without ketchup."

"Exactly my sentiments."

"Stuff it, Doris." Sandy giggles, a sound not unlike the one my fifteen-year-old daughter, Debbie, frequently emits when talking over the phone with her friends. "Are we a little drunk, Rog?" she asks.

I puff on an imaginary cigar and do my Edward G. Robinson getting tough routine with Claire Trevor in *Key Largo*. "You may be drunk, sister, but I've never been drunk in my life. I don't get drunk!"

"You can't always be so perfect, Rog. Perfect men

wind up sleeping with their students."

The piano player has run out of Gershwin tunes and swings into a few Cole Porter oldies. Personally I prefer Gershwin, but Sandy doesn't mind. Pretty soon she is humming *"Begin the Beguine,"* and we are rubbing knees as we did when he played *"Someone to Watch Over Me."* Sandy has divine knees. She is a divine person, courageous, sweet, intelligent. I find myself intensely jealous of Harry. Harry has had sex with Sandy, maybe thousands of times. My taste of honey would probably never be more than the smell of her hair and the memory of her cheek rubbing against mine while we danced.

"Twenty-two years I've known you, but I don't really know you," Sandy says "Where've you been, Rog?"

"Being dependable."

"To tell you the truth, Rog, I didn' really like you very much when I firs' married Harry. You were always so serious, so worried that everythin' should be *poifect.* You'd make me feel like my stockings weren't on straight. I'd wonder if you and Harry were really brothers."

"Everybody loves Harry. Why is that?"

"Harry can be everythin' to everybody, cause Harry doesn' give a damn. You get my meanin', Rog? Harry doesn' give a damn. Maybe you're the only person left that he cares about."

"Harry doesn't care about me."

"Harry loves you, Rog. He's always braggin' to his friends what a great doctor you are. 'You got some-thin' the matter with you, you go see my kid brudder.' Then he starts in with the degrees. Harry must have told nine milli'n people that you graduated from the Univer'sty of Chicago Medical S''ool."

"He brags about me?"

"Every chance he gets."

"Jesus, I feel like cryin' when I think of what a lousy person I am, sittin' here with you, not givin' a damn about my brother."

Sandy moves into the chair next to mine and leans against me. She kisses me behind the ear. "You're special, Rog. I jus' never realized it." She throws an arm around my shoulder. "Don' think about Harry? Harry's gone. He's never comin' back."

"But you don' understan' about Harry."

Sandy's mouth is running around my neck. She starts to sing, "'I've got you under my skin.'" It isn't fair. *What about Izzy Horowitz, Sandy? That isn't Harry's fault.* "'I've got you deep in the heart of me.'"

The salads arrive along with the jumbo shrimps. The sight and smell of the food seems to have an immediate sobering effect on both of us. In a flash Sandy detaches herself from me and grabs her fork. "Eat, eat!" she commands. We are ravenous in our appetites, all the time smiling perversely at each other between bites. After we polish off the shrimp, we order one more round of martinis while waiting for the entrees.

"I'm going to think about tonight for a long time, Rog," Sandy says. She belches gloriously. "I'm goin' to think about drinkin' with you, and eatin' shrimp with you, and dancin' with you." She puts her hand on my knee and runs it up my thigh until she touches my erection. "If you had met me when you were twenty-one, before you met Doris, could you have loved me?" She begins a gentle little massage of the bulge, then starts to unzip my fly. The waiter saves my life when he arrives with our next round of drinks and Sandy withdraws her hand to fondle the stem of the cocktail glass. "Do you love, Doris?" Sandy asks.

"I loved Doris more before they invented microwaves."

"I hate microwaves. Some day I'd like to cook you my pot roast, Rog."

"I've eaten your pot roast. How do you make it so delicious?"

"You gotta give it a lotta of love."

"Love, plenty of love, that's the secret. Maybe Doris doesn't love her pot roast."

"Maybe she loves her roast beef."

The Maitre D' passes by leading another couple to a table. He lights their candle with more showmanship than he did ours. I want to ask him how much this other couple has tipped him to get him to do this extra little song and dance for them. Not that it matters. I just want to know. Maybe Harry would have asked him. There are no rules for Harry. Maybe that's why Sandy loves Harry.

"What are you thinking about?" Sandy asks.

"Harry."

"Don't think about Harry," she says fiercely. "Think about me."

"Harry's my brother and you're Harry's wife."

"You think Harry gives a damn." Sandy starts to laugh hilariously. After she quits she says, "Poor Rog. You care more 'bout Harry than I do."

Sandy is going crazy, too. She's drunk, but she's going crazy and I'm responsible. Love is what she needs. Harry will never be able to give her that sort of love anymore. She doesn't know that, and I can't tell it to her. I think of Mom. Once she was a young woman and her husband had killed himself and her brother-in-law wanted to love her. Now Mom is dying, and Joseph wants only to say goodbye, but Mom probably wouldn't even know who he is. She remembers only Izzy, even though Izzy has been dead for forty years.

The waiter brings us our entrees. We eat, drink more dry Martinis. Afterwards we go into the Venetian room and dance. The piano plays along with a bass, and a saxophone. We want to hear more of the piano player. He is special. He belongs to us, not the saxophone player, who plays too loudly, or the bass player who is so bored he looks as if he is going to fall asleep standing up. The combo plays monotonous music and young couples dance apart, moving their bodies freely, independently of each other. Only Sandy and I hold on to each other. We dance slowly, the same step, the same beat no matter what is being played. We might never go home. We might stay and dance until we both drop from exhaustion, like the dancers in those thirties dance marathons. I want to die with Sandy in my arms. I don't know how I will ever be able to tell her about Huntington's Chorea. I would sacrifice my life, if it could spare her the pain she will feel when she discovers that Alan has a fifty-fifty chance of dying from a disease that causes you to shake yourself to death while you are becoming crazy."

The parking attendants have all gone home by the time we stagger out into the parking lot. Fortunately, there are only four cars left in the lot and we have no trouble locating ours. We come to my Mercedes first.

"Don't leave me, not yet," Sandy begs.

"We have to go home, sooner or later."

"No, we don't." She slides her arms around my neck and puts her mouth against mine. I don't know how long we stand next to the car, kissing, holding each other as if we are about to be separated from each other for the rest of our lives.

I unlock the back door to the Mercedes, and we crawl into the rear seat. Within moments Sandy's green chiffon dress is curled up around her neck, and my pants are draped around my ankles. We are both bloated and drunk, and cramped by the closeness of the small back seat. It doesn't matter. We could have been jammed into a telephone booth and we would have somehow managed to discover an intimacy that goes beyond our experience, one that wipes out all usual standards of behavior. We make love out of sheer desperation of will and desire. And when we are finished, we are half on the seat, half on the floor, still tangled up as one. We smile into each other's eyes and seal the moment with a long, wet kiss.

Afterwards, we decide that I will drive her home and she will taxi back to the restaurant in the morning to pick up her car. As we speed down the highway, Sandy stretches out in the front passenger seat and lays her head in my lap and dozes. I stroke her cheek as I would a sleeping child's. I smile inwardly as I think of what we have done in the back seat of a car, like teenagers after a prom. The surprising thing is that I don't feel the least bit guilty. I mean how can you feel guilty for doing something that was more fun than anything you have ever done before in your entire life?

CHAPTER EIGHT

Can't Go Home

In the large cafeteria on the first floor of the County Mental Hospital, most patients sit by themselves, drinking coffee and smoking. Those few who choose to gather at the same table with others could just as well be by themselves, for there is little conversation, virtually no interaction with each other. The patients are black and white, male and female, young and old, pot-bellied, edentulous, slovenly. Some bend forward, their chins almost touching the tables. Others exhibit more rigid postures. The only common characteristic are their vacant, empty stares. Abe Epstein, my neurologist friend, tells me that the majority are chronic schizophrenics, many of them *lifers.*

Abe and I stand behind a glass wall that separates the tables from the counter waiting for our sandwiches and coffee. After we are served, we go into the staff dining room, where the tables are made of thick mahogany and the seats are newly cushioned. Flowered plants of white roses and pink chrysanthemums hang on walls painted sky blue. One can't help but contrast the bland, depressing appearance of the patient's dining room with this one.

"For Christ's sake, the paint is peeling off the walls," I say to Abe.

"This is a county institution, Roger. We're so broke we may have to shut down the Art Therapy department the first of the year. You want us to spend money decorating the walls of this smokestack?"

During my residency, a bearded psychiatrist, nicknamed "*Siggy*" because of his resemblance to the

Great One, once remarked to me that you never knew what might make a difference with mentally disturbed patients, so you had to try everything. I want to ask Abe how much a coat of paint costs, but Abe has been kind enough to cut several hours out of a busy schedule to accommodate me, and I decide to keep my opinions to myself.

"The only HD patient we've got right now is on the ward in the basement," Abe says. "He's mixed in with the chronics. As soon as there's an opening, we'll move him to another building where the more medical cases are."

I had called Abe last week and told him that one of Doris's male cousins had been tentatively diagnosed as having HD. He immediately barraged me with questions. He wanted a family history, signs and symptoms, what kind of tests had been taken, who was treating him. I described Harry's personality change, and fabricated a family history of parents killed early in life in an automobile accident and a grandfather who had committed suicide under peculiar circumstances. Finally I told him that members of the family had asked me to examine this cousin to confirm the diagnosis.

Abe suggested that I should meet him at his office at the hospital. I thought I detected a certain skepticism in his voice. He wasn't a man you could easily deceive.

"I'd be interested in seeing what tests they ran on your cousin," Abe says. "Can you get me a copy of the record?"

"I don't see why not. What should I be looking for when I exam him?"

"Early in the disease these patients often begin to have problems with visual processing. You show them a picture and they might have difficulty recognizing and naming items in the picture, or perceiving objects in three-dimensional space. There could be problems in understanding and differentiating the nuances of speech. We do better with PET scans and CT scans, but only after onset of real symptoms. Am I being helpful, Roger? Frankly, I don't really know how you can expect to diagnose Huntington's without a comprehensive family history and some real experience with these patients."

Abe Epstein is a short, stocky man in his late fifties. He contracted polio early in life and walks with a leg brace and a cane. He can be irritable and impatient when confronted with the sort of ignorance that I appeared to be showing.

"Bear with me, Abe," I say as amiably as I can. "There are children involved, as well as a brother and sister."

"A PET scan is Positron Emission Tomography," he explains. "It measures caudate, hemisphere glucose metabolism. Once the disease has begun to progress, we can demonstrate hypometabolism in the affected cells. A CAT scan will show you areas that are shrinking, particularly in the caudate nucleus and putamen."

"How is that different than in Alzheimer's?" I ask.

"In Alzheimer's you see a much smaller brain everywhere. In HD you are looking for the area that affects coordination of movement, but the rest of the brain works moderately well until the later stages-- though not necessarily."

"So altogether how many stages are there?"

"Five. At first your cousin might have problems in work and coordination, but still be fairly functional. He might be forced to move to a lower level job. Ultimately, he'll be unable to work on a regular basis, though he could still handle things around the house and do a lot of routine activities. I knew a brilliant mathematician who in the second stage of HD couldn't add two digit numbers."

"Where is he now?"

"He died of heart disease. In the later stages HD patients can burn as much as six thousand calories a day. It's like running a marathon all day long. Eventually your cousin will start having real problems around the house. He may need help in getting dressed. He'd still be aware of the world around him, though many of these patients are often quite depressed. It's a double whammy. He may suffer not only a reactive depression knowing how sick he is, but from the disease itself."

"And at the end?"

"It's what you'd expect. Progressive chorea, and dementia. It can take ten to twenty years from the onset of symptoms until death. Even longer in some cases. Your cousin will probably die with HD, not from it, like my mathematician friend."

On Ward 32 water pipes run up the drab cream colored walls in the hallway leading to the lounge. Between two windows barred on the inside is a large painting--a lake, leaves and algae, hanging branches, a background of rolling hills. Not quite a Monet, but the painting offers color in an otherwise dreary environment.

Abe leads me into a cheerless room with a high vaulted ceiling, and huge yellow unwashed windows, the sort you might find enclosing an old YMCA swimming pool. The air is musty and I wonder why someone doesn't start the two large floor fans in the corners. Six men are sitting around. Several are watching a movie on television, the others, except for the man with HD, stare with lifeless eyes at the floor.

A small black man runs up to Abe and pokes

him gently in the chest. "Go home, go home," he says, all the time smiling broadly, showing brown gums instead of teeth. The back of his T-shirt reads *I'm lucky*

"Go home yourself, Charles," Abe says.

"Can't go home. Can't go home." Then the little man sits and starts a conversation with himself.

Abe warns me not to pass too closely to one patient, who is slumped forward at a forty-five-degree angle. He will not move from his seat but on occasion, like a caged animal, will lash out unexpectedly and grab hold of a passerby. We stand off to one side and observe the HD patient. He is a tall, thin man, more alert than the others, the chronic schizos. He continually crosses and uncrosses his legs, while moving his right hand to his forehead, smoothing his eyebrows, returning the hand to his lap, then repeating the movement, but this time gliding the hand across the forehead as if he is wiping away beads of sweat, then once again bringing the hand back to his lap, then back up to his eyebrows and so on, never stopping for a second, never altering the pattern. There is a curious grace in his movements, almost as if he is a pantomimist performing for an audience.

Later Abe tells me that he sits almost the entire day like this. In spite of medication he is unable to control his movements, and tries to mask his loss of voluntary control by converting the involuntary movement into a seemingly functional act, thus the smoothing of the eyebrows, the wiping of his forehead, the natural way he crosses and uncrosses his legs. If you were on your way to a table in a restaurant and happened to observe him for a few seconds, you'd probably imagine that he was quite normal.

Abe takes me over to the hospital library where

we find a slew of articles that have been written on HD in the last ten years. "Look them over," he advises me. "A lot of good stuff here . . . Arrange for me to examine your cousin. Be sure and get the medical records."

I thank him, and he limps away, leaving me alone in the library with hours of reading material.

I settle in and do my homework: "--involuntary movements that seem purposeless and abrupt, but less rapid and lightning-like than those seen in myoclonus . . . Somatic muscles are affected in a random manner and choreic movements flow from one part of the body to another. Proximal, distal, and axial muscles are involved . . . In the early stages and in the less severe form there is a slight grimacing of the face, shrugging of the shoulders and jerking movements of the limbs. Pseudopurposeful movements are common in attempts to mask the involuntary jerking. As the disease progresses,waking is associated with more intense arm and leg movements. There is a dancing, prancing, stuttering type of gait . . . Mental effects involve progressive dementia, memory loss, impulsive or aggressive behavior, chronic depression . . . George Huntington wrote in 1872: "We suddenly came upon two women, mother and daughter, both tall, thin, almost cadaverous, both bowing, twisting, grimacing . . ." Huntington observed that the disease came on gradually but surely, increasing by degrees, and often occupying years in its development, until the hapless sufferer was but a quivering wreck of his former self.

There is more. Differentials, treatment, recent studies on PET scans, genetic codes and genetic mapping. I am reminded of Harry as I read an article on Woodie Guthrie, who was thought to be using alcohol and drugs because of his slurred speech and unsteady gait. An historical suggestion that HD victims were hanged as witches in Salem in 1692 invokes for me a vision of my father swinging by his suspenders from the rafters of his lonely cell.

A couple of hours pass, and I am intellectually and emotionally drained. I return the medical articles to their shelves and leave. On my way out of the hospital, I pass by the corridor leading to Ward 32 and think about the HD patient, his endless, unceasing movement, his desperate effort to mask the embarrassment and pain of no longer being in control of the movement of his limbs. And I think of Harry, Alan, Phyllis, Debbie, myself, our brains demented, our skeletal muscles out of control, lurching about like drunks, dancing what one theologian of the 17th century had called *The Dance of the Devil.*

It is a tight fit but we finally manage to maneuver our bodies in such a way as to be reasonably comfortable. Sandy is sitting on my thighs, her slender legs wrapped securely around my waist. Our arms are spread-eagled against the sides of the bathtub.

"Is the water too hot?" I ask her. "I read in the Health Section of the *Times* that ninety-eight degrees is the optimum temperature for a bath."

"You're a genius," she says.

She leans forward and places her hands on my shoulders, then pushes up against me until we are butted together like Siamese twins. She kisses me on the lips. Her mouth is a soft, moist sponge that tastes like peppermint toothpaste. When we break apart, I splash water on her breasts. She drops one arm and splashes me back.

"How is this happening?" I ask. I am discovering feelings I didn't realize were possible for me, that no one would have thought possible. All who knew *Dr. Dependable* knew a man who had made sure he had married a Jewish woman with a college degree, whose bills were always paid on time, who lived in a suburban community where there was plenty of trees and grass, and the school system was top ten percent in the state, and above all, who always came straight home from work, rain or shine, good times and bad.

She begins to soap my chest, working her way down my trunk, my nipples, my hair, rinsing generously as she lathers. She wants to explore all the bumps and crevices of my skin. She is especially intrigued by my navel, gently pushing an index finger into its opening, measuring its depth as if there is some meaning in the discovery. Finally she encircles my torso with her arms and lathers my back. We are so close I can hear her heartbeat, or is it my own?

"Now it's my turn." I start with her breasts, small, pointed, virginal, only the large pink nipples are womanly. I hold them in the palms of my hand, soaping them, kneading them with care.

"Don't be so professional," she says with a grin. "Am I too small?"

"Perfect appetizers." I splash off the soap, then run my tongue around each nipple. She pushes my head against her chest, then leans forward, tilting her face and laying a cheek on the top of my head. I am drowning in the softness of her body.

She washes the back of my neck, behind my ears. Not since my mother had bathed me as a child has another human being cleaned behind my ears. I may lie in her arms forever. "We've just begun and already I'm worried about the end. When I think about that, I almost wish we had never started in the first place," I say.

"Let it be Rog. Just see where it takes us. Otherwise, we'll go bananas."

Two hours ago we had met in the lobby of the motel. She had been five minutes late and I was already making excuses why she wasn't going to come, preparing myself for a disappointment that I was sure was going to happen. I signed the register as Mr. and Mrs. John Robinson, made up a phony address in Newark, then paid the bill in cash. Earlier, I had checked the telephone book in Newark. I had found four pages of Robinsons, a perfect name, common but not likely to raise an eyebrow like a Smith or a Jones. To complete the subterfuge, I carried an empty valise. The clerk, a young man with a bored look, smiled politely. "Enjoy your stay," he said and handed me the key.

Sandy, who had been standing behind me, took my arm and said, "Come, dear, I do want to freshen up before we drive into the city."

We had not seen or talked to each other for eight days, not since our dinner at the Pines. Just thinking about calling her terrified me. When she didn't call me, I decided that our little misadventure that evening had meant nothing to her. She had been lonely; we had both drank too much. The whole affair was one of those crazy indiscretions that can occur in one's life, which at the moment seems so right, *so appropriate*. It is only later, on reflection, that you begin to feel that you had behaved like a fool, and you wish it had never happened. Nevertheless, last night, after everyone in my office had gone home, I decided that if I didn't at least call her, I would go mad wondering what she was thinking.

Without as much as the formality of a "hello," she asked me if I'd meet her Saturday afternoon at the Holiday Inn in Kenilworth.

"What time?" I asked straightaway.

"One. Don't be late," she said, then hung up so abruptly you'd have thought she had been talking to a bill collector.

We dry ourselves, and she starts to dress, until I push her back on the bed and pull off her panties and unbuckle her bra. For the third time in two hours we exchange bodily fluids. At the age of forty-one, I have broken my record for orgasms in one day. Afterwards we lay on the bed, enjoying the pervasive smell of sweat and semen that has invaded our senses, and are content to stare at an empty TV screen, while still rolled up within each other.

"I have to go," Sandy says. "I promised Alan I'd be home by four. We're going to barbecue spare ribs and eat chocolate cake."

"When am I going to see you again?"

"I don't know."

"How about next Saturday. I could tell Doris that I'm taking off the day to play a round of golf with some colleagues. If that's no good, we could see each other Sunday when the girls are swimming."

"Sunday is better. On Saturday I've enrolled in an all day seminar on real estate."

"Real estate?"

"I know a couple of teachers who make piles of money selling real estate in their spare time. Harry left us nothing. I owe Sears, the electric company, Alan's violin teacher, and two months on the mortgage."

I slide off the bed and reach into my inside suitcoat pocket, pull out my checkbook and a pen, then write her a check. She looks at the amount and whistles. "Five thousand dollars. Do you expect me to accept this?"

"We're family."

She tears up the check. "Two weeks ago we were

family. Today we are strangers fucking like rabbits in a motel room."

Fucking like rabbits. The woman is a wonder. Her look is almost pristine. I immediately have another erection. Quickly, I write a second check. "Three thousand. Consider it as an interest free loan."

"Rog, I can't take all this money. Just help me pay for Alan's violin lessons. I'll manage the rest."

"But you need the money."

She fingers the check." This is not exactly change."

"I can afford it."

"What if Doris finds out?"

"We have separate accounts. When she runs short, I transfer funds from my account into hers. She never looks at my bank statements. I've written this check to CASH in the unlikely event that she does come across it." But you could see that she's not exactly happy, and I wonder if I've made a mistake offering her such a large sum of money. The result is that I begin to dwindle. *So much for money and love.* "Pretend you're my mistress and I am blanketing you with diamonds and furs."

She tosses the check aside and takes my poor, tired organ in her mouth. For a few excruciating seconds her lips and tongue are gloriously kind. Then she withdraws her mouth and sits up. "I've got to go. I mean I've really got to go. This was just a preview of coming attractions."

I pick up the check and offer it to her once again. "Please take it," I say.

She ignores me and dresses. "Come on," she says. "We've got to go downstairs together."

She brushes her hair, pins it up neatly, fixes her face. While I am in the bathroom, she tidies up the bed, smoothing out the wrinkles on the covers with particular care. By the time we are ready to leave, we have destroyed all evidence of our prurient behavior.

In the elevator I press the check in her hands. This time without a word, she opens her pocketbook and drops it in. "I'll deposit it tomorrow," she says. "It'll cover all my bills and I'll be able to put in a new muffler on my car before some unforgiving cop gives me a ticket. Whatever's left over I'll save for Alan's lessons. I'd ask my parents for help, but they're barely making it on their social security. This is all wrong, but I'm going to take the money for Alan's sake."

The clerk, who is reading a comic book, hardly seems to notice us as I plunk the key down on the counter. "We've changed our plans, and decided to drive on."

"Everything satisfactory, sir?" he asks without bothering to look up.

At the door I note that he is staring at us. The clever dog knows perfectly well what has been going on in Room 208 for the past two hours. When Doris sues me for divorce, will this clerk, who spends his leisure moments reading *The Adventures of Captain Marvel,* be a competent witness? I grab Sandy's hand and we hurry outside like thieves leaving the scene of the crime.

Standing next to her car, Sandy puts her arms around my neck, checks the parking lot, and kisses me goodbye. Then she unlocks her door and slips behind the wheel, her dress sliding up above her knees as she settles herself in. She unrolls the window and says, "Go home, Rog. I'll call you at your office tomorrow." She starts the engine and pulls away, waving her hand as a final parting gesture.

Driving home, I am concerned that some horny truck driver will ogle those beautiful bared thighs while stopping at a red light next to her. Go ahead and stare, you lascivious bastard. Eat your heart out. Too bad she's all mine. Today, we did it three times in two hours, a feat that will not be inscribed into the Guinness Book of records, but not a bad day for *Dr.Dependable.*

Doris is in the kitchen dicing carrots, while listening to the radio. I sit and watch her, hoping to engage her in some cheerful small talk, but she ignores my presence, a happening that has become standard since the night I staggered home at three in the morning smelling of alcohol and Sandy.

Given that I have never lied to my wife in twenty years of marriage, what is most remarkable is how the next morning, I had managed, without a moment's hesitation, to adlib a fairly reasonable story.

I just had this craving for a decent meal, so I went to the Pines and bumped into Ben Lowenstein and his wife. You remember Ben, don't you. He's the urologist in Livingston, whom I sometimes referred cases to. (Introducing a real person was a major flaw in my lie, but Doris had never met Ben, and it was quite unlikely that she ever would. I suppose even the best liars must be forced to take risks now and then.) *The perfume smell on my shirt and jacket must have come from dancing with Ben's wife. She puts it on a little thick. Hey, you drink too many martinis and you wind up half-drunk and lose track of time.* (I emit a little phony chuckle.) *That doesn't make you a candidate for Sing Sing.*

Doris is no blockhead, but I'm pretty sure she believed me. How could she do otherwise, given my spotless record of love and fidelity in twenty years of marriage? I decide that the cold shoulder she has been giving me of late has been her way of chastising me for indiscrete, inappropriate behavior. After all, suppose I had been observed by friends staggering across a dance floor with another man's wife.

"What smells so good?" I ask.

"I thought I'd try a pot roast for a change."

"You don't love pot roast. You love roast beef."

"I'll make roast beef another time. Tonight the menu is pot roast." She turns around. She has this concerned look that always precedes trouble. "Roger, where've you been? I called your office earlier and your receptionist said you had canceled your afternoon patients."

"Don't you remember I told you I was going to play golf today."

"Golf? Since when do you play golf?"

"Are you crazy? I'm a great golfer."

"You don't even own a set of clubs."

"Which I'm going to rectify as soon as possible. You're always telling me I need to exercise more."

What is most interesting, I am rapidly discovering, is that to get away with a really good lie isn't altogether unpleasant. No wonder kids lie so much to parents. Unfortunately, my overdeveloped superego refused to allow me to enjoy that pleasure since I was never able to lie to my parents, unlike Harry, who lied to them about everything.

At dinner, Doris's overcooked pot roast tastes like shoe leather smeared with gravy. To be kind, I dig in and eat more than my digestive enzymes ought to be asked to manage. I am tempted to tell Doris to ask Sandy for her pot roast recipe, but think better of it, especially after the girls excuse themselves from the table without as much as a bite, content to nibble on a few half-cooked hash brown potatoes and lots of canned apple sauce that Doris seems to think automatically should be served with pot roast. Doris herself nurses one hunk of meat during the entire meal watching me curiously while I eat like a pig. She continues her basic silent treatment toward me, which I don't mind, since my thoughts are elsewhere.

In our bedroom before retiring, she disappears into the bathroom for a good ten minutes, to emerge dressed in a lacy, pink shorty nightgown, instead of her usual plaid cotton pajamas. She has brushed the artificial curls out of her hair, giving it a wild, feral look, and scented herself with one of her expensive perfumes. Within moments after we turn off the night light, she drapes an arm around my chest and butts up against me. She massages my chest, my stomach, then in the surprise of the year, unceremoniously grabs my penis.

"What's the matter?" she asks.

"I'm a little tired, I guess. It's been a long day. Can you give me a rain check?"

"This isn't a baseball game!" She gives the poor little fellow a hostile squeeze and withdraws the hand.

"I guess I'm getting old." Actually there is a rather sensuous aroma sifting from her warm, womanly body. I rub my nose between her breasts, try a little self-arousal. But alas, I am hopeless. Nothing will work. My manhood has been used up, consumed this afternoon at the Holiday Inn by my rapacious, greedy sister-in-law. I'm disappointed in myself, sad for my disappointed wife. "Tomorrow," I say. "I promise."

"Tomorrow I might be dead." She rolls over and hugs her pillow. Within minutes I can tell she is sleeping by those sometimes harsh, irregular breathing sounds that I have been listening to for several decades. Because of Sandy our connubial life will never quite be the same again. Forgive me, Doris. I touch her shoulder ever so gently. She makes a little murmuring sound, but doesn't awaken. What dreams will she have tonight? Will I be a part of them? We are so tangibly locked into a life together that for me to dissolve that life seems impossible, yet that is exactly what I am contemplating.

CHAPTER NINE

Trouble in Newark

Mitzi calls me during working hours, something she's never done before. She is borderline hysterical. I am immediately plagued by fears that Harry has committed some God awful offense since he returned to Newark last week.

"He came in and socked Mom right in the face," she says.

"Harry hit your mother?" My worst fears have materialized. Harry has gone completely mad.

"Not Harry--my father! You've got to come over, Uncle Rog, and get me out of here."

Her father--John Whalen, the famous religious zealot who had once threatened to prune Harry's dick? "Where's Harry?" I ask.

"Upstairs with Mom. I'm calling from a downstairs apartment."

"And your father?"

"Please come, Uncle Rog. Right away." There's a commotion and the phone goes dead.

On my way to Newark I can already hear Doris telling me that the Whalen's smacking each other around is none of my business. *Why do you believe you have an obligation to protect Mary Lou Whalen from her drunken husband?*

Three days ago Harry had called me to inform me that, like Douglas MacArthur, he had returned, and was back living with Mitzi and her mother, who had moved in while Harry was gone. I tried to imagine who might be sleeping where in that dingy tiny attic. The double bed occupied more than half the space of the room. A third person would have had to sleep either on the laundry bag, or the luggage.

"You heard about Mom?" I had asked him.

There was a silence, then he said, *"'Who ran to help me when I fell,/And would some pretty story tell,/Or kiss the place to make it well?/ My mother./'"* Mom was dying of cancer and the *fucking* guy was quoting some English poet with about the same degree of emotion as if I had announced to him that she had hemorrhoids.

"She wants to see you, Harry."

"I'm through traveling for a while."

"She's dying, for God's sake!"

"'I was shapen in iniquity; and in sin did my mother conceive me.'"

"Stop it!" I shouted at him. "Don't you want to see her before she goes?"

"'Goes.' Too prosaic, Rog. Let's try *parting* or *departing.* How about *passing away, expiring, perishing, fading into the dusk."*

"Fly down tomorrow. I'll arrange everything."

"Seeing me will not cheer her up."

"You must at least call her, Harry. Do you hear me? Call her!"

He must have dialed my parents' condo a hundred times in his life, but I had to repeat the telephone number to him three times. The third time I pronounced each numeral very slowly, the way you'd tell a child something you wanted him to memorize. "Did you write it down?" I asked. "Read it back to me." I corrected one digit. "Are you okay, Harry?"

"I was thinking about running the Boston Marathon this year."

"Come in and let me examine you." He actually made an appointment for the next day, but as I expected, never showed up.

*   *   *   *   *

A police car and an ambulance are already in front of the tenement when I arrive. I double-park, then puff my way up the four flights to the attic apartment.

A brawny Newark cop greets me at the top of the staircase. The apartment looks as if a giant wind had scattered just about every unfastened item--books, magazines, clothes, toilet articles--all over the place. A medic is wiping off caked blood from around Mary Lou's lips. There is a dark lump the size of a small plum on her left cheek below her eye. Harry sits in the corner on a suitcase, his tee shirt half-torn from his body. The knuckles on both his fists are bloody. His face is scratched, his right eye half closed. Mitzi sits on the bed talking to another policeman, a young, blond fellow, who is asking questions, jotting down her replies in his notebook.

I learn that John Whalen and Harry had fought like pumas, wrestling, punching, scratching, biting. Neighbors first called the police, but before they arrived, Whalen had left the apartment shouting wild threats of revenge.

I sit next to Mitzi on the bed, and put an arm around her shoulder. Her face is smudged with dirt; there is a small bruise on her forehead. Her cheeks are wet from crying.

"Are you okay?" I ask her.

"I thought Harry and Dad were going to kill each other," Mitzi says.

"Does anybody want to press charges?" the blonde policeman, who is taking notes, asks, looking from Mitzi to Mary Lou, then back to Mitzi. Neither women responds. You could see he is growing im-patient. What good is the law if he can't run somebody in?

"No," Mitzi finally says.

The policeman addresses Mary Lou, "How about you, lady? It looks like you were hit with a sledge hammer."

"The sledge hammer was her husband, my father," Mitzi says.

"I thought *he* was her husband." The policeman points toward Harry.

"Harry's my daughter's boy friend," Mary Lou chimes in. "John came busting in here, drunk as a skunk, and attacked Mitzi and me." She goes on to explain that Harry, who was in the bathroom down the hallway, heard the commotion, and ran back. When he saw Whalen hitting Mary Lou, he threw his typewriter case at him before attacking him with his fists.

"Do you want to press charges?" the policeman asks Harry.

Harry draws himself up. "S-S-Sure. So then we'll all wind up in some domestic court where one of the County's distinguished judges will fine us a million dollars, and warn us that if we ever come back to his court he'll have us castrated. I have a better idea. Why don't we find Jack Dempsey and throw him in the Passaic River with all the other garbage?"

The policeman looks over his notes. "I thought the perpetrator's name was John Whalen," he says.

"Harry's a comedian," I explain to the policeman who looks genuinely confused. "Jack Dempsey was a boxer."

Harry curls his hands into fists. "Tunney hits him with a left, then a right, smack, smack, crash, bang. The Manassa Mauler is down, folks. And it doesn't look like he's gonna make it."

The policeman nods, then puts down his pencil

and says to no one in particular. "From what I can gather this John Whalen came up and instigated the fight. He wrecked this room, inflicted serious bodily harm, and disturbed the peace of the neighborhood. You want him to get away with this?"

"Dad didn't know what he was doing," Mitzi says. "He was drunk."

"You have a right to press charges and being drunk is no defense." The cop once again turns to Mary Lou. He appears almost desperate to make an arrest. "What do you say, Miss. It looks like he tried to kill your daughter's boy friend, not to mention what he did to you."

Mary Lou touches her bruised cheek. "You think it's the first time he's beaten me up, the lousy bastard. Go ahead and get him. It'll serve him right."

"I'll take you down to the station house and you can file charges against him." Hope glows in his pale, blue eyes.

"Don't do it, Mom," Mitzi pleads. "You know how he is. Tomorrow he'll be all sorry and repentant. What good is putting him in jail?"

"That's where he belongs."

Mitzi points a finger at her mother. "Are you and Harry any better?" Then, unexpectedly, she clutches her abdomen, and sits on the bed.

"Are you okay, Miss?" The policeman motions to the ambulance driver. "I think you better take her over to emergency."

"It's okay," she says. "Baby kicked a little. Too much excitement, I guess."

I intervene. "I'll take care of her."

Mitzi reaches over and grabs my hand. "He's my doctor," she is quick to explain.

"She'd be better off at the hospital," the ambulance driver says to me. You could see that he, too, needs to do his job, save a life, haul somebody away in his ambulance. Apparently both Harry and Mary Lou have already refused to go to the ER.

"Please, get me out of here, Uncle Rog," Mitzi says.

I look toward Harry. "Do it," Harry says to me. "The *Great Avenger* has struck, but we have survived." He walks over and sits next to us.

Close-up I can see how badly bruised and swollen his knuckles are. The injuries to his face, however, are nasty but not serious. His right leg begins to jerk around. He crosses the leg over his other one and presses down on the knee to try and stop the involuntary movement, and I am reminded of the HD patient I had observed at the County Hospital.

"Go, Rog, please," he says to me. "T-take care of Mitzi."

"Let me help you, Harry," I plead.

There is an anguished look on his face. "Nobody can help me, little brother," he says, then stands up and walks over to Mary Lou and puts an arm around her. It is time to leave.

Mitzi grips my forearm tightly as we walk down the stairs, a delicate step by step descent. After we are on the sidewalk, she lets loose and immediately brightens up. "Thank God, I'm out of that hell hole," she exclaims joyously. "Let's get moving, Unc."

"Moving? Where?"

"Anyplace."

I am not overjoyed at leaving Harry, but the medic will clean up his wounds better than I could, and at the moment Mitzi seems to be the one who needs me the most. The girl leans heavily on my arm as we make our way toward my car.

Once out of Newark Mitzi slumps back against the car seat, a huge grin on her face. "What a relief to be out of that dump," she says. "You don't know what it's been like. I don't ever want to see either one of them again."

I learn that yesterday Mitzi caught Harry and Mary Lou in bed in the middle of the afternoon. It turns out that it was Mitzi, herself, who called her father. "I wasn't thinking straight," she said. "I should have called you instead."

"Harry was. . .was. . . with your mother?" Harry has descended to new depths of depravity. And what about Mary Lou Whalen? What has happened to her sanity? "Do you have any friends you can stay with?" I ask.

"Not really."

"Aunts, cousins?"

"You're the only one, Unc. It's you or the street."

At what point in our relationship did I somehow manage to convey to Mitzi the impression that I was obliged to look after her forever? Yet who could not feel real empathy for this nineteen-year-old pregnant girl, who had left the comfort and safety of her home to live with a man, who was now sleeping with her mother.

"You could still go home and live," I say impulsively. Then to compound my stupidity, I add, "Your father might surprise you."

"My father! Are you out of your mind? Did you see what he did here today? You can't ever trust him, Uncle Rog. Especially when he's drinking."

I stop at a Burger King off the highway. While Mitzi is enjoying a Whopper and a double order of fries, I call Doris and explain the situation to her. "I thought we might put her up for a day or two until I can make a better arrangement," I say.

"Harry ought to be arrested and put in solitary for the rest of his life. Let him quote Shakespeare to the rats and cockroaches."

"We have to do something."

"Our home is not a boarding house for wayward girls. If you bring that girl here, on my sacred honor, Roger, I will pack my bags and leave."

I do not take Doris's threat seriously. Still how can I place Mitzi in such a hostile environment, even for only a day or two? "I'll take her elsewhere," I say.

"Where?"

"You needn't concern yourself. Your *sacred honor* is intact." I hang up, a criminal act, which I will be tried for later on today.

Through the large glass window I observe Mitzi happily slopping down fries with a giant Coke. She looks like any other pregnant adolescent who might have a family that loved her, and a life with a future. If my parents had been Mary Lou and John Whalen, I don't think I would have waited until I was nineteen to do something desperate. Her biggest mistake was in picking Harry to save her. I ring up my last hope.

Sandy's "Hello" is more than enough to uplift gloomy spirits. Without fanfare I explain to her my predicament. And without being asked, this remarkable woman, this extraordinary woman, who more than anyone else in the world has the right to hang up on me, volunteers to put Mitzi up for a couple of days.

"You'll do it," I exclaim, hardly able to believe how readily she has agreed.

"Someone has to deal with Harry's bastards," she says before I have a chance to thank her. "It would appear that you and I have been elected."

Harry's bastards? Could there be others? Is it possible that my deranged brother has already spewed millions of genetically flawed spermatozoa into a multitude of unsuspecting hosts, that he has been breeding carriers of Huntington's Disease for untold future generations?   I am horrified at such a prospect.

"I'll try to find a more permanent arrangement for her as soon as I can," I assure her.

"Just bring her over," she says. "I'm dying to meet this little twerp." And on that unctuous note our conversation concludes.

CHAPTER TEN

She Had Two Sons

Mom died at five-thirty this afternoon in a nursing home in Boca Raton. Dad had promised her that he would never put her in a nursing home, but for the past month even with a full time's nurse's aide, he couldn't manage her at the condo. Her legs had swollen three times their normal size. To go to the bathroom she had to be lifted off the bed onto a wheel chair, then from the wheel chair to the toilet seat. Every time she was moved she cried from the pain in her bones. If she weren't moved fast enough, she would defecate or urinate on herself.

After being placed in the nursing home, she refused to talk to anyone, including Dad, who sat by her bedside, day and night, reading to her, playing tapes of the Puccini operas she loved best, talking to her about her children, grand-children, her old friends. He sensationalized the news, invented racy stories about neighbors, anything, in an attempt to arouse a response from her. She laid there hour after hour, staring into space, continually gulping and swallowing her saliva, her breathing heavy and ir-regular. Aside from a little orange juice, she refused to eat or drink. An hour before she died, she broke her silence and whispered to him that when she felt better she wanted to go home. Then she asked him to call Harry. She wanted to see him right away.

Why Harry? Didn't she have two sons? Wasn't I the good son, the obedient son, the one who always did the right thing? Why did Dad have to tell me that it was Harry she had wanted to see in those final seconds of her life? Dad's voice had wavered badly in the telling about her last days. I suppose, on reflection, he was too distraught to worry about placating feelings, that he was merely reporting to me events like a good journalist, more concerned about the truth, than the emotions his story may evoke. I suppressed my feelings, asked him if there was anything special he wanted me to do. Come down as soon as possible, he replied, and help him with the funeral arrangements. Before he hung up, he said, "You're a good boy, Roger. I don't know what I'd do without you." He was trying to be kind, but somehow I wish he hadn't said that to me.

I take an evening flight to Fort Lauderdale. Doris, my two girls, Sandy and Alan are going to fly down the next day. I have no way of reaching Harry, since he and Mary Lou have left no forwarding address after being evicted from their attic in Newark following the fracas with John Whalen. I have asked Mitzi if she wishes to come to Florida with us, though I haven't quite figured out how I would explain her pregnancy to Dad. But, as it turns out, she prefers to stay in New Jersey and take care of the dog and the parakeet.

The day after I had delivered Mitzi into Sandy's hands, I had made several inquiries into special *homes* that cared for pregnant women. The cost was higher than I expected, but the alternative would be to put her up in a motel or abandon her. A few days later I discussed it with Sandy. She caught me off guard when she said that she thought that Mitzi should remain at her house until she had her baby. I reminded her how Mitzi had all but wrecked her life.

"Don't be in such a rush to spend thousands of dollars to make somebody miserable. She can stay with us."

"It's you and Alan I'm thinking of."

"It isn't Mitzi's fault that Harry is such a bastard."

Five days passed before I called Sandy again and asked her if she might have changed her mind."

"No," she said most definitely.

I was irked. I don't know why. It just seemed unnatural. "What about Alan?" I asked. Doesn't he have a vote in this?"

"Since she's come, Alan's a different person. He doesn't run around at nights anymore. He's stopped drinking beer."

"Because of Mitzi?"

"It's a friendship between teens. Alan is teaching her to play chess. She listens to him practice the violin. They cook for themselves, even clean the house together."

"How about you? How do you feel about her?"

"To tell you the truth, I like her. She's bright and considerate. She's as much a victim as I am."

"What happens if her father comes around?"

"He already has--twice."

"The man is crazy. I mean *crazy*."

"Not crazy. Just obnoxious. When I threatened to call the police, he left without a fuss."

"You should have called me."

"What for. Yesterday, I went to the police and asked for a restraining order. While I was there, I filed an application for a handgun. After I get it approved, I'm going to use your money to buy one."

I was appalled. "You're going to shoot him?"

"I might," she said coolly. "I might also shoot Harry if I get the chance." I was discovering a part of Sandy I hadn't realize existed, which had the unexpected reaction of making me love her even more.

"You don't know anything about guns."

"I'm going to learn."

Doris was shocked when I told her about Mitzi moving into Sandy's house. No one in our family had any special obligation to serve Mitzi, especially Sandy, she said. Mitzi was old enough to know what she was doing when she began to sleep with Harry. After she learned she was pregnant why didn't she have an abortion? Who was going to take care of her and her baby? Did she intend to go on welfare? Another unwanted child for the taxpayers to support. Chances were the child would grow up and repeat the mistakes of the mother. He could easily wind up a junkie and a thief. Why didn't someone inform Mitzi, when there was still time for an abortion, that the yearly cost of supporting an inmate in a state prison was greater than the tuition of an Ivy League school?

You couldn't blame Doris for blowing off like that. Still, you have to wonder why Doris, the ex-social worker, this really compassionate and decent human being, was so nasty and unforgiving about someone she'd never met, particularly after Sandy had explained to her over the phone that the girl was not such a bad person.

Doris has been especially feisty with me these days. Maybe I am being too naive in believing that she doesn't suspect that something's going on between Sandy and me. If I come home fifteen minutes later than I had promised, she gives me the third degree. I have in turn become a *liar supreme*. I will sometimes lie even when I don't have to, almost as if I need to keep practicing, like an athlete needs to stay in shape during the off-season.

There are moments when I think how great a

relief it would be to be able to look Doris straight in the eye and tell her the truth, admit that I am a chronic philanderer, a hypocrite without a conscience. But, I will never do that. If I tell her the truth, I'd either have to stop seeing Sandy, or leave Doris, both unacceptable alternatives. I see no way out of my dilemma. I will keep on seeing Sandy until I get caught, and then I will deal with whatever is left of my battered sense of morality.

The grave diggers lower Mom into the earth. In accordance with tradition Dad shovels the first scoop of dirt onto the coffin, Alan, substituting for his father, the second, the last one, I do myself. My children throw pebbles, which bounce aimlessly off the coffin. Then the Rabbi says a few final prayers before we all recite the *Kaddish*, the Prayer for the Dead. Alan and I flank my father. Alan is a good boy, tall and straight, and I love him, but I wish it were Harry standing next to Dad, reciting with me the *Kaddish*. A brother can have all sorts of envies and a lifetime of accumulated angers toward you, but when they are shoveling dirt over your Mom's coffin, he is the only one who really knows how you are feeling at that moment.

Dad insisted on picking me up at the airport yesterday. On the drive back to his condo he wanted to know why Harry wasn't coming to the funeral. I could think of no lie that would make any sense, and wound up telling him half-truths--Harry had moved again, and we didn't know where he was living, making no mention of either Mitzi or Mary Lou. I felt obliged to tell him, however, that he had quit his job. To soften this upsetting news, I explained that he needed more time to work on his latest book, and that once it was published he would probably go back to teaching again.

"How is he feeling?" Dad asked.

"He seems no worse." Then I asked him not to mention to the family anything about Israel Horowitz, that I would do it at a more suitable time. He seemed to think that was a pretty good idea.

Earlier in the day, I had a talk with Doris, the girls, Alan and Sandy, and cautioned them not to discuss Mitzi or Mary Lou with Dad. Doris initially objected, feeling that Dad had a right to know what was going on in our family, but in the end even she agreed to cooperate in my manipulations of the truth, after I asked her to reflect on Dad's depressed state of mind.

"And how are you feeling, Roger?" Dad asks me, as we make our way back to the limos.

"Does it look like there's something the matter with me?"

"You're different."

"What do you expect? My mother just died, and I have recently discovered that I had a father who died of Huntington's Disease."

We rest for a moment under a large palm tree that provides a modicum of relief from the tropical, Florida sun. It is late May. The sky is a solid, deep blue, broken only by an occasional swirl of thin white clouds that drift slowly across the expanse. The temperature is almost ninety. I loosen my tie and remove my jacket.

"I must tell you something that's been on my mind all day," he says. I am not in the mood to hear more confessions, but I don't know how to shut him up. "I had certain doubts about marrying your mother. An hour before the ceremony I became so sick we almost had to call off the wedding. I loved her more than my own life, but I was terrified thinking about the day when I would have to tell you and Harry about your father's disease."

"Last month when you told me about Israel, why did you omit the part about Huntington's?"

"I thought Mom ought to be the one to tell you, and if not her than let it be Joseph Horowitz. I knew that if I gave you his name you'd look him up. It was cowardly. Forgive me. I was all mixed up with Mom in the hospital."

"When did you first discover the truth?"

"A month after I met your mother, Joseph wrote me a short letter asking me to meet him at a cafe on West Seventh Street in the Village. When he told me about Huntington's Chorea I thought he was being spiteful, because Mom had rejected him. At first I refused to believe him. 'I will give you the proof,' he said somberly. We took the subway to Queens, then rode the trolley down Roosevelt Boulevard near to the cemetery where your father and grandfather were buried. At their graveside, he said that if that wasn't proof enough, he would introduce me to his mother and sister. On the ride back into the city, I asked him why he felt this compelling need to tell me these horrible facts about his family. 'Esther never will. You have a right to know.' he said. I guess he figured that now I would back out of my promise to marry your mother, and *he* could marry her. I told him that nothing on this earth could stop me from marrying her, and that it might be better if we never saw or heard from him again. Once he saw how determined I was, he agreed. To his credit, except on *Rosh Hashanah* when he would send us a New Year's card, he never called or tried to make contact with us, until a few weeks ago when he flew to Florida to visit

Mom.

"Do you have any regrets?" I ask.

"Because of you and Harry? Never. I'm grateful that we had so many wonderful years together as a family."

We resume walking. He moves slowly, each step an effort, as if everything inside him has temporarily shut down. Next week he will be seventy-five. He is developing a small cataract in his left eye and his right knee is slightly arthritic, but his heart, lungs, kidneys, are all perfect. He has never raised his hand or said a harsh word unjustly to either Harry or me in our entire lives. I thank God Sam Stone had married Mom and adopted me, and I pray he will live to be a hundred.

We sit *Shiva* for three days. There isn't room for all of us to sleep at Dad's condo, and Sandy and Alan stay at a nearby Holiday Inn. On one occasion while everyone is at the condo, Sandy asks me to drive her over to her motel to pick up a change of clothing. Once inside the motel room, I lock the door, and without a word we begin to grab at each other. In thirty minutes we climax twice.

The next day, while at the airport waiting for our plane to Newark, I sit between Sandy and Doris. The three teenagers sit opposite us. I envision myself as a sort of *Grand Patriarch* of the family, responsible for the lives of Doris, Naomi, Debbie, Sandy, Alan, Mitzi, even Harry's unborn baby. I confess, to my dishonor, that the idea has a singular appeal. In this broader context sleeping with both Sandy and Doris seems more than justified, almost as if it is my legal right. I will, of course, keep these thoughts to myself, but simply realizing who I am these days is enough to make me smile now and then for no particular reason.

CHAPTER ELEVEN

Stanley

We have recently installed a computer system in the office for record and billing purposes. Though our bookkeeper had quickly mastered the system, I sign up for a Tuesday night computer course at the New School in New York. Now Sandy and I will be able to spend at least one night a week together without my having to concoct for Doris some half-witted excuse for staying out late.

Being fifty-fifty to come down with a disease where the only cure is death, I consider a reasonable justification to live recklessly. As long as you don't abandon your responsibilities in the process, whom does it hurt? I am earning more than enough to provide for my family, and still be able to help out Sandy, Alan, and Mitzi, as well. I am even helping Harry and Mary Lou pay their rent at one of those seedy motel-apartments off Route one.

Last month Mary Lou called me at my office to borrow a few hundred dollars, promising to repay me as soon as she started her new job at a deli in Rahway. When I asked how she and Harry were doing, she said, "It hasn't been easy." She wasn't exactly complaining, but the next morning as I dropped a check in the mail, I wondered how long it would be before she left him.

This morning I made dinner reservations at a Polynesian restaurant that Sandy especially favors. After dinner we will be driving into the city to listen to Van Cliburn in an all-Mozart concert at Carnegie Hall.

I decide to call up Sandy to arrange to meet her at five instead of six, which will allow us time to go to a motel before dinner.

"Meet at five? Did you forget?" she says.

"Forget what?"

"You don't remember my telling you last week that I wouldn't be able to make it tonight." At that moment I should have realized that I had lost all control of my life. "The detective, Rog. I made a date with him tonight . . . Now you remember?"

"No, I do not," I say emphatically. I am not exactly lying. Granted that in the middle of a rather pleasant conversation she had for no particular reason begun to talk about this *very interesting* Westfield detective who had been invited to lecture to her class on drug and alcohol abuse. Without my asking she had described him as a Vietnam veteran with a little scar across his right eye, who spoke to the kids *right from the heart.* I suspect that I stopped listening to her after the 'little scar over the eye' part, and thus never heard her say that he had asked her out.

"He had a couple of free tickets for the New Jersey symphony," she says, then what is most disconcerting, adds, "I promised him."

"What about Van Cliburn?"

"Van Cliburn?"

"I bought the tickets a month ago. I might add that they were not handouts, that I paid for them with hard cash. Mozart. Van Cliburn. Can't you break the date?"

"I hardly know the man. It doesn't seem quite fair."

And she promised him! "Fair! Who cares about fair?" Have a heart, Sandy. Doesn't she realize that I put myself to sleep each night thinking about being with her on Tuesday evening?

"Please, Rog. You, yourself, told me that I should begin to go out with other men."

How could she have taken me seriously? We had been lying in bed, resting, our naked bodies still solidly butted up against each other, and in a moment of twisted kindness I had blurted out, "I want you to start seeing other men. You're a young woman. You've got your whole life to live. We both know that one day this has got to end between us."

My receptionist pokes her head inside the office door: I have two patients waiting, including Maria Rodriguez, my all-time crazy. Last week Maria had called to inform me that the melanoma on her arm, which, I had diagnosed as a freckle, had metastasized to her hip.

"Tell them to hold their horses," I snap at Charlotte, an even-tempered, resourceful woman, the heart and soul of our office for the past fifteen years. She storms out of the room in frustration, and to my discredit, I don't give a damn. Sandy has unbalanced me. I whisper frantically into the receiver, "Please!" When you begin to beg all is lost, yet I cannot help myself.

"He's really very nice, Rog," is her icy response. Does she realize how much she is making me suffer? When she adds, "I know you'll like him," I realize that she is serious about this Westfield cop. "Bad enough that you like him. Now I'm supposed to like him," I blurt out like a rejected adolescent.

But she is not listening to my agony. "Two years ago his wife died of breast cancer," she says. "He told me that I was the first woman he has asked out since the funeral."

Calm down, I lecture myself. This may all be nothing, a momentary uplifting of an ego that had been damaged by a wayward husband. What she is saying may have little real significance. "Does he have children?" I ask. Maybe five or six, I pray. Hopefully at least one has Downs Syndrome.

"A boy in his early teens, a girl of nine. He showed me their picture. The boy looks exactly like him."

This man whom supposedly she hardly knows has been showing pictures of his motherless children to her. What's next? "Yeah," I say. "He sounds like a terrific person. You're lucky to have found him. I wish you both a lot of happiness."

"My God, Rog, I'm only going to a concert with him."

"Today it's a concert. Tomorrow you're married and the mother of two depressed children. The next day this pillar of the law gets killed chasing a bank robber and you've got yourself a lifetime responsibility raising orphans."

"Nobody robs banks in Westfield. It's a very peaceful community."

"You never know. Bank robbers, muggers, car thieves. Don't you watch TV? Read the papers. Crime in the suburbs is as bad as in the cities."

"I won't marry him. I promise. I'll go to this concert with him and we'll just be friends. Okay?"

"Do you still love me, Sandy?" I ask out of desperation.

"I think about you all the time, Rog."

I am being conned. I can feel it all the way down to the corns on my big toes. "You sure you can't break this date?"

"I don't want to hurt Stanley's feelings. You can understand that, Rog."

The impersonal *he* has, without warning, turned into a first name. I have a strange feeling that I am losing more than my pants. "Does Stanley have a last name?" I might as well know it all.

"Applebaum."

Mrs. Stanley Applebaum. How do you damn up a river before there's a flood, and not let the river know you are doing it? "How come Stanley isn't taking you bowling? What's all this symphony *shit?*" My vocabulary is deteriorating in direct relationship to my sense of reason.

"He loves classical music." In love with a Jewish cop that likes classical music and has a scar above his eye, a wound he probably received while carrying a comrade two hundred yards across open terrain under deadly fire. *I am a goner.* "I have to get ready to go," she says. "I'll call you tomorrow."

"It's only three-thirty. The concert doesn't start for another five hours."

"He's taking me out to dinner."

She requires two hours to get ready to go out to eat? I imagine her lying in a bubble bath scented with lilac, scrubbing away all the messy, foul smelling infidelities of her recent past life with me. All that elegance and sensuality lost forever. *Cold steel in my gut.*

"I'll call you tomorrow, Rog. Stop worrying so much." Final obligatory words of consolation to a loser in the only race he will ever run for the rest of his life.

Maria Rodriguez points to her right hip. The pain is excruciating, she says. There is an elaborate bandage on her forearm covering her *melanoma.* Once again she insists that I send her for biopsy. I exam her hip. I tell her that in my opinion the *freckle* on her arm has not yet metastasized. I warn her that her next cancer is going to be her last as far as I'm concerned. She starts to cry, and I apologize so vociferously that she becomes frightened and begs me to calm down. Though I know it is pointless, I give her the telephone number of a phobia clinic in Millburn.

After Maria leaves, I phone Doris and tell her that I am cutting my New School class. Lionel Phillips, the detail man from Merck has given me two tickets to Carnegie Hall where Van Cliburn is performing an all-Mozart concert. Did she want to go? I am learning that cheating successfully on one's wife requires a scrupulous attention to details. It is as much science as art.

"What about the girl's swim practice?" she asks.

"Can't you get someone else to take them?"

"Who?"

"For Christ's sake, after all these years, didn't you ever set up a car pool?"

"You're giving me a very last minute notice, Roger. Why didn't you call me earlier?"

"I just got the tickets." A mistake. Suppose she checks and discovers that the Merck detail man always comes in the morning. I begin to think of ways to cover up the lie.

"I promised to take the girls to *Larry's* for dinner after practice."

"But it's *Van Cliburn.*"

"I hate driving into the city. All that traffic and noise. Let's do it another night. I'm really not in the mood. I'll leave you a nice dinner in the microwave. See you later."

I redial Sandy, but hang up before the second ring. No need to be TKO'd twice in the same fight. I wonder what Stanley Applebaum looks like, aside from the scar over his eye. Probably a tall, good-looking guy with a great physique. I pinch the little roll of blubber occupying my middle. No more red meat, no more chocolate cake, no more slabs of Portuguese bread between patients.

I kick off my shoes and lay down on the floor and do fifty sit-ups. Tomorrow I'll do fifty-five and within a week work my way up to a hundred. I turn over to do pushups. After ten I collapse and fall on my face. I'll bet that Harry, more dead that alive, could do twenty. And Stanley Applebaum? He could probably do twenty, one-handed.

Fifteen minutes ago I was enjoying the prospect of an evening with Sandy, dinner, concert, making love. Now I am a maze of anxiety, more concerned about the little roll of fat around my waist than I am about my family. It is that lousy cop, Stanley Applebaum, who has put me on the floor where I am grunting and groaning like a wounded animal. Suddenly all I can think about is Sandy, bathing, then putting on her black lace panties and bra, combing her hair, fixing her face, making herself beautiful for Stanley, who probably has a shlong the size of a giant sausage.

I am alone, abandoned. Sandy has deserted me for another man; my wife prefers the company of our children to me. Right now the one person I would want to be with more than anyone else is my brother, Harry. Harry never paid much attention to me when we were kids, but whenever I was down, when nothing seemed to go my way, he would be the first to put an arm around my shoulder. "You and me, little brother," he'd say, "we were born special and don't ever forget it." And I'd believe him, and whatever was bothering me would just disappear as if he had waved it away with a magician's wand. Harry could do that for you. He had the knack.

CHAPTER TWELVE

Brothers

Doris and I are watching on the TV the replay of the rally earlier in the day in front of the Lincoln Memorial, where a quarter of a million people protest Ronald Reagan's cutbacks in social programs. Doris thinks we should have been there. What has happened to our sense of social justice? She reminds me of *The March On Washington* in 1963 and how we had listened to Rabbi Joachim Prinz, and the Reverend Martin Luther King, who according to Doris, will be remembered in future generations as *The Great Black Emancipator.*

"I'm into tax-free bonds now," I say. "You can't always be a dumb college kid." These days I frequently demean myself in Doris's eyes. This self-debasement started after Sandy had begun to go out with Stanley Applebaum about a month ago. I am hoping that Doris will eventually become so disgusted with me that she will kick me out of the house, and divorce me, so I would then be able to marry Sandy. I could, of course, simply confess to her my adultery, but I must regretfully admit that on that score I am somewhat lacking in courage. I am in a word, the *pussy,* which Harry has always claimed I was. In the long run such a course of action would be less cruel, and certainly more honest, but when it comes to honesty, I haven't been winning any gold medals this past year.

Doris reaches over my shoulder to answer the phone. "It's that woman," she says handing me the receiver. *That woman* has to be Mary Lou, a name she refuses to pronounce.

Mary Lou cries out: "Harry said he was going out

to buy a shotgun and shoot John."

"*Shoot John?*"

"Last week John came to the diner, drunker than usual. To avoid a scene in front of customers I went out into the parking lot with him."

"Did he hurt you?"

"He shoved me around a little. Two truckers saw him and did a little shoving of their own. I made a mistake telling Harry what happened."

"Where's Harry now?"

"I don't know. Once Harry's made up his mind about something, there's no stopping him."

Driving south on Route One toward Linden, I pass transient motels that advertise DAY RATES and IN-HOUSE MOVIES including the Royal Motel, one which Sandy and I have frequented on several occasions. We like the seedy joints, a preference that probably has something to do with the illicit nature of our relationship. I envy Stanley Applebaum. He can simply send his children off for the night to friends and perform all sorts of indecent, carnal acts with my *beloved* in the comfort of his home.

The apartment-motel, in which Harry and Mary Lou are living, looks, with its broken down fake brick facade, as if it is about to collapse from the next high wind that sweeps down the highway. The clerk, a beefy, middle-aged man with tattoos on his forearms, sits behind a bullet proof glass enclosure viewing a ten-inch black and white TV. He looks over the registration book. No one by the name of Harry Stone is registered. After going through the book together, we discover that Mr. and Mrs. W. Somerset Maughn are in Room 119.

Upon entering Room 119 I am greeted by Mary

Lou along with a pungent, ropy odor, a mixture of marijuana, stale beer and cigarettes. The window air conditioner is so weak and ineffective that it does little but recirculate the spoiled, offensive air.

"Thanks for coming," Mary Lou says. Her hair is wet and tangled as if she has just crawled out of a washing machine. She is wearing a loosely drawn terrycloth, and with a beer can in one hand, and a cigarette dangling from her lips, she is Ida Lupino in "High Sierra."

She shuts off the TV, and offers me the only chair in the room, a frayed leather easy chair that squeaks when you sit on it, like an old car with bad shocks. Mary Lou settles on the edge of the bed and crosses her legs, revealing plump white thighs and a little tuft of dark pubic hair, which, to my great relief, she quickly covers by bringing together the sides of her robe.

"He's been gone over an hour," she says. "I'm worried to death. Want a beer?"

"No thanks."

"How about a reefer?"

"I don't smoke."

"No vices. Good for you. When Harry gets high, I get high. It's become a way of life for us, which I'm not too happy about. But I always say, 'if you can't beat em, join em.'" She finishes off the can of beer and places the empty on the floor next to the bed. "How's Mitzi doing?" she asks.

"Why don't you call her and find out for yourself?"

"She hangs up on me. I wish I could let her know how sorry I am. Would you talk to her?"

"I could try, but you can't expect her to feel kindly toward you after what happened."

"I want you to know that sleeping with Harry was no spur of the moment decision. For weeks he had been pestering me. I said to myself, 'What in hell is Mitzi getting herself into with this man.' She's young, she's got her whole life to live. She sure as hell doesn't need him."

"Are you telling me that you slept with Harry for Mitzi's sake?"

"I know it was a hurtful thing to do to my own daughter, and I'm probably going to regret it for the rest of my life, but at the time I thought I was doing the right thing."

"What about your own life? Your marriage?"

"That's been dead for years. The only reason I stayed with that bum was because of Mitzi."

"Mitzi's finished with Harry. Your plan worked perfectly. So why hang around with Harry?"

"That's the craziest part. There's something really sad about your brother. I can't explain it. It's like he's carrying the whole world on his head and it's burying him. Once he was an important person, and now he can't even dress himself properly. I just can't walk out on him. I think maybe I even love him." She squashes her cigarette butt on the empty beer can at her feet and gives me a nice glimpse of cleavage before straightening up. "Please tell Harry's wife that I appreciate what she's done for Mitzi. She's some woman to take her in like that." Mary Lou is a better person than I had given her credit for, though she has this major personality flaw of picking the wrong men to love.

"What do you want me to do about Harry?" I ask.

"Not much, I guess. I really don't see how he can buy a shotgun at this hour of the night, unless he finds a pawnshop in Newark or Elizabeth. What do you think?"

"I don't have any opinions, Mary Lou." I really don't, other than I'm sorry I made this trip. I remind myself of Doris's admonitions about minding my own business. "So what exactly happened tonight?"

"We're watching TV, having a few beers, when Harry stands up and tells me that he has decided to shoot John. With Harry you never know if he's kidding or not. He just blurts out any damn thing that's on his mind, most of which makes no sense. Suddenly, he's dressed and has the car keys in his hand. 'Going to buy a shotgun,' he announces, and out he goes."

"Did he have money?" I ask.

"Took my last twenty."

"I don't believe you can buy a gun with twenty dollars. At least not one that shoots bullets. How's he been feeling lately?"

"He's got the shakes. I told him to cut down on the booze. That'll do it to you. Most of the time, he sits around and watches TV and rambles on without bothering to breathe between words."

"Does he try to write?"

"Last week he pulled out his typewriter, but gave it up after five minutes. He tried writing with a pencil but kept dropping the damn thing until he finally flung it across the room." She pulls out an opened pack of cigarettes from the bathrobe pocket, but can't find a match and tosses the cigarettes aside. "Talk to him. Harry will listen to you. Get him to stop drinking so much."

"What makes you think he'll listen to me?"

"Just the other day he said you were the only one in the world that he could really trust."

"Yeah, well, we're brothers, and brothers are supposed to look out for each other."

"Suppose he really does shoot John."

But, as it turns out, Harry is not in his shooting mode tonight. He comes stomping in carrying instead of a shotgun, a six pack and an Italian rye. I hardly recognize him. His face is drawn, almost skeletal. His thick black hair has grown down to his shoulders. He hasn't shaven in a week. He wears an old corduroy jacket, torn at both elbows where once there had been leather patches. His jeans have grease stains at the knees.

He looks at me and breaks into a huge smile, then drops the six pack and hugs me as if he hasn't seen me in years. Surprisingly, there is still power in his arms, though I can feel the bones of his rib cage as I hug him back.

"Mary Lou called me," I say to him. "She was worried you were going to buy a gun and shoot John Whalen."

Harry starts to laugh, but the laugh soon turns into a hacking cough so violent that he is forced to his knees. Mary Lou is quickly down beside him, smacking him on the back, holding him until the cough finally subsides. She helps him to the bed where he begins to breathe more normally.

"Are you okay?" I ask him.

His facial muscles begin to twitch on one side of his face. He throws an arm around Mary Lou and squeezes her. "F-f-feel great," he says.

"So you've decided not to shoot poor John after all," I say.

He makes a gun out of an index finger and thumb. "Bang, bang." Then he says, "*In the long run men hit only what they aim at'*. Th-Thoreau, Rog. My aim ain't so good these days. What would be the point in trying?" Mary Lou drops her head on one of his bony shoulders, just lets it lay there like a small sack of potatoes, a neat, little contented grin on her face. You have to be a little moved by the way that she seems to care about Harry.

Harry pulls out two cans of Bud from the carton

and pops them both open, handing me one and giving the other to Mary Lou. He reaches over and smacks one of my knees affectionately. "I'm really glad to see you, kid."

"Are you hungry?" I ask him. He looks as if he hasn't eaten in a week.

"Al-always hungry," he says. He reaches for the loaf of bread, and tears off a chunk, offering it to me.

"Always," Mary Lou agrees.

I remember Abe Epstein telling me that HD patients could burn up to six thousand calories a day, that it was possible for them to literally starve to death, though surrounded by food. "Why don't we go out for a while?" I suggest. Between the odor of cigarettes, marijuana and beer, I am ready to throw up. "I know a diner not far from here."

"We're being invited to dinner," Harry says to Mary Lou. "Get dressed, Babe."

Mary Lou declines. "You brothers should have a chance to be alone together." Without waiting to be asked a second time, she goes into the bathroom, and begins to draw herself a bath.

We take my car since Harry says his Mazda is having carburetor trouble. Soon as he finds a job, he's going to buy a new car, so why waste money fixing up the old one.

At the diner Harry orders two jumbo cheeseburgers and a double order of fries. I decide on the apple pie, having already sampled the cake two nights ago with Sandy, which had tasted like soggy cardboard soaked in chocolate syrup.

While we are waiting for the food, I ask Harry about the two ten-thousand dollar tax-free bonds that Sandy told me was missing from their bank vault.

"I've got them," he admits. "I'm saving them for Alan."

"Why not give them to him now? He's going to need the income when he goes to college."

"S-Sandy's liable to cash them in for herself."

"She wouldn't do that, Harry."

"I'll be dead, then it's all his." He jerks his hand to his ear, then scratches it, and once again I remember the HD patient I had observed at the hospital who transformed involuntary movements into seemingly social acts.

"Were you really thinking of buying a shotgun and shooting Whalen?" I ask.

"If not Whalen then myself," he says with a nasty grin. "What else is there to do? I've seen just about every old movie on TV."

"You can be helped," I say.

"Don't kid a kidder. Inside I'm dead already. Nothing works right--my arms, my legs, my brain." He reaches out and touches my arm. "What's happening to me, Rog?" He presses his fingers into my flesh until I can see their imprints. "Tell me, for Christ's sake. D-don't worry, nothing can spoil my appetite."

"You can live another fifteen, twenty years, Harry. It'll get worse, but very slowly. Medicine can help the shaking."

"And my head? I wake up mornings and can't remember going to sleep. You hear the way I talk."

"You've got Huntington's Disease."

He actually seems to be relieved that I've given what ails him a name. He lifts his hand from my arm, and says jocularly, "Sounds contagious."

"Not contagious. Genetic."

When I tell him about Israel Horowitz, he has no visible reaction at all, just sits and stares at me as if I were telling him that it was going to rain tomorrow.

"A-again," he finally says. "Tell it to me again so I can understand what you're saying."

I give him details, explain to him where Israel came from, his profession, how he met Mom, how he was arrested and hung himself in prison. I tell him about our uncle in Bayshore, our aunt, our cousins, our grandparents, all buried in that overcrowded cemetery in Queens near the U.S.Open Tennis center. When I am finished, he still shows no perceptible signs of emotion, until he begins to shake his head. The muscles under his eyes begin to twitch uncontrollably. I reach out to him, but he doesn't seem to feel my touch upon his arm. At last he sits up, settles back in his chair and raises a middle finger. "So be it," he says calmly. *"If I chance to talk a little wild, forgive me;/ I had it from my father./"* He grimaces. "Harry Horowitz. A rather nice alliteration, don't you think?" Another silence. He grows pensive, then he says, "Funny thing. But sometimes for no reason at all I'll have this daydream. I see a coffin being lowered into the ground. Mom is standing next to me crying. I want to make her stop, but I don't know what to say to her."

"Am I in this dream?"

"Just me and Mom."

"Israel Horowitz's funeral, Harry. You were a toddler. I wasn't even born. You could have remembered."

"I press up against her and she pats me on top of the head. Then I start to cry. But I don't know why I'm crying."

The waitress brings the food. Harry pours huge globs of ketchup inside the bun of one of the giant cheeseburgers, then presses down on the sandwich with the heel of his hand, the ketchup squirting out from all sides. He tears into the sandwich savagely, the ketchup drooling out of the corners of his mouth and rolling down his chin, making it look as if he has a gaping knife wound. I toss my napkin at him, but he ignores it and continues eating.

After he finishes the sandwich, he drinks a glass of water, then sits back and stares at me with a sharp, almost schizoid look. "Who's fucking Sandy these days?" he asks.

"I wouldn't know."

"How about the gym teacher?"

"There never was a gym teacher, Harry. You imagined him."

Harry devours a handful of fries. "N-not bad if you're into soggy pieces of shit." He pours the remaining half of the bottle of ketchup onto the rest of the fries, then shimmies one out of the dark red pool with his fingertips, and slowly slurps it down.

"So you think I imagined the gym teacher," he says.

"It's part of the disease."

"You're telling me that this disease is making me crazy?"

"Yes."

"H-how crazy?"

"I don't know. How crazy are you, Harry?"

"How would a crazy man know how crazy he is? If I knew that I wouldn't be crazy."

"You're pretty crazy. And you've got no manners." I reach across the table and try to wipe his face with the unused napkin in front of him, but he brushes me off and somehow manages to do it himself.

"Y-y-you know I never really wanted to hurt Sandy," he says. "I was doing her a favor running out on her. Sooner or later she would have left me."

"She never would have left you, Harry."

"You're wrong. Mitzi had nine orgasms a day listening to all my dumb stories, the same ones that made Sandy want to run to the bathroom and puke.

She was tired of me, Rog. It took her twenty two years to discover what a phony I am."

When Harry talks about Sandy, I cannot look him in the eye. I make several decisions. I will love her for both of us. I will never be jealous of Harry, though I will always envy him all those good years he had with Sandy.

"What about Mary Lou?" I ask.

"N-not a bad woman to have around when you've got a disease that's so boring that you can't remember what it's called." Again he grins that awful grimace that seems to mock you. "How does it work, this disease? W-why do I feel like I'm a piston inside a smoking engine?"

"It destroys the cells in your brain that act like brakes to your muscle movements."

"You said you can give me medicine."

"Yes."

"How much do you take? How long does it work?"

"I don't know."

"The boy says he doesn't know. Will I ever be able to teach again?"

"I doubt it."

"I-I shouldn't have bothered asking. How can you teach when you not only can't remember the names of your students, but even what you had prepared that day to teach? The kids were beginning to think I was some sort of freak."

"You're not going to get any better. There are no cures, but you can still live a long time."

"What a blessing. Hun-Huney's Disease? Who was Hunney?"

"George Huntington. In 1872 he published a paper, *On Chorea.*"

"On Ch-chorea. Sounds like a college football song. Cheer, cheer for old Chorea. Good old

George. When is it your turn, Roger?"

"It's fifty-fifty, Harry."

"Fifty-fifty. Like shooting crap. Don't worry, kiddo, I've got the fifty part for both of us." He stares at me and you could feel the muscles just beneath his skin contract around the bones of his skull. "I'm glad it's me and not you, little brother." He means it. If we were on a sinking ship, and there was only one life preserver, Harry would strap it around my waist and throw me into the sea.

Two customers at the counter are gaping at him. "Mind your own business," I say to the closest one, a burly fellow dressed in overalls and a sweatshirt. He looks at both of us, shrugs and goes back to his steak.

"You're the crazy one," Harry whispers.

"I can always count on you protecting me," I say.

He starts on the next cheeseburger. After he polishes that one off, he continues munching the fries. "W-w-we don't tell anybody about my little problem," he says. "Make up some fairy tale for Alan and Sandy."

"I was thinking about Multiple Sclerosis. The symptoms are actually quite different. But nobody will realize it."

"M-m-multiple Sclerosis sounds a lot more interesting than Hunney's Disease."

"How long are you going to live in that crummy motel?"

"We're looking for an apartment."

"Find yourself a decent place. I can help you with the security deposit and the rent."

"Alan's fifty-fifty, too, isn't he?"

I wondered how long it would take him to realize that awful truth. "One day they'll come up with a cure. If Alan ever gets it, he'll probably be able to take a pill every morning and be perfectly normal."

"Y-y-you're not making it up?"

"I'm giving you a money back guarantee," I say without hesitation.

He slumps back against the chair and seems to unwind--first, a slow, settling of his facial muscles, then, his whole body, until he appears to be not much more than a collapsed skeleton.

"Let's get out of here," he says. "Unless you want to watch me eat another double cheeseburger."

"Yeah, that was great fun."

Outside the diner, while walking to my car, Harry begins to lurch crazily, a lilting, off balance gait, his arms flailing about. I grab hold of his arm, try to steady him, but he unexpectedly brushes me off and straightens up like a marine sergeant on parade. He begins to whistle the Colonel Bogey March, and with the same determination as Alec Guinness in "Bridge Over the River Kwai," staggers like a drunken tin soldier toward the car.

CHAPTER THIRTEEN

The Briss

While in labor, Mitzi's blood pressure elevates to dangerous levels, and a Caesarean is decided upon rather than risk a stroke. The surgery goes well, and the baby is born unblemished and in perfect health: eight pounds, seven ounces, Mitzi's blue eyes, Harry's black hair. However, the day following surgery, Mitzi runs a temperature, and there is concern about pneumonia.

Sandy stays at the hospital sixteen hours a day, caring for Mitzi, bottle feeding the baby. I offer to pay for special duty nurses, but Sandy refuses.

"I want to," she says to me when I ask her why she is doing this. "It's for Harry."

Harry? Some bizarre identification as the mother of Harry's baby? Alone in bed at night, would it always be Harry she longs for, no matter that she is sleeping with Harry's brother?

After three days, Mitzi's fever drops to normal, and she begins to breast feed the baby. She has decided to name him Herschel Mordecai Stone, the second. When I point out to her that it isn't in the Jewish tradition to name a son after his living father, she replies, "Wrong. That's the *Ashkenazai* tradition. However, Sephardic Jews do. We are simply up-holding Sephardic tradition. We'll do the naming at the *Briss*."

"You cannot have a *Briss*," I say. "Jewish law will not sanction it. The baby was born out of wedlock, and you are not Jewish."

"Wrong again. His father is Jewish, and I'm in the process of converting. As far as Heshey being born out of wedlock, we are no longer living in the Dark Ages."

"You are converting to Judaism?"

"I wanted Orthodox, but it didn't work out. I mean I don't mind keeping a *kosher* home and everything, but going to the synagogue to take a bath after having my period is a bit too much."

"What are you talking about?"

"*Mikvah*, Unc. Seven days after you have your period, you've got to cleanse yourself by taking a special bath."

"*Mikvah*?"

"I fired my orthodox *reb* and found a nice reformed one. He gave me the name of a *mohel*. I was hoping you'd call him and make the arrangements. Sandy said she'd be happy to have the *briss* at our house, and Alan said he'd make sure we had a *minion*."

A *mikvah*, a *mohel*, a *minion*. It's just a matter of time before Mitzi will be speaking perfect Hebrew and observing the Sabbath. Her father is a religious fanatic, so I suppose one might have predicted that Mitzi would become one, too. If you're religious, you're religious, whether you're a born-again Christian, or a converted Jew. In years to come, Mitzi would learn to make a good *seder,* and Herschel would go to Hebrew school and be *bar mitzvahed* when he turns thirteen.

On the eighth day after Herschel's birth, there is a *briss* just as Mitzi planned it. Sandy has arranged the catering, Alan has invited every Jewish friend he knows who has been *bar mitzvahed*, and I have hired the *mohel*, who, for the sum of two hundred and fifty dollars is happy to perform the ceremony for us. "It's the spirit of the law that counts," he says. "I admire your daughter-in-law." According to the *mohel*, Mitzi has now become my daughter-in-law, which makes Harry my son. Interesting that I don't bother to correct him.

It is more of a teen-age party than a religious ceremony. The house is crowded, not only with Alan's friends, but also Naomi's and Debbie's. Aside from Mitzi and the *mohel* the only adults present are Doris, Sandy, Stanley Applebaum, myself, and Harry and Mary Lou. Inviting Harry and Mary Lou was my idea. Surprisingly, Mitzi and Sandy offered no objections. Doris thought inviting Harry was in bad taste, but she was smart enough not to voice her objections too vociferously.

Before the ceremony begins, I observe Stanley Applebaum and Harry engaged in conversation, and worry that it will end in a shouting match, or even a brawl. Stanley Applebaum turns out to be not the big, brawny, tough-looking cop which I had imagined him to be. He is, in fact, quite the opposite: a short, chunky man with straight brown hair parted down the middle, and a round, pleasant face that seems to have a perpetual smile planted on it. He is dressed in a tan gabardine suit, with a white silk tie and a large pearl tie clip, and shakes everyone's hands as if he is running for public office. Harry, on the other hand, is his usual dark and surly self. His thick, black hair is all tangled and wild. He needs a shave. A half-made tie sticks outside his frayed shirt collar like a hangman's noose. If they had met on the street, Stanley would have either greased Harry's palm with a quarter, or run him in as a vagrant.

My fears turn out to be baseless, for whatever passes between them appears friendly enough. They even shake hands before Stanley sidles his way through the crowded room to find his *beloved* Sandy.

Later Stanley and I are standing in the dining room serving ourselves fruit punch while waiting for the *mohel*, who is in the baby's room inspecting Herschel's penis. Stanley must have thought that I was the *mohel* since he asks me if I was reformed or conservative.

"I'm a conservative," I say, "but I voted for Jimmy Carter."

Stanley raises an eyebrow, but laughs good-naturedly. Then he whispers confidentially, while wagging a finger in Harry's direction. "Who exactly is that fellow?"

"He didn't identify himself?"

"He claimed he had a diaper service and was looking for a new account. He's a bit of a strange duck."

"That's the father."

"Harry? I thought he was an English professor." Stanley is plainly confounded, but quickly recovers his poise. He then asks me, "Who is the woman with him? She looks half-drunk."

Looking over at Mary Lou and Harry, it's hard to figure which one is holding up the other. "That's the grandmother."

Stanley is confused, but he politely nods, then leaves me to shake someone else's hand.

Before the service begins the *mohel* tells us that the circumcision will be accomplished in a matter of seconds and the baby will feel no pain. If Herschel had a say in the matter, I have a feeling he might voice a different view and vote to postpone this snipping off of the foreskin of his penis for another day. But as it turns out, he is a good patient, crying only briefly when his arms are strapped down, which I suppose is a necessary precaution to prevent the baby from thrashing about during this *innocuous* surgical procedure. I am reminded of those old civil war movies in which the gallant wounded soldier is held down by his comrades while the army surgeon amputates his leg without anesthesia to save his life against the complications of gangrene. A young man standing next to me cups his privates during the cutting part, something I felt like doing myself.

After Herschel is named, I join Doris and Sandy at the serving table, and pour myself a glass of red wine. The women seem oblivious to what they have just witnessed and I would like to ask them how they might feel if Herschel had been a female and tissue was being resected around her nipples.

"What's the matter with Harry?" asks Doris. "I could hardly recognize him when I first saw him. And why does he keep smiling like a clown?" Then, as she is prone to do, she answers her own question before I have a chance to respond. "It's his conscience," she says. "It's eating him up alive."

"Why don't you shut up?" I say to her.

Doris reels as if someone has thrown a chocolate cake in her face. I am immediately sorry that I have insulted her publicly, something I have never done in twenty years of marriage, but I don't feel like apologizing. Doris turns beet red, then without a word, executes a perfect one hundred and eighty-degree pirouette and bulldozes through a group of young people toward Naomi, the closest friendly face. Later, in the privacy of our home, I will hear it from her. But I'm not too worried. She will be reduced to tears when I inform her that Harry has Multiple Sclerosis.

Managing Sandy is more complex. You cannot lie to your mistress the way you lie to your wife. When Sandy asks me why I am being so rotten to Doris, I reply that "I felt like it," which is not exactly a false-hood, unless you consider telling half-truths to be just as immoral.

"It's supposed to be a happy occasion," she reminds me.

"Then why did you invite *him*?" I make a hitchhiker's motion with my thumb toward Stanley Applebaum.

"He asked if he could come. Mitzi likes Stanley."

"Who's paying for all of this?"

"This isn't like you, Roger."

I am antagonizing the two women I care most about, a disastrous course for a man trying to live a double life with those very same women. Realizing it doesn't seem to help.

"I'll call you tomorrow," she says, then brushes up against me, and with the back of her hand touches my fly for a split second, which has the immediate effect of turning me into a normal person.

I make my way across the crowded room to be with Alan and Mitzi. Mitzi, still recovering from the Caesarian, is the only one in the room sitting, unless you count Herschel, who is cradled in her arms. She is rocking him, trying to lull him into sleep, perhaps in her motherly way trying to get him to forget about this unexpected insult to his young manhood.

"What's up, Unc?" asks Mitzi. She is more cheerful and radiant than I have ever seen her before. It would appear that the *Briss* has given her an official *entrée* into our family, which she is clearly enjoying.

I reach down for the eight-day old infant. "Can I hold him for a second?"

Herschel is *a Harry baby picture*, beautiful, round cheeks, unclouded eyes, perfectly clear skin, unmarred by the usual birth trauma because of the Caesarian birth. "I'm your faithful loving, Uncle Rog," I say. I tickle him under his chin. "Gootchy, gootchy, goo." As I rock him, I cannot help but reflect that we may be bound by the same genetic flaw, that little Herschel is also *fifty-fifty*.

After I return Herschel to Mitzi, I spot Harry standing in the corner by himself, alone and dejected, and go to him.

"Why don't you hold the baby?" I ask him.

"I'm afraid I'll drop him."

"It'll be okay. I'll help you."

"M-M-Mitzi might not like it." He tries unsuccessfully to loosen his tie. I reach over to help him, but he grabs my wrist with a remarkably strong grip. He quickly lets me go, and without a word I remove his tie for him, and stash it in his suitcoat pocket. "I-I-I shouldn't have come," he says.

"You're the father."

"I'm no one's father any more." He takes my arm and leads me to the outside door. "Let's take a walk," he says.

His gait has become noticeably more awkward, Once on the sidewalk, he wants to walk without my help and lets go of me. But he stumbles over a crack in the sidewalk and almost falls. This time I grab his arm, guiding him as I would a blind man.

"*To Be or Not to Be?*" he says. "Not to be, methinks."

I remember the despondent, wretched expression on Joseph Horowitz's face during his recounting of how his father, my grandfather, had taken a walk into the forest, and blown out his brains--the act, so traumatic that my grandmother had refused to leave the house for the next two years. How Israel, our father, had bequeathed to my mother a lifetime vision of a man, his neck broken, swinging from the rafters of a dark, lonely cell. I can hear Uncle Joseph's voice as if he is standing next to me: *Please God, no more suicides,*

"It's the disease, Harry," I say. "It can make you confused. I can give you pills that'll help you to feel better."

"I'm a freak, Rog. D-D-Didn't you notice everybody in there staring at me?" He takes his hands out of his pocket to demonstrate the involuntary jerking movements that he can only partially control by pressing his hands together until his skin blanches. "One day I won't even know who I am. Then it'll be too late. I'll live on for years, a F-F-Fellini monstrosity to be mocked and jeered. While I'm still able and have the will, I've got to end this." Then he asks me the question I most dreaded hearing. "Will you help me, little brother?

I answer without hesitation, "I'm a doctor, Harry. I took a sacred oath to preserve life, not to destroy it." I do not tell him the bigger truth--*I don't have the guts to help him kill himself.*

"I hallucinate, Rog. I see myself sinking into q-q-quicksand. The other day I almost choked to death eating a beet. It's only going to get worse. My life is over, Rog. I know it. You know it."

We have wandered into a small park in the center of town. Small children are throwing bread to ducks in the pond. We stand under an enormous elm that casts a long shadow over the lake. I have a childhood memory of walking along the lake in Weequahic Park watching Harry whip rocks across the water, our mother behind us, sitting on a bench, speaking with other mothers. I ask Harry to show me how to throw a rock the way he does, so it'll skim halfway across the water's surface. We search for flat stones. He doesn't let me give up, until I finally throw a good one.

Harry stares into the water as he speaks. "The w-w-ways to kill oneself: jump off the roof of a five-story building, lock yourself in a garage and turn on the car motor, hang yourself, slash the veins in your wrist, swallow a bottle of sleeping pills, step in front of a train like Anna Kerenina. The b-b-best would be to shoot yourself. Quick, clean, with your own hand. What do you say, Rog? Get me a gun. I'll do the rest."

"Get your own gun, Harry."

"I left out walking into the sea like Virginia Woolf."

"The lake's in front of you. Start walking."

"It's a low choice. I-I-I'd rather blow out my brains."

Two boys stand twenty feet from us and stare at Harry. "Go away," I tell them brusquely, and they run back to the water's edge.

"Kids will stare at a freak, Rog. You can't get mad at them for it." Harry takes his hands out of his pockets and clamps them between his knees. "Why does Sandy sleep with a man who parts his hair down the middle?"

"How do you know she sleeps with him?"

"He looks like he belongs in a Barber Shop Quartet. What's his name?"

"Stanley Applebaum."

"H-h-how does Alan feel about Apples?"

"I don't know."

"Alan is ashamed to look at me. Have you told him anything?"

"Not yet."

"Tell him about that other disease I'm supposed to have. Maybe then he'll talk to me."

"How do you think he'll feel if you kill yourself?"

"Y-Y-You'll explain it to him." He puts a hand on my shoulder. "Suppose it was the other way around, Rog. Suppose you were the fifty percent. What would you do?"

"I don't think about it."

I lie. I'm so scared that sometimes I'm even afraid to fall asleep. Day dreams are bad enough, but one night I dreamt that I saw my father lying in a coffin, his face contorted, his eyes bulging out of their sockets, his tongue hanging lifelessly out of his mouth. When I awakened, I realized that it wasn't my father, but myself.

"Now it's my turn," I say. "Would you help me kill myself?"

"'Doomed to death, but fated not to die.'"

"Answer my question." He stares at me. Beneath the grimace he manages a smile, then grabs my hand as I help him to his feet. "In a million years you wouldn't do it," I say.

"I might."

"You're full of baloney."

Arm in arm, we start back to the house. We are brothers, comrades who share a common grief, and we walk like wounded soldiers finding our way back from the trenches.

CHAPTER FOURTEEN

Alan Fiddles Away

Two weeks after the *briss*, I inform the family that Harry has Multiple Sclerosis. We are having dinner at Sandy's house. Present at the table are Doris, Naomi, Debbie, Sandy, Alan, and Mitzi. Herschel is sleeping in a portable crib in the living room. On hearing the news Sandy covers her face with her hands. The rest of the family, with the exception of Doris whom I have already told, appear numbed by my disclosure, and I wonder how they could not have suspected that there was something seriously the matter with Harry, given the way he had been lurching about at the *briss*.

"Can't you make him better?" my daughter Debbie, the eternal optimist, asks.

"No, but he could live for years and not get much worse," I say. Debbie shrugs. Not much of an answer from a man, whom she has always believed could cure all the ills of mankind.

"He's skin and bones," Alan says. "And the way he stutters."

"What about Herschel?" Mitzi asks me in all innocence. "Will he get it some day?"

All eyes rivet on me. I am quick to respond: "It doesn't run in families. Herschel will be just fine." I don't know if I've convinced anyone. "Hey, look, I'm fine. And so is Alan. So stop worrying."

"When did you find out?" Alan asks.

"I've known for a while. I just wanted to be sure before I told you."

"Maybe that's why he left us," he says.

"Could be?" I look toward Sandy and wonder how she will react on the day I tell her the bigger truth about Harry.

"Why don't we eat our dessert?" I say. "Then watch the football game." But the chocolate cake and apple pie go untouched. When we separate, we are a downhearted, miserable bunch.

Two weeks later Sandy marches angrily into my office just as I am about to leave for the hospital.

"I'll come straight to the point," she says. "You won't believe what's going on." In a hoarse whisper she says, "Mitzi and Alan have been sleeping together." Before I could begin to frame a response, she departs from the whisper and blurts out, "Don't you dare say, 'like father, like son.'"

"How do you know?" I ask judiciously. "I'm sure they didn't tell you."

"Empty condom packages all over the place. You can just see it--the way they slobber over each other."

"I hadn't noticed." Actually I had, but, simpleton that I am, I thought they were just being affectionate in a brotherly-sisterly way.

"And here's the worst--Alan is talking about going to Rutgers instead of Harvard."

"Why?"

"I don't know why," she says angrily, then immediately calms herself and continues, "I try to talk to him and he puts me off. 'Later.' 'I'm too busy.' 'Why can't it wait? ' 'Why do you always have to bother me?' You've got to talk to him, Roger." She is now more frustrated than angry, a concerned mother seeing her son's life going down the tube.

"Maybe he just wants to be near Mitzi."

"Is he going to wreck his entire life because he has found out about sex?"

"That can do it for you," slips out of my foul mouth.

Once again she's in a rage. "I could kill that girl. I'm throwing her out of the house *tonight.*"

"You're being irrational."

"Irrational? What's irrational about your house being turned into a brothel behind your back. I feel betrayed, Roger."

"If you throw Mitzi out of the house, what will happen to Herschel? Where are they supposed to live? With Harry and Mary Lou? Or perhaps with her father, the *Great Avenger?* Don't do anything you might regret."

"I've been so desperate that I've been tempted to talk to Harry. Maybe he'd knock some sense into Alan."

"Harry?" The old Harry, right. The Harry you see sitting in your living room, Sandy, has a problem trying to remember to flush the toilet. How she could have supposed that Harry could possibly help her? What is it about my brother, that even half-dead and seriously deranged is still able to arouse such powerful sentiments? "I'll speak to Alan, I promise. But you must promise not to say or do anything rash."

"All right, I won't throw her out tonight. But I'm not making any promises about tomorrow. How could she do this to me?"

"I wouldn't take it personally. And it won't last. They wanted to be found out. Otherwise why would they leave empty condom packages lying around?"

"Actually there was only one," she says sheepishly.

"One!"

"I found it in the waste paper basket."

"You check the garbage?"

"It was quite by accident, I assure you," she is quick to reply.

"Alan has probably been carrying around that

condom in his wallet for months, and finally decided to throw it away."

"Why would Alan carry a condom in his wallet?"

"In college I carried one around for four years before I used it."

"On whom," she demands to know, with a sly, little grin.

"*That* is none of your business."

"Doris is the only woman you've ever slept with, Roger. So don't give me any of your bull." Interesting that she says *only woman you've ever slept with*, as if what *we* have been doing together this past year were imagined, illusory acts.

She is right, however, about my sexual history. Doris is the only *other* woman I have ever slept with. The first time it happened between Doris and I, we were in my dormitory room studying together, and began to fool around. In a rare moment of passion we undressed each other. I reached into my wallet and pulled out a condom that I had been carrying around for years. Unfortunately, when I tried to use it, it shredded like wet tissue paper, but we did it anyway. When Doris realized that she could become pregnant, she called me a *selfish rat* and refused to speak to me until she had her period. So she managed to ruin what was, on reflection, probably the only instance of absolutely uninhibited sexual behavior between us in the entire twenty-two years we have known each other.

"You must convince Alan to go to Harvard, Roger," Sandy says. "I don't care if I've got to work three jobs." She pulls out a Kleenex and begins to wipe away tears that have begun to flow for nothing. "I'm sorry," she says. "Lately, I've been dreaming about Harry. It's put me a bit on edge."

Bad enough I have to deal with Stanley Applebaum, now there's her dreams about Harry.

She blows her nose. "Last week. I tried to talk to him. He stared at me and gave me that strange smile of his, but he said nothing, as if I had never existed for him. What's in his heart, Rog? Does he have any feelings at all for me? Why won't he at least talk to me?"

"He's very sick, Sandy. Maybe he's embarrassed that you see him this way."

"Please don't bring him around any more."

"Mitzi asked me. Since the *briss* she's got this idea about everybody loving each other." Mitzi *loving* the world does not bode well with Sandy, who presses her teeth against her lower lip.

Sandy stands up. "I'd better get going. You'll talk to Alan, then."

"I promise."

I accompany her back through the office and into the parking lot. "I'll see you tomorrow," I say, as she opens her car door.

"Tomorrow? Didn't I tell you that I won't be able to make it?"

Every Tuesday, Sandy, it's automatic, I'm about to remind her, when she says, "I have to attend a PTA meeting." Perhaps she has noted my stricken look. "It's my job," she is quick to add.

"Can't we make it later, after your meeting?" How that woman can make me beg.

"I'll call you and we'll arrange something," she says to my enormous relief.

She drives off and I walk slowly over to my car. As I start the engine, I am stuck with this feeling that I am a man walking a tightrope a hundred feet above a pit of rattlesnakes. How nice it would be if I never had to lie anymore, to become once again, old, dependable Rog. I likened my need for Sandy to being addicted to heroin. There's no cure but death, or cold turkey, and you could die of that, too.

Alan's room is almost Spartan in appearance: a single bed without a headboard, a bureau, a music stand, a violin case, a bookcase, an old mahogany desk and chair. The floor is bare except for an inexpensive throw rug. No clutter, no socks or shoes lying around. The bookcase is neatly packed with textbooks, art books, a few novels, biographies of famous musicians. On the desk is an Apple computer and an Epson dot matrix printer. Instead of rock musicians and movie stars that blanket the walls of my girls' rooms, there is a small unframed picture of Jascha Heifitz thumbtacked over the desk. Alan's only concession to youth is a large photograph of Elvis Presley hanging on the wall above his bed.

Alan offers me the one chair in the room, then stretches out on his bed. In the past we have always managed to get along amicably as uncle and nephew, but in the roles of father and son, we are both a little uncomfortable.

"You want to talk about Rutgers?" he asks, wading right in. His tone, while not exactly belligerent, is hardly condescending.

"How many high school graduates from New Jersey this year were admitted to Harvard?" I ask.

"I don't know, and I don't care."

"You study your butt off for four years, so that you can go to Harvard, and now you don't care. Would you be so kind as to explain that to me?"

"What difference does it make?"

"How would you feel if you were asked to play second violin in the orchestra, and other players, lesser talented ones, who never practiced a tenth as hard as you have all your life, played first."

"That's not the same thing."

"You're the concert master. It's where you belong because you've earned it."

"I've got my reasons why I don't want to go to Harvard."

"Your mother doesn't think they're very good."

"She has no idea what's going on in my life."

"She knows more than you think."

"How could she know anything? She's always with *Smiling Stanley.*"

Thank you, Alan, for the rabbit punch. I struggle to regain my poise, to remember my mission. "Your mother came to my office yesterday. She was pretty upset." He seems to be attentive, but with teens you can never be sure. They have this knack of hearing only what they wish to hear. "You've got to give me something to tell her, some intelligent reason why you would prefer to go to Rutgers instead of Harvard."

He sits up at the edge of the bed. "I want to be near Dad," he says.

Dad? What happened to Mitzi, to sex? "But you never talk to him."

"I haven't told anybody, but I've been driving over to his apartment a couple of times a week to see him."

"In Rahway?" There can be no more surprises left for me today. "What do you talk about?" I ask rather stupidly.

He shrugs. "Not much." That I believe. Lately, Harry has become extremely reticent, and when he does speak, he is difficult to understand. "He asks me the same questions over and over. You know, stuff about school, if I've got any girl friends, questions about Mom. I don't think he listens very much to what I'm saying. But I know he likes to have me over.

Sometimes we just sit around and drink a beer, or smoke a joint, and don't talk at all."

Drink a beer? Smoke a joint? Now that's one for the imagination--Harry and Alan lounging in Harry's three room hovel, getting high, the air choking with that ropy, chemical smell from a burning reefer; Alan wondering how long his father will live; Harry praying that his limbs don't start flailing about; a father and son sharing final moments together, a rare communion of blood and love.

"Did you tell him about not going to Harvard?"

"I did. You know what he said to me? I quote: '*A foolish son is the calamity of his father.*' The man can hardly put five words together to make a decent sentence, but he can still quote you from the bible or Shakespeare."

"You know that he wants you to go to Harvard."

"I've made up my mind. I'm not leaving him now."

"Your mother thinks that the one you don't want to leave is Mitzi."

His demeanor, dead serious up to now, unexpectedly brightens. "That's wild," he says. He actually cracks a smile.

"She thinks that you're sleeping with her."

I wait for a profusion of denials, but he maintains a stony silence. Finally he says, "That's none of her business." What a marvelous kid. How could you not love him? No beating around the bush, no phony disavowals, no apologies. "Mitzi has nothing to do with Rutgers," he says. "And Harvard will still be in Cambridge after Dad dies."

"But he could live for years. When you're thirty it's going to be a little late to be an Ivy Leaguer."

"I don't believe you, Uncle Rog. I don't think he can live much longer."

Alan is too smart to be tricked for long. Soon I

will have to tell him the truth. When informed that he has a fifty-fifty chance of developing HD, how will he react? Probably better than I have. There is something tough about Alan, something spiritual. You always have to remember that he is Harry's son.

"After a year or two, I could transfer," he says.

"Your mother may not see it that way," I warn him.

"Talk to her. She'll listen to you."

"She might be uncompromising, make things difficult for you."

"Then I won't go to college at all," he says defiantly. "Mitzi and I will find an apartment and we'll both go to work."

"Sure. You could always deliver pizzas."

"We could move in with Dad and Mary Lou." He is dead serious. So much for believing that Alan has intelligence beyond his years. "Dad can watch the baby. It'll be something for him to do."

Picture that one friends: the five of them crawling all over that tiny three-room apartment like a den of snakes: Harry changing Herschel's diaper; Mitzi dragging the wash in from the laundromat. And Mary Lou? Half-dressed, a reefer hanging from her lips as she watches *Jeopardy* on TV, while Alan fiddles away like Nero.

"Are you in love with Mitzi?" I feel obliged to ask.

"We've been messing around a little. It's no big deal."

No big deal! I'd like to see the expression on his face if I'd say to him, "Your mother and I have been messing around a little. Heck, it's no big deal." But then, who knows, maybe he wouldn't give a damn. He might even go out and *buy me* a packet of condoms. A couple of months ago Doris and I saw a revival of Death of a Salesman on TV. Biff, the oldest son, surprises his father, Willie, while he is with *another* woman in a hotel. The son becomes permanently traumatized by his father's fall from grace. If Arthur Miller wrote the same play today, he'd be laughed out of town.

"I'll tell your Mom that you denied sleeping with Mitzi, and that I believe you," I say. "But you've got to promise me that there'll be no more *messing around* in this house."

"Suppose Mom asks me herself? I'm not a very good liar."

"Start practicing. Look her straight in the eye and tell her you've got a girl friend and you didn't want her to wind up the way Mitzi did. Which accounts for the empty condom package she found."

"I don't have any girl friends."

"Make up one for chrissake. Someone your Mom couldn't possibly check out." It occurs to me that I ought to write a book on *How to Lie.* I could index a whole slew of lies for every possible lying situation. Just consider how children lie to parents, pupils to teachers, workers to bosses, clients to lawyers, lawyers to juries, *husbands to wives,* politicians to everyone. The book would be an instant best seller.

"You really think Dad could live a few more years?"

"Absolutely. Who knows? Tomorrow they could find a cure. Anything is possible."

Why am I leading him on? We are no closer to finding a cure for Huntington's Disease than we are to finding a way to end war. "What's it going to be?" I ask.

"I'll cool it with Mitzi. I promise."

"And school?"

"Rutgers this year. Next year I'll transfer to Harvard."

"If they'll take you."

"So I'll stay at Rutgers. I can get into medical school just as easily from Rutgers as from Harvard."

"Medical school? When did you decide you wanted to be a doctor?"

"Since Dad became sick."

Another boy might have said that he wishes to emulate his uncle, embrace his profession. Alan is too honest. He is going to be a doctor because he wants to save his father. Dead or alive, in any competition with me, Harry always wins.

CHAPTER FIFTEEN

Tired of Livin'

For the past two weeks John Whalen has been stalking Mitzi. While Sandy was at work, and Alan in school, he'd park his car on the opposite side of the street, and stare at the house until Mitzi would call me, then I'd call the police. In each instance (there were four altogether), Whalen would drive off when he saw the police coming. Today, after the most recent occurrence, I call Bob Handleman, my lawyer.

"The police cannot presume that a man sitting in a parked car is about to commit a criminal action," Bob says in his usual, detached, highly professional manner. "You've got to obtain a *Restraining Order* against him before the law can take an appropriate action, which means that Mitzi will have to appear before a judge in a Domestic Court."

"I'll have Sandy file the papers right away."

"Good. There could be a problem, however, if he decides to contest the order. He's a father and a grandfather, and the court may feel that he has some rights of his own."

I give him a quick history of John Whalen's abusive nature.

"Can you prove any of it? Has either his daughter or his wife ever filed a complaint against him in the past? It's his word against theirs. He could retaliate, file a complaint of his own demanding to see his grandson."

"What happens then?"

"Possibly an expensive court fight."

"Maybe he'll get run over by a bulldozer."

"That would be your best bet." Not even a

chuckle. The guy is a robot.

After office hours, I call Whalen at his home. The phone rings at least a dozen times before he picks up.

"Whoz ziss?" Whalen asks.

He sounds half-drunk, and I have a tough time identifying myself. Once he realizes who I am, however, he becomes aggressive, and blurts into the phone, "You tell your fuckin' brother that one day I'm gonna fuckin' kill him."

Nothing like talking to a belligerent sot. If I shout and curse at him, he will simply hang up on me, and I'll have contributed ten cents to Ma Bell stockholders for nothing.

"What about Mitzi? Do you want to kill her, too?" I ask.

"I'm gonna tear that bastard apart with my bare hands. You tell him that."

"I'm talking about Mitzi, you loathsome ape." A marginal insult by any standards under the circumstances.

"Mitzi?" There's a pause, then finally: "Why don' Mitzi wanna see me? I'm her father. She's got a liddle boy. Why don' she let me see him? Why she being so mean?" His voice has degenerated into an infantile whine. I think I liked him better when he was more combative.

"You've been going over to her house and frightening her. That isn't very nice, now is it?"

"I din' do nothin'" Once again he becomes contentious. "There ain't no fuckin' law 'bout sittin' in a car. I was minding my own fuckin' business."

Whalen obviously knows more about the law than I do. No need for him to call a Bob Handleman who bills you a hundred dollars a second and offers advice proposed mostly for his own amusement. "I thought you loved Mitzi," I say.

"I jus' wanna talk to her, see my gran'son. Hey, Buddy, you got a gran'son?"

"No, I don't." How have I suddenly found myself on the defensive with this moronic dipsomaniac?

"You gotta have a grandson, then you'd know what I was talkin' about."

"The next time you go near that house, the cops are going to arrest you."

"Cops! You think I'm scared of cops. I know lots of cops. Cops believe in God. God knows I'm right. The devil's in Mitzi's heart, not mine."

With God and the devil making a grand entrance into the conversation, I figure it's time to hang up. Anyway, by tomorrow he probably wouldn't remember a word of what we said. I am wasting my breath. John Whalen is a pathology that will not go away without radical surgery.

"I'll speak to Mitzi," I say in a final, desperate attempt to communicate with him. "She'll let you visit the baby if you promise to behave yourself. But there'll be conditions." I decide that for the moment the best course of action is a delaying one. Later I could try and work out a permanent solution on how to deal with John Whalen.

Whalen actually begins to cry. "I wanna see my liddle boy," he wails between sobs.

"Stop crying, you idiot, and listen to me," I shout into the phone.

"I wanna tell Mitzi how sorry I am for everythin'."

"The Devil's not in Mitzi's heart, John, he's in your heart. It's the devil that's driving God out of your heart. It's the Devil that's making you frighten your daughter. You don't want to hurt anybody, John, because then you'd be hurting God."

Whalen lapses into a long silence during which I can hear his rasping, drunken breathing. Hopefully,

I have nailed a stake into his *wicked soul.* I wait patiently for his parting words. "Talk to Mitzi," he says just as I'm about to hang up on him. "God will bless you for eternity."

"I'll call you in a few days. In the meantime you're not to go near the house. Do you understand?" When he doesn't answer, I shout into the phone. "You get me, John?"

"Yeah, yeah, I getcha."

I slam down the phone with an *Amen* hanging on my lips.

An hour later I'm at the hospital doing rounds when I'm paged on the staff intercom. It's Mary Lou Whalen. What now? I wonder. The Whalen family has become a permanent noose tied around my neck.

"About an hour ago, Harry sliced the veins in his left wrist," Mary Lou says. "I found him in the bathroom sitting on the toilet seat, bleeding, singing at the top of his lungs. I wrapped up the wrist and stopped the bleeding. A few minutes later he snuck out of the apartment." She is calmer than you'd expect. I guess when you live with someone like Harry long enough you either shoot yourself, or learn to philosophically ride through his ups and downs, which now includes self-mutilation.

"Do you know where he might have gone?" I ask.

"Probably over to the park. Three days ago the cops found him wading in the lake trying to feed the ducks. When they brought him home, they told me that the next time they find him wandering around they're going to take him over to Elizabeth General."

"I'm on my way."

*   *   *   *   *   *

The doorbell doesn't ring. I'm about to try another apartment when I realize that the downstairs lock is broken. In front of Harry's apartment, I knock on the door, wait a moment, then try the knob, remembering that Mary Lou usually doesn't lock the door since she told me that Harry has a problem fitting the key into the keyhole. It's amazing that the apartment has been ransacked only once, the thieves probably deciding that a second walk up and down the three flights of stairs would be more trouble than it was worth. They wound up stealing a half- smoked joint, two cans of Bud and a watered bottle of Vodka. They somehow missed Harry's air force binoculars, and didn't bother with the 12 inch black and white TV.

Mary Lou is sitting in the kitchen dressed in a white waitress's uniform listening to rock music and smoking a cigarette. She looks up and greets me, then says, "I can't take much more, Dr. Stone. I drove around looking for him until the car overheated. I don't even know how I'm going to get to work, and I've got to get back to the deli in twenty minutes. These days I'm working double shifts, and we're still barely able to pay the rent for this dump. He's your brother, Dr. Stone. I'm just along for laughs." For the past year she has always addressed me as "Roger." Why the formality? Is she preparing herself psychologically to walk out on Harry, and wishes to distance herself from me as well? "There's something else," she says. "Last week John showed up again. He didn't do anything, just sat in his car across the street for about half an hour, then drove off. Two days ago he came back. Harry keeps threatening to go after him with an iron pipe."

"Call the police."

"A lot good that's gonna do. I think I'll hit him over

the head myself."

Even Bob Handleman agreed that the best way to deal with John Whalen would be to run him over with a bulldozer. I wonder how old Bob would feel about Harry hitting him over the head with an iron pipe instead.

After dropping off Mary Lou at the Deli, I cruise up and down the side streets, then drive down St. George's Avenue until I come to Rahway Park. I circle half the lake, then park, and start to walk along the water's edge. The area is deserted except for a few after-work joggers and a group of teenagers, who are horsing around, smoking, drinking beer.

I locate Harry on a swing in the Children's Playground, soaring like a big bird, his legs extended, his arms outstretched, singing away: *". . .You and me, we sweats and strains/ Body all breakin' and racked with pain./ Tote 'dat barge./ Lift 'dat bale./ Ya gets a little drunk an' ya lands in jai-ul./"*

Not a trace of a stammer in his speech while he is singing. I make a mental note to call Abe Epstein and ask him what medical significance that might have.

Harry laughs when he sees me. "Hey, Rog," he says. "Out for a little stroll in the park?"

I sit on the swing next to him and extend my legs, kicking hard, gradually increasing the arc of the swing, until I am flying in tandem with him. Quietly at first, then at the top of my lungs, I warble along with Harry. *"But ole' man river, he jus' keeps rollin' a-long."* We are a little out of synch, but only the ducks are listening.

We try the see-saw. I have to slide up the seat to get a better balance between us, since, for the first time in our lives, Harry weighs less than I do. Bouncing up and down like children, we stare at each other, not exactly laughing, just making stupid, idiotic faces.

With a running start I get the merry-go-round going. Harry falls onto the dirt trying to jump on, and I have to stop it and help him up. I make sure he is holding onto the iron railing before I start again, whipping around wildly until I become a little dizzy.

"One more time, Rog," Harry says after I quit. "You can do it."

"I'm going to have a heart attack."

Harry shouts, "Hi yo Silver," as I exhaust myself pushing the merry-go-round to roll once again at a decent speed.

Sitting behind him, I notice a cut behind his right ear, the blood oozing down the side of his neck, which must have occurred when he fell. I wipe him clean with my handkerchief as I would a child. His sweater is torn at the elbows, probably from other falls. A portion of the bandage that Mary Lou had wrapped around his left wrist protrudes under the sweater.

He is reluctant to return to the car and go home. "I like it better out here," he says.

"The cops will arrest you, Harry. You'll wind up in the psycho ward at Elizabeth General."

"Where I belong."

We drive home without a word between us. There isn't much to be said that we haven't already said to each other in a lifetime of being brothers. On the FM the Jupiter Symphony is playing. When he switches to a rock station, I allow him to have his way, as always.

Once in his apartment Harry slides his binoculars from under the sofa and positions himself at the window. "Nothing much doing," he says as he scans the neighborhood below.

"Take a bath," I say to him. "But keep your wrist

out of the water."

"Wh-Where my wrist wishes to go, that's where it will go. Go home, Rog."

"I think I'll stay a while."

"Don't worry, I'm not killing myself any more to-day."

"What about tomorrow?"

"Tomorrow the Knicks are playing the Lakers. I might kill myself the day after tomorrow." He puts down the binoculars and turns. "Cutting my wrists was practice. To do it right, I'm going to need your help."

"I told you. I'm not in the suicide business." I try talking tough, but up against an older brother who has always been my boss, I have a hard time keeping a poker face. Still, I am determined to remain reso-lute in my refusal to help him. "I'm warning you, Harry," I say. "You're going to wind up in a straight jacket. They'll connect your brains to electrodes and zap you good."

"Who knows, zapping could turn out to be a new cure for Hunney's Disease." He grins, but you can't be sure if the facial expression is involuntary. After a moment, he says, "You heard about *Sir Lollipop* dangling his sweet presence around the apartment?"

"You mean John Whalen?"

"You know how he tried to beat up Mary Lou at the Deli, and that he's after Mitzi."

"I heard. We'll go for a Restraining Order against him. If he shows his face, he'll get arrested."

"We've got to get rid of him *p-p-permanently*?"

"And how do you propose to do that?"

"We get him to kill me."

"That shouldn't be hard to do. The next time he comes over, just lie down in front of his car."

"Not bad. I hadn't thought about that. On the

other hand, you can't be sure that he might not botch up the job and I'd wind up with broken fingers and a crooked dick." He drags himself over to the kitchen table and sits opposite me. He leans forward until his face is less than a foot from mine. "F-f-first we buy a gun," he says. "Then we go down to the reservoir and I shoot myself. You fire a second shot in my head, so it looks like murder. Then you drive over to his house, smear blood all over his car, hide the gun in the trunk, and the cops do the rest." As he outlines his plan, he becomes excited. This genius, sick brother of mine is mixing up fact and fantasy the way he has always done when writing his fiction.

I clap loudly. "Great idea, Harry. And the best part is when I shoot you in the head."

"The best part is when the cops arrest that bastard and he doesn't know why. I want you to take a snapshot of him and airmail it to Hell." He grabs my wrist hard.. "Mary Lou told me that he always leaves the car in the driveway. She's got an extra key, which I'll get from her, just in case it's locked. All you've got to do is follow him around for a few days and figure out his nighttime habits.. In court Mary Lou will testify how he beat her up, how he threatened me. We've got last year's fight, the gun, and all the blood evidence." His voice has turned into a conspiratorial whisper. It would appear that there's still plenty of grey matter left in Harry's brain.

"What happens if he pleads temporary insanity." I point out to him, as I shake loose from his grip. "'Ladies and Gentlemen of the jury. Put yourself in the defendant's place. Harry Stone, this corrupt villain, this unworthy educator of our youth, impregnates his daughter, then seduces his wife and runs off with her. For months the defendant broods, until his mind cracks and he takes his revenge.'" I can't believe that I am actually discussing his crazy idea in a rational voice, giving it a certain stamp of credulity that can only encourage him to pursue it even further.

Harry is quick to pick up the debate. "Very good, counselor," he says, "but the beauty of the plan is that since he really didn't do it, he's not going to try for an insanity plea. He's going to insist that he was framed."

"How do we get a gun?" If you're dumb enough to get sucked into someone's fantasy, you might as well go all the way.

"On Forty-second Street you can buy a phony driver's license for just about any state. Y-you drive to Virginia, and using the phony I.D. buy yourself a gun."

"How do you know all this?"

"It's no big secret. Last year I was having a beer and some wise guy was shooting off his mouth. "

"Suppose the cops trace the gun."

"There's the phony I.D. And nobody gives a damn about guns in Virginia. The dealers don't even bother registering them. I read that there are places outside of Norfolk where the people don't know how to write two sentences in a row, and there's a gun shop on every corner. The Feds have about four hundred agents to keep track of two hundred million handguns."

"Did Mary Lou help you with this idea, or did you figure it out all by yourself?"

Harry held out his wrists. "You know, Rog, eventually I'm going to be in a bed jerking around like a battery-powered toy gone berserk. I'll have tubes stuck up my dick and down my throat. In the morgue, they'll probably have to identify me from whatever teeth I've got left."

"Who made you an expert on HD?"

"Y-y-you think I've forgotten how to read. Even in

Rahway they've got a library."

"For chrissakes, Harry, if you read about it, then you must realize that you could live for years this way. You've got Mary Lou, Alan, Herschel. They all love you, Harry. I love you."

"Get serious, Rog. I-I-I'm a teacher who can't teach. A writer who can't write. There's nothing left but the contemplation of nothing? No hope. No salvation. You know it as well as I do. We could do this little job together. A-A-A sort of final sharing, *pardner.*"

I stand up. "I've got to get going, Harry. I'll call you tomorrow." He is back viewing the sidewalk through his binoculars by the time I reach the door. I say, "goodbye," but I don't think he hears me.

Downstairs on the sidewalk, I look up in his direction. The binoculars appear attached to his face, making him look like a giant space bug. I walk to my car and without realizing it begin to hum *Old Man River* I think of the movie *Showboat,* and Paul Robeson. Robeson is standing in the stern of the riverboat, its propellers churning up the river into a great white foam, and singing in that rich, thick basso voice that belonged only to Robeson. ". . . *I'm tired of liven', and scared of dyin'* . . . ," and I start to cry, not a great, sobbing cry like someone in a lot of pain, more like a deep, choking sound that gets stuck in your throat and doesn't want to go away.

The Range Rover is in the garage. Two suitcases are standing like sentinels against each side of the hallway leading in from the garage. I have no way of knowing that they are filled with my belongings as I pass into the kitchen. The table is clean, no plate setting, no salad, even the fruit bowl is missing. I look in the microwave. Nothing. Had I forgotten that we were supposed to go out to eat tonight?

Doris is waiting for me in the living room. She says that she canceled the girls' swim practice and drove them to friends, so they wouldn't be forced to witness the spectacle of *parents ending a marriage.* Then she speaks as if she is reciting lines that she has memorized for an acting tryout, "All my life I have done my best for you, Roger, and if that wasn't good enough, why couldn't you have been decent enough to face me and tell me the truth about how you felt?" Her arms are folded across her chest, her posture is ramrod straight, and I am reminded of Miss Hollock, my eleventh grade biology teacher, moments before she threatened to jump out of the second floor window because we were whistling "*Hold That Tiger,*" while she was trying to teach us how to pith a frog.

"What are you talking about?" I ask. I actually sound offended by her accusations, which proves only that I don't even realize what a liar and cheat I am. I make a move toward her, though I have no plan. Perhaps if she would have allowed me, I might have hugged her, begged her for forgiveness, but before I've taken a second step, she raises a hand like a traffic cop. "Don't come near me, you *adulterous reprobate,*" she shouts. "I don't want you ever to touch me again."

"I think there's been some tremendous misunderstanding here."

"How long did you think you could keep it a secret from me? What a fool I was to keep hoping that you'd somehow end it and come back to your family. But today--" She stops herself, almost as if it is too painful for her to go on. I hold my breath. "--I know who the woman is, Roger, so I don't want to hear any more of your lies . . . I feel so humiliated . . .

You're such a bastard. I can't believe you're the same man I have loved and cherished these past twenty years." Suddenly she looks infinitesimally small and defeated. I am prepared to confess to anything, submit to whatever punishment she chooses. "You want to tell me about Maria Rodrigues? Who is this *hussy*, this slut who would destroy people's lives, without the slightest problem of conscience?" She snaps her fingers with a resounding *crack, crack.* "Just like that."

"Who?" I am flabbergasted. *Maria Rodrigues Not Sandy?* The only Maria Rodrigues I know is my crazy, cancer-phobic patient. "I don't know whom you're talking about," I say with righteous indignation. Doris has made a grievous error. It is waltz time. I am being given a second life.

"Please don't insult my intelligence, Roger, or I'm liable to do something desperate."

"Give me details. I insist that you give me proof." With Maria Rodrigues named as the other woman, I automatically revert back to my old deceitful self, and become bolder, more confident.

But Doris is an abused woman, full of fight. She shouts at me: "Proof! I'll give you proof, and then I want you out of this house!"

I cross my arms arrogantly. "So let's hear it," I shout right back at her.

"For starters, your precious Maria called earlier this evening and after having the arrogance to give me her name, demanded--not asked--*demanded* to speak with you. What happened? You, two, have a little lover's tiff. 'Can I take a message?' I asked politely, though inside I was burning up. She insisted on speaking only to you--can you imagine such nerve?--then hung up. Fifteen minutes later the phone rang again. When I picked up, the phone went dead."

"Maria Rodrigues is a patient of mine, Doris. A patient!"

"It's not the first time that woman has called this house. She just never gave me her name before. Apparently, now she doesn't even care if I know about you and her. What's happening? Are you getting ready to run away with this . . . this--" She is in such a rage she cannot complete her sentence. Her complexion darkens. For a moment I worry that she might have a heart attack or a stroke.

I try to be as conciliatory as possible. "She must have somehow got hold of our unlisted number from the exchange, or maybe from the receptionist. Believe me, she's only a patient. I swear it."

"A wife of a lifetime knows when she's being cheated on. At least have the decency to admit it."

"Maria Rodrigues is an obsessive-compulsive personality with a death phobia. She gets a mosquito bite and she thinks she's got skin cancer."

"Your bags are packed." I can see that no matter how much I protest I will not win this battle. There are no second chances for an *adulterous reprobate*. Her woman's instinct has emerged. She knows what a phony I am. That she's twisted things around is irrelevant. She points a chubby index finger toward the door. "Leave through the garage--immediately."

"But you've made a terrible mistake."

"I've already spoken to Bob Handleman. If you refuse to leave, he said that he would obtain a court order and have me removed."

"Bob said that?" Was that before or after he told me to obtain a *Restraining Order* against John Whalen? Tomorrow, after I call my answering service and threaten to sue them for a million dollars for handing out my home phone to Maria Rodrigues, I will call my ex-lawyer, Bob Handleman, and offer him a few choice words of advice, which I will have the decency not to charge him for. "I still don't see why I have to leave tonight, for cryin' out loud. Have a heart."

"Are you prepared to drive me out of my own house because of your ill-begotten misbehavior?"

Ill-begotten misbehavior. The words have a softer, less pernicious ring than *adulterous reprobate.* Encouraged, I decide to plead my case one last time. "You've got to listen to reason," I say. "Call Maria Rodrigues. Ask her yourself about this supposed affair I'm having with her."

"Roger, I'm not a complete fool. If you have any feelings left in your heart for me, then please leave quietly. Allow me to salvage a bit of dignity out of this." Then to my horror she starts to cry like a child. The last time Doris cried was fifteen years ago when she broke her wrist trying to swat a mosquito with a newspaper, and fell off a chair.

I stand up and walk over to her. Her shoulders are hunched, her head is bent. I run my fingers over the top of the head. "Okay," I say. I am down for the count. *Totally Vanquished.* "Now please stop crying," I beg. "I'll go. Tomorrow I'll call you. Hopefully by then, you'll have come to your senses."

"I hope you and Maria will be very happy," she blubbers between sobs. Then suddenly she perks up and adds, "Scram, Roger. I want to get on with my life."

On my way to the motel, I flip on the radio. I don't bother changing Harry's station and listen to the loud, raucous music that my children and now, even Harry appear to enjoy so much. I decide that the music isn't really all that terrible, and if I give myself half a chance, I might even come to enjoy it. Music like life

196

comes in all shapes and forms, and I remember Harry once telling me over a beer, "You gotta learn to dig it all, little brother, because, though you may not realize it at the moment, it's all good."

CHAPTER SIXTEEN

Shootin' Up

The first thing you hear when you shut off your motor are the distant crackling sounds of firing guns. Sandy is waiting for me just beyond the graveled parking lot at the start of a long concrete walk that edges a grassy mall three times the size of a football field. She greets me with a little sisterly kiss on the cheek, which I am not sure how to interpret.

"Are we really going to shoot guns?" I ask.

Life is full of surprises. Not all pleasant. The day after being thrown out of my house by Doris, I called Sandy from my lonely room at the Holiday Inn. Instead of rushing over to cheer me up, she offered to meet me at the Sportsman's Pistol and Rifle Club Saturday afternoon, three days hence.

"A pistol club? Who are we shooting?" I asked.

"I need to practice." Stanley Applebaum has bought her a gun, registered it for her, and begun to teach her how to shoot it. A woman living alone is automatically a victim, according to Westfield Township's *Law Enforcement Officer of the Month*.

"I'd like to speak to you," I said, "and not between gunshots."

"We need to speak, and not on a bed," she replied, then gave me directions before I could protest any further.

Rain slaps against an overhead corrugated tin roof as we walk past shooters lined up behind a wooden platform about four feet high. The targets range in distance from about thirty feet to over a hundred yards. Beyond the farthest targets, at the perimeter of the range, the ground slopes upward about ten feet, a design apparently intended to stop errant bullets from flying into someone's back yard.

"Couldn't we at least have met at some nice quiet restaurant?" I ask.

"Stanley says that until I'm proficient with my weapon, I must practice at least once a week. We can eat later."

Proficient with her weapon! Now she is even talking like Stanley. "What kind of Jewish mother goes to a pistol range and shoots guns? Stanley has made you crazy." I know that my denouncement of Stanley Applebaum falls on deaf ears, but I am guided by emotion not logic.

"Unfortunately, we live in an age of unpredictable violence. Consider John Whalen, for example," she quite properly reminds me.

"But why do I have to shoot with you?"

"I'm very busy these days. I've decided to go back to school and finish my Master's. In addition Stanley has enrolled me in a martial arts class. Time for everything is becoming a problem for me. Anyway I wanted to show off, show you how good I am." *Everything?* I have been reduced to an impersonal pronoun.

She leads me past a large green quonset that looks like an old air force hangar, which turns out to be the indoor shooting range. Without being asked, she explains that unless the weather is really bad, the members prefer to shoot outside where the noise isn't as deafening, and the smell of gunpowder as noxious. I tell myself to be patient. Show a little enthusiasm This woman you love is only trying to impress you with this strange new world she has recently discovered.

She hands me a pair of ear protectors, then we walk to the end of the platform, about fifty feet away from the nearest shooter. She opens up the rectangular wooden box she is carrying and shows me her gun. "This is a Detective Special, the Colt 38," she informs me with the aplomb of a connoisseur.

"Very nice," I say. "But if I can take your mind off six-shooters for a while, please tell me what I'm going to do about Doris? She really believes that I've been having an affair with a patient of mine. What happens when she finds out the truth?"

"Maybe we should stop seeing each other for a while." Sandy expresses this earth shaking sentiment with about the same degree of passion as if she is informing a waiter that her steak is too well done. "Now let's get to business." She then proceeds to show me the different parts of the pistol: barrel chamber, firing mechanism, breech, grip. "Each part is meticulously crafted for its singular purpose," she adds. My love has metamorphosed into a Marine sergeant lecturing a raw recruit.

I would like to tell her that my life, which at the moment happens to be in crisis, could stand a little *singular purpose,* namely a little serious affection from her. Instead I benignly ask: "Do we really have to talk about guns *meticulously crafted*?"

"Yes." She gives me a lopsided look before strapping a holster around her deliciously curved hips. Then she breathes deeply and carefully guides her gun into it. *Talk about your Freudian symbolism.*

"I'll divorce Doris and marry you," I say.

"Great idea, but first, let's shoot." She practices drawing from the hip. "You cock the pin as you clear the holster. Watch. See. The gun then fires with a gentle squeeze of the trigger." *Click, click.* She hands me the pistol. "If you pull the trigger without cocking it, it takes a lot more force." (Does she really mean *cocking*?")

"I mean it. I want to marry you."

I finally seem to have distracted her, at least momentarily, from her shooting mania. "Yesterday, Stanley asked me to marry him," she says rather triumphantly. "Not bad. Two proposals in two days for a woman who's already married."

"But you don't love Stanley," I say with little real conviction in my voice.

She eyes me suspiciously and commands me to concentrate on what I'm doing. "That's no toy you're holding," she reminds me.

"All right. Let's get this over with." Impatiently I pull back the pin and squeeze the trigger. *Child's play.*

Sandy picks a bullet from her box and holds it up for inspection. "You see, a spring drives the firing pin through the flat part of the bullet into the primer, which causes a jet of flame to ignite the gun powder. The gases explode and the bullet is ejected from the barrel. And that's all there is to it."

This absolutely gorgeous woman, this sex goddess whom I have worshiped for more than a year has turned into a ballistics article from *World Book.* I give her back the gun. Carefully, she places six bullets into the breech, then snaps it shut. "The safety always stays on until you're ready to fire," she warns me.

"So will you marry me?"

"First we shoot, then we talk."

She lays down the gun, takes from her box six small red bullseyes and walks out onto the field to a large, circular target about fifteen yards away. She pastes the bullseyes on the target, then returns and picks up her gun. We put on our ear protectors, then she releases the safety and cocks the pin. Standing sideways, feet spread, body erect, she squints with her left eye and pulls the trigger. Flames leap out of the barrel and the sound echoes like a distant explosion through the protectors. She fires five more times, then lays down the pistol. (*Shane blows away Wilson and the Riker brothers. His eyes become slits. He is all business, the consummate gunfighter.*) Together we walk over and examine the top right target. Five of the six shots are in the red, the sixth slightly off to the left in the black. I am flabbergasted. For the past year I have been making love to *Annie Oakley.*

Back on the firing line, Sandy opens the breech and ejects the empty cartridge cases, then reloads, making sure that the safety catch is on. She hands me the gun. "Your turn," she says.

"What do you mean, 'We'll see.'? Why would you want to marry Stanley and not me?"

"I didn't say I would marry anyone. Now shoot," she commands.

Obediently, I pick up the gun and sight the target. I am surprised to discover that my hand is shaking. "Shoot for the middle target," she says.

I slowly release the safety catch, pull back on the pin, then squeeze the trigger. The gun kicks more than I would have expected. It occurs to me that I have just done something that has always been an absolutely repugnant idea to me--fired a gun. The wonder is that I am trembling with excitement.

"Nine o'clock, in the white. Aim slightly to the right," she says. I fire again. "You're in the black at three o'clock. Back to the left a hairline."

I fire four more times in rapid succession, no longer caring whether or not I hit the target, each time waiting for the gun to kick back on me like a nasty act of protest.

We check the target. Sandy is delighted. "You hit the red twice," she says ecstatically.

"Great. Now can we talk?"

"No. We have to practice more."

"Why can't we talk now, and practice later?"

"Stanley told me that when you have a gun in your hand, think about nothing else."

"Stanley is a one-dimensional human being. If you marry him, your vocabulary will consist entirely of words like *weapons, perps* and *victims.* Sex will become *fornication between consenting partners.*"

"You don't know Stanley, so please clam up and shoot."

In spite of my objections we spend the next hour firing at targets at varying distances. Sandy continues to hit bullseyes, even at greater distances and with smaller targets, while I never again managed a single bullseye. What I have learned the first time I fired the gun was more than I would ever need to know.

We wind up talking in my car in the parking lot after Sandy informs me that she won't have time to lunch with me after all. She has a date with Stanley.

"What about the shoot first, eat later promise?" I try not to show my outrage at this latest betrayal of our love.

"The *later* didn't mean, *right away later.*"

When your honey starts doubletalking, you know you're in big trouble. "Couldn't you break your date?" I beg. "I could really use the company."

Living by myself is not quite what I had anticipated. I had hoped that the solitude would have allowed me time for serious reflection on what I wanted with my life (or whatever was left of it). Away from Doris and the girls, I could be more objective, try to understand what really matters. I had also hoped to spend time with Sandy, leisurely, not having to worry about being late, about lying to Doris. Instead, I find myself dining alone at the hotel restaurant and, mindlessly scanning the TV schedule between courses. In my room after hours of watching TV, I will sometimes do a newspaper crossword puzzle, or read a boring detective novel. For the past week since leaving my house, I've slept badly, lost my appetite, am constipated, and am no closer in discovering any great truths about myself than when I was living a double life with my family.

I call home daily. Doris still refuses to speak with me. I ask the girls about school, swim practice, remind them to walk the dog. They give me answers like "okay," "sure," "right." Neither girl seems particularly interested in what I'm doing, or if I ever intend to come home again. I wonder what their mother has told them, but am afraid to ask.

"I'll try and make it tomorrow night," Sandy says. "But it's going to be the last time."

"We haven't had a first time since Doris kicked me out of the house," I say.

"I want you to call Doris tonight. Promise her that you're going to stop seeing this other woman, and that you want to come home."

"You want me to admit that I've been having an affair with a patient who belongs in a mental institution."

"She knows that you've been unfaithful with someone. Let her think it's this woman. It solves a lot of problems for us."

"I want her to discover the truth. I want her to file for a divorce and let Bob Handleman squeeze me out of my life savings. I no longer give a damn."

"What about Naomi and Debbie? They'll care plenty."

"Did you read last month's issue of *Psychology*

Today? There's an article on children of divorced parents. Kids learn to accept what has happened, and go on with their own lives, which are a lot more important to them than ours, anyway."

"What about Doris? She's a person, you know, not a slice of Swiss Cheese."

"Bob Handleman will see to it that Doris will be rich. She's only forty, still in her prime. Before you know it, she'll find someone who will love her more than I do. Maybe we can fix her up with Stanley." I can hear the popping of gunshots in the background and roll up my window. I'm grateful for the silence.

"Please try and understand," she says.

"Do you love him?" I ask knowing full well that like a boxer in a fight for the championship, I am leading with my chin. "I mean really love him. Even more than you love me."

"I'm supposed to give him an answer today," she says too casually. "What you don't understand, Rog, is that you and Harry aren't quite real. You both live inside me like dreams." She smiles self-consciously. "Yesterday, at the supermarket, I thought I saw Harry bending down by the frozen vegetable section. I wanted to go to him, put my arms around him, tell him not to worry, that I'd take care of him. Instead of Harry a young man looked up at me. 'Are you okay, Lady? he asked." *She is hallucinating Harry. It's all over between us.* "The other day I was watching TV. Something about Chicago. All I could think of was Harry and I walking across the Midway. He stops and says that he'll marry me if I'll agree to stop writing bad poetry. An icy wind sweeps up from the lake, and we duck under a small bridge crossing. We wrap our arms around each other for warmth. Then he kisses me, and I think I will never love anyone else for the rest of my life."

"Why bother coming to the motel tomorrow? We can end it right now."

"Shut up, Roger. Tomorrow, we'll end it." Then she does the unexpected. She kisses me, a beautiful, soft, loving kiss, her hands resting on my shoulders, her eyes closed. Was this the way she kissed Harry under the bridge crossing the Midway twenty-three years ago? After we separate, she rubs her knuckles across my face affectionately, and gives me one of her shy, little grins. "Did you have fun today?"

"Yeah, I love being Wild Bill Hickock."

"It grows on you."

"I'd rather take an enema."

She opens the door and slides out of the car. Off to see Stanley Applebaum, the guy who parts his hair down the middle, and is always smiling. *Diner, motel. The old routine. Our routine.*

I start the engine, shift into DRIVE. In thirty minutes I'll be back in my room at the Holiday Inn, back to the *Ledger's* daily crossword puzzle, which I had almost completed before meeting Sandy. In thirty minutes the most important thing in my life will be to figure out what Fred Astaire movie starts with a T and has six letters? T-O-P-H-A-T, of course, you dummy. On my way back to the motel, I think I will stop and pick up a *Times*. If I could solve their daily puzzle, who knows what worlds I might yet be able to conquer?

CHAPTER SEVENTEEN

Brother's Keeper

I wake up in a sweat. In my dream Sandy is firing at my chest. My heart is the bullseye. *My life is over.* I am grateful to be awakened by the telephone.

Mary Lou must have a cold. Her nasal pitch with its knife-like edge cuts through my already embattled nervous system. "Harry never came home," she says."I called the cops a couple of hours ago, and they just called me back." The fluorescent dial on the motel radio alarm reads: Two-thirty a.m. "There's a corpse at the morgue at Elizabeth General." She starts to cry. Between sobs she says, "Someone's coming over to pick me up. Would you meet me there?"

In every motel room in America is a bible. I am not religious by nature. I can't recall ever believing in the existence of God. Nevertheless, I scan the book of Genesis until I come to: *"And it came to pass, that Cain rose up against his brother and slew him. And the Lord said unto Cain: 'Where is Abel thy brother?' And he said: 'I know not; am I my brother's keeper?' And He said: What has thou done? The voice of thy brother's blood crieth unto Me from the ground."*

"But you have done nothing wrong," I say to myself. Another voice whispers: "You may have done nothing wrong, but what did you do right? *What did you do to try and save your brother?"*

Mary Lou falls against me when they wheel out

Harry's corpse and roll back the sheet. She cannot voice a simple yes, or no, not even a nod, in response to the sheriff's questioning. I escort her to a bench in the corridor than return to the examining room. It's up to me to make the identification.

The top of Harry's head has been almost destroyed, but there is enough left of his face to make a positive ID. A detective from the Union County Sheriff's office introduces himself as David Wan. He informs me that in cases where the face had been even partially damaged, fingerprints, and dental x-rays, if they are available, are required to confirm the identification. Detective Wan speaks without emotion. Another bureaucratic zombie, I decide.

"Don't waste your time," I say. I point to the scar on Harry's lower right quadrant from an old appendectomy, and the small but highly visible birthmark on his inner right thigh. "Call my father, if you doubt my word," I say, knowing that he won't bother. I bid farewell to Harry, then follow the detective and the Medical Examiner out of the room.

Outside the morgue, in the corridor, I fill out a form and sign my name. Wan relates to me that Harry's body had been found by a young couple around eleven p.m. near Sunrise Lake in the Watchung Reservation after they had heard two shots. The Medical Examiner confirmed that Harry had been shot through the head at close range. After the body is autopsied they will have a better idea as to the exact cause of death.

"Is there a doubt?" I ask.

"You never know. He could have been poisoned, then dragged down to the lake and shot."

"Poisoned?"

"Just speculating. In this business anything's possible."

Wan is dressed neatly with a suit and tie. He has a slight pot, not unlike my own, and wears round, steel-framed glasses. One could have just as easily thought him to be a bank teller, or a nuclear scientist, instead of a homicide detective from the Sheriff's office.

"Can you help me out at all?" Wan asks.

"I'll do my best." What else can you say?

"Was your brother depressed? Did he ever talk about killing himself?"

"He talked about suicide all the time. Last month he cut his wrists, but he didn't do a very good job of it."

"The problem is that it's not so easy pulling a trigger a second time after you've already put the first bullet in your head."

"Isn't it possible that the second shot went off as he was falling, or that he was just practicing with the first shot?"

"Not likely, if we are to believe the preliminary report. Though, anything is possible. I guess we'll just have to wait for the final autopsy."

"Right now I'm not feeling so wonderful. If you don't mind, detective, I think I'd like to take Mrs. Whalen home." I look toward Mary Lou, who is sitting on a bench, bent over, holding her head in her hands, sobbing quietly, her face a mess from eye mascara smearing with the tears.

"Sure, I understand. Just one thing, if you don't mind." Before I can raise an objection, he says, "I understand there was bad blood between your brother and Mrs. Whalen's husband."

"Who told you that?"

"Mrs. Whalen. In the car on the way down here."

"You were questioning her before you realized that it was Harry in the morgue?"

"It's the job." He makes a little self-conscious grin, an apology of sorts, I guess.

"Can we talk about it another time?" I give him my card.

He pockets it with a little slight of hand. Then he says, "Sure, Doc, I understand. In the meantime, do you think Mrs. Whalen can give me her husband's address and phone number?"

Mary Lou begins to cough hard, a deep-chested hacking sound that doesn't want to quit. Finally she catches her breath and I hand her the back of another business card along with a pen. "I hope he goes to jail for a hundred years," she says as she neatly prints the information Wan has requested.

Wan perks up. "You think your husband did this?" he asks her.

"Who else?" she says, and starts coughing again.

I return the card to Wan. "Thanks," he says. "We'll be in touch."

Wan is distant. He is being deliberate, or as my daughters would say, "playing it cool." Perhaps, he already knows more than he is letting on. At the moment I am not interested in what he knows or doesn't know. What I know is that my brother Harry is lying in the next room, *dead as a mackerel.* Harry's blood will never again flow threw his arteries and veins; he will never again open his eyes and see color and forms, or listen to a Mozart quartet, or quote a soliloquy from Hamlet. I will never see him again. He can never be anything but memory. I can barely hold back my own tears as I grab Mary Lou by the arm and lead her out of the hospital.

In front of her apartment house Mary Lou asks me if I'd like to come upstairs with her. "Just for a while," she begs. "I don't think I can stand being alone right now."

Once we are inside the apartment she starts to cry again, and flings herself against me, throwing her arms around my neck while resting her head on my shoulder. She is wearing a thin, cotton blouse, and I can feel a dampness around the line made by her brassiere strap. I don't have the heart to push her away. Instead I guide her over to the couch and sit next to her. She blows her nose twice, then coughs in my face. Once settled she lights up a cigarette and takes several long inhalations, the expired smoke half choking me to death. She needs to be lectured on the sin of smoking, especially when you've got a cough so violent that half the time you can hardly breath, but I say nothing, grateful that she has at least stopped her incessant bawling.

"You want a drink?" she asks. She goes into the kitchen and returns with a newly opened bottle of gin and two glasses. "Best medicine for a chest cold," she says, then hands me a glass and fills it half up before pouring herself a drink. "Thanks for coming up." She sits back down next to me. "We'll have a few drinks and then I'll feel better." She belts down the undiluted gin as if she were drinking soda pop, then pours herself another. "Harry was a very sick man," she says. *Sip, sip.* "So what if he tried to kill himself. That didn't give John the right to shoot him. John should rot in hell."

"Maybe it wasn't John. Harry could have been wandering around. Maybe he was attacked and robbed."

"How did he get over to the Reservation?"

"He could have taken a taxi."

"Harry was a good man," Mary Lou says. "But he'd think too much. He could drive himself crazy thinking about things. He always seemed to blame himself for anything wrong, and then he'd want to write about it, as if that would make it okay. It didn't matter what it was. Somebody in Texas could shoot his grandmother and Harry would think it was his fault." She leans back against the couch and crosses her legs, revealing bare, plump thighs. Drink in one hand, cigarette in the other, she is more relaxed, less edgy. She says, "Then there are men like John. Always blaming others because they could never have what they want." Her speech is becoming slurred, but she has stopped coughing. I must remember in the future to prescribe gin instead of cough medicine to patients with upper respiratory infections.

"Maybe John didn't do it," I interject. "You can't be sure."

The possibility that John didn't do it seems to enervate her. "Yeah, maybe he didn't. When you get right down to it, John's no worse than most. He always hated being a trucker. Hated going out on the road days on end, sleeping on the run, worrying about his rig breaking down, whether he was going to deliver his goods on time. He did it for his family. Trucking is all he knows how to do." She becomes misty-eyed again, and gives me the once-over. "You're lucky, Roger. You help people. Everybody loves you. You walk down the street, people notice you, look up to you. 'There's the young Doc. He takes care of me and my family, he keeps us alive.' That's what they're saying. You don't need to get drunk like

John so you can feel important."

I am astonished by her unexpected show of affection for her husband. It could be the gin. Or maybe a decimated pride that wishes to salvage a portion of itself, no matter how minimal, from living with a man she had once loved.

"We'll have to bury Harry," I say, also starting to feel the effects of the gin.

"Why don't we just cremate him? Toss him in the oven and put his ashes in some pretty urn. I'll put it on my night table, next to my bed." She places her hand on my one of my knees and gives it a little squeeze. I don't bother removing the hand, though it feels like a dime store suction cup.

"Can't cremate him," I say. "It's against Jewish law."

"Sorry. I forgot the law."

She removes the hand and pours me another drink. The gin is vile. Mary Lou's breath reeks of tobacco and alcohol. With each cough and sneeze she spews millions of pathogens into the air. Nevertheless, I continue to drink with her, because, like her, I don't want to be alone. We are an odd couple to be sitting *shiva* together.

"Whom I goin' to take care of?" Mary Lou asks me through misty eyes. "No more Harry. Mitzi don' wan' me around. I didn' mean to hurt Mitzi. I swear I didn'. I was jus' so tired and lonely and sick of livin' with John. I deserve to rot in hell."

"Mary Lou, we have to bury Harry. It's the law. Harry was my brother. I'm going to have to stand up and say *'Yisgadal v'yiskadash shmey rabbah'*. . ."

"Shimmy who?"

"It's the mourner's prayer."

"What's it mean?"

213

"I don't know, but you still gotta say it."

"Say it for Harry, Roger. He deserves the *shimmey* prayer."

She tips the bottle before she realizes there is nothing left in it. Then she arises and goes into the bedroom, to return a few moments later with a marijuana cigarette. She lights it and inhales deeply, then hands me the burning joint.

"Drag on it, taste it in your throat," she instructs me.

I have an odd sense that my brain is being stretched like a giant elastic band, then the sensation ceases abruptly, and I begin to feel jittery, though not unpleasant.

We smoke the joint to the end, then another, until I lean back against the couch and close my eyes allowing the *Cannabis* to slowly work its way through my already intoxicated brain. The last thing I remember before passing out is Mary Lou's hand lying indifferently on my crotch.

I awaken with a splitting headache. I am surprised to discover that I am still in Mary Lou's apartment, lying on the couch, fully clothed except for my shoes. A blanket is draped over me and a small throwaway pillow is stuffed under my head. I toss off the blanket and sit up, almost stepping on Mary Lou, who is sleeping on the floor next to the couch.

Guided by moonlight that slants through the shadeless window, I make my way to the bathroom and switch on the light. In the mirror I see a worn, middle-aged man, eyes all bloodshot, hair messed up. I have pronounced people dead who looked more alert.

Pills galore in the medicine cabinet, but not an aspirin for a headache. I wonder how long I've been sleeping and check my wristwatch--it's a little after five. I wash my face and comb my hair with Mary Lou's hairbrush, then make my way back into the living room where I look for my shoes and suitcoat.

Mary Lou is curled up in a foetal position, clinging to a sofa pillow, her face in sleep quite innocent, almost angelic. The last of Harry's girls, I think.

On the street I discover that my car has been broken into--the driver's window smashed, my hi-fi radio with its eight track tape player torn out of its shelving, the side pocket jimmied and insurance papers and maintenance receipts strewn all over the front. If I weren't an atheist, I would think the break-in as an act of *Divine Retribution* for my getting high with Mary Lou.

Like a homing pigeon I drive to my house in Scotch Plains. Nothing but darkness inside and around the house. I dread returning to the motel, to be alone in that tiny enclosure with only a TV, a bible, and an unfinished crossword puzzle for company. But I lose my nerve and turn around. Tomorrow I will call Doris. After she finds out about Harry, she will welcome me back into the house.

A light rain begins to fall, moisture spraying in through the broken window. Tomorrow I'll notify my insurance company of the break-in, put in a claim, arrange to have the car repaired. I make a big decision. After I bury Harry, I will settle in, give up Sandy, go back to my old prudent life. Being *Dr Dependable* is who I really am. The rest has been a fantasy.

CHAPTER EIGHTEEN

Pizza with Wan

There's a decent Chinese restaurant a block from my office, but Detective David Wan says he prefers Italian, and we decide on Pizza Hut on Route 22 in Union.

While waiting for our pizza, Wan asks about my family. What kind of doctor is my father? Myself? He writes memos on a pad with a small pencil, the sort of stubby, red pencil golfers use to keep the score. When the point begins to wear, he pulls out another pencil and slips the old one in a side pocket.

"What did the autopsy reveal?" I ask.

"I haven't seen the full report. I was hoping you might be able to help me out." He eyes me quizzically, sizing me up, it would appear. The best I will give him is a little non-committal shrug. He goes on: "Mrs. Whalen told me that your brother was quite sick, that he'd shake a lot. Were you his doctor?"

"As much as he'd let me."

"What was the matter with him?"

"I'm not sure. I think he probably had MS. Multiple Sclerosis."

"That's pretty serious, isn't it?"

"It's the sort of disease that comes and goes. When you suffer an attack, you become weak, your vision deteriorates, you have trouble walking, talking, sometimes thinking. When you're in remission, everything becomes normal. Remissions can last a long time."

"How long?"

"I've seen cases where patients have gone without symptoms for more than ten years. But there are no guarantees."

"How do you treat it?"

"Physical therapy, good diet, vitamins, plenty of rest. There are no medicines. No magic bullets."

"How sick was your brother?"

"Bad. Within five years he probably would have wound up half blind, incontinent, bedridden. But like I said you never can tell with MS." At this point I think I have almost talked myself into believing that Harry really had Multiple Sclerosis. I suppose the mark of a good liar is if the liar gets to believe his own lie.

"You seem uncertain."

"I'm not a neurologist, and Harry refused to see one."

"Could he have had another disease?"

"He refused to go for a brain scan. He wouldn't even let me take blood. There was always the possibility of a brain tumor or a CVA, but the symptoms all pointed to MS."

"What's a CVA?"

"A stroke. You must look to the autopsy for more definitive answers." I am representing half-truths as medical gospel, but not without some trepidation. Without concern I can lie to my family about Harry's medical condition, but lying to the police is withholding evidence. I could use the doctor-patient relationship as a legal way of concealing information, but if Wan discovers the truth, that Harry had Huntington's and I knew about it, he would be bound to ask embarrassing questions. He might even begin to regard me as a murder suspect, particularly if he found out about Sandy.

"Like I said, the Medical Examiner is still working on it, but he doesn't think he's going to find much considering how much damage has been done to the brain. One thing is clear, however, both bullets were shot into his head. The first went through just above the right ear and the other into the back of the brain." He doesn't need to remind me that this finding disproves my theory that Harry shot the gun once for practice, or that after he had shot the fatal bullet, the gun had fired accidentally as he fell.

"How could he tell which bullet was shot first?" I ask.

"I don't know. But he was pretty positive. It's almost like your brother shot himself first, then someone else fired the second bullet."

"Why would someone shoot him if he were already dead?" You find out about yourself in moments of crises. I am cool as a cucumber. I am so cool that right now I could probably beat a lie detector machine.

"I wondered about that myself. . . By the way you don't happen to know if your brother had a life insurance policy, do you?"

"I have no idea."

"Did you know that some insurance policies don't pay off on suicide?" Again Wan eyeballs me, then he pulls out handwritten pages of notes from an inside pocket. He flips through several sheets before settling on one. "The Rahway police reported that on three different occasions this past month your brother was found wandering around the streets at night." He reads silently to himself, before saying, "Last Friday, he jumped into the lake at the park."

"He was probably drunk."

Wan nods. Without comment he flips to another page. "I understand that last year your brother ran off with one of his students. Did he ever discuss with you his reasons?" So Wan knew about Mitzi. He could have found out from Mary Lou? Or John Whalen might have told him. Or even Mitzi herself, which means he must have already spoken to Sandy, too. If that was the case, why hadn't she called me? Several times I went to the phone to call her, but decided against it. You never knew who might be monitoring your telephone conversations. Perhaps, she also thought it might be best to see me alone first.

"Harry was in the midst of a mid-life crisis," I say. "It happens all the time these days. Don't you ever watch TV?"

"I like to watch the wrestling, and once in a while an old movie," says Wan. "Never having been married, I don't think much about infidelity. Tell me, how long was your brother married?"

"Twenty-two years."

"How long a professor?"

I give the question a moment of thought, as if I want him to believe that I am not all that involved in Harry's life. "About fifteen years," I finally say.

"Why did he quit?"

"He said he needed more time to write. Harry was a novelist, you know. Maybe you've read one of his books."

"To tell you the truth I don't read a lot of fiction. I'm a sucker for those books that tell you how to get on in life. Once in a while I like to settle in with a good biography. Why don't you write down a few titles for me? I may want to borrow one of them from the library."

"How is that going to help you find the murderer?"

"You never can tell. I like to know everything I can about a murder victim. A man writes a book, he reveals a lot about himself. Last year I read a biography about Ernest Hemingway. His idea of a *man* was someone who wasn't afraid to die. So he wrote about bullfighters and hunters and men at war. He was in love with death. When he got old, and there was nothing left to prove, he killed himself. You see, if I were on that case, I wouldn't have had any doubts about the cause of death."

We split a meatball, onion pizza. The crust is too thick, and the meatballs taste as if they are eighty-percent breadcrumbs. For the past year or so, since Harry became ill, my gut has been less than kind to me, especially after I eat junk food. I should have insisted that we go Chinese, and not worry about whether Wan might think I am racially insensitive.

"Tell me, Doc, how did the university feel about your brother sleeping with one of his students?"

"I never asked."

Wan tears into his half of the pizza with gusto. Nothing the matter with his intestines. After he chews and swallows a huge piece, he sums up, "Married twenty-two years, a professor for fifteen. A pretty solid citizen. Then he runs off with a student and quits his job. Lately, he's been taking hikes after dark, and midnight dips in a county lake." He finishes off another piece, then half a Coke. "He sounds like a candidate for a rehab."

"You think Harry was using drugs?"

"Or alcohol. Hey, I don't know, Doc. I'm just poking around, hoping you might be able to help me out a little. His girl friend admitted that once in a while they did a little grass."

"Millions of people smoke grass. I bet you've

smoked a few joints yourself in your life."

"Not me. I'm a very solid citizen."

"How could I have thought otherwise?"

Wan breaks his solemnity and tenders a modest little grin. I judge him to be cagey, but not deceitful. Probably not a bad fellow when he isn't doing his job. Still he makes me uneasy, and I am eager to get out of here and back to my office, where I can finish my paper work before going to Newark Airport to pick up my father.

"When you admit a little, it could be the tip of the iceberg," Wan says.

"What's the iceberg?"

"Heroine, cocaine, speed. You tell me."

Good cops, like social workers, probably recognize the symptoms of drug addiction more readily than your average MD, who rarely sees a case in his office. But, when you've got a framed degree hanging on a wall in your neatly paneled, carpeted office, your pride is at stake. Thus, I speak with confidence:"I examined him less than a month ago. If he had been using hard drugs, I think I would have been able to tell."

Wan executes one of his annoying little shrugs, then pulls out another pencil and scribbles on his pad, no doubt some nasty aside on my attitude. "Let's go on . What can you tell me about Mary Lou Whalen?"

"Harry had been living with her for over a year. She's Mitzi's mother."

"Mitzi?"

"Mitzi Whalen, the student, the girl who Harry ran away with."

"Sure, now I see it," he says. "I just didn't realize that she's the one living in Harry's house? Wow!" He smacks his forehead in astonishment. I'm not sure if he isn't putting on a little production for me. The guy is tricky. "And the baby? Don't tell me?" He picks up his pencil poised to do some serious scribbling, perhaps make some sense of what he has just learnt. "Let me sum up," he says. "Harry left his wife to live with Mitzi Whalen, who is the college student, and then left Mitzi to live with Mitzi's mother, Mary Lou Whalen, while Mitzi and the baby, who I assume is Harry's, are living with Harry's estranged wife, your sister-in-law, Mrs. Sandra Stone." With his mouth slightly agape, Wan has the uneasy look of a patient on his way to the operating room for bypass surgery.

"It happens every day on TV. But how would you know, since you only watch wrestling and old movies. If you want to learn what's really going on in the world, you're going to have to change your viewing habits." Then I tell him about the fight between John Whalen and Harry last year, and the circumstances leading up to it, and why I took Mitzi over to Sandy's house. "It was only supposed to be a temporary arrangement until I found a shelter for Mitzi."

Wan goes back to writing in his notebook. He finally says, "Ten years a cop, and never have I heard a humdinger like this one. So tell me: how does Mitzi feel about Harry sleeping with her mother?"

"How would you feel?"

"Is it possible she might have lost her cool?"

"You think she killed Harry? Not possible."

Could Mitzi have been the one? She must have known about Sandy's thirty-eight special. Sandy might even have taught her how to use it to protect herself against her father in an emergency. Still it's hard to believe that Mitzi would ever have agreed to help Harry. She's a little crazy, a girl with this beautiful vision of a perfect world in which people love and take care of each other and it's all free. Not exactly the type to blow out someone's brains. If not Mitzi, then who? Sandy? Mary Lou? Take your pick: A, B, C. Maybe none of the above. It was naive of me to believe that just because I had refused to help Harry, he wouldn't have been able to find someone else.

"What about Harry's son?"

"Alan's got a Bhuddist's mentality. He wouldn't swat a mosquito, let alone shoot his father."

"Alan and Mitzi were home by themselves at the time of the death." Wan pauses, then adds in a slightly, nasty voice. "That is--according to them." When I make a face, he says, "I'm not accusing anyone, Doc. Just reaching for straws. Both had motives, and don't forget, they're each others' alibis." Wan has a sudden brainstorm and begins to scribble frantically until he breaks his pencil point. He tosses the pencil aside in disgust and begins poking around in his pocket for another one, calming down only after he finds a new one. "Last year I had a case where a son tried to kill his father because the father was fooling around with his girl friend," he says. "You don't seem too interested, Doc. Okay, let's talk about John Whalen, Mitzi's father, the guy with the big temper."

"Why would you suspect him just because Harry had impregnated his daughter and was living with his wife?" In spite of myself, I am playing a role that Harry knew I would. Ironically, I feel no guilt.

"Two detectives are checking on him right now," Wan says. "By the way, did you know that your sister-in-law bought a gun this year?"

"Lots of people own guns." How did he find that one out so quickly? Did Sandy volunteer the information? Did he check with the Westfield police?

"We borrowed the gun, and handed it over to ballistics."

"Believe me, she had nothing to do with it." And if it was Sandy's gun? But that didn't necessarily mean she shot Harry. Everybody in the house must have known where the gun was kept, including Stanley Applebaum, the guy who bought it in the first place. Smiling Stanley--now that was a thought. He probably hated Harry more than anyone. He must have known about the enmity between Harry and Whalen, and that the law would immediately go after Whalen. Unwittingly, he could have been Harry's accomplice, and Harry didn't even have to ask him. He didn't even have to use Sandy's gun. Everybody knew that cops owned extra guns that were untraceable.

"Wives shoot ex-husbands on a daily basis," Wan says. "And you can't rule out the girl friend either."

"Why would Mary Lou want to kill Harry?"

"Maybe Harry had another woman, someone we don't know about. It would appear that your brother was quite a Don Juan. He might have even started up again with Mitzi, or even his wife." Wan smiles, an annoying little smirk. "What do you think?" he asks.

"You're wasting your time. Each one of these women loved Harry."

"*Love, hate.* I may like to watch wrestling on TV, but I also listen to the lyrics of the songs people sing." He pauses, once again as he checks his notes, then says, "I understand your brother was in a motorcycle accident last year."

"He lost control of the bike because of a sudden weakness in his limbs, which caused him not to brake fast enough."

"Could he have been on drugs?"

"In my opinion it was due to his MS, which we didn't know about at the time."

"The hospital records showed that there was no blood test."

"Harry refused to take one."

"And you didn't insist?"

"He wasn't my patient. My sister-in-law was upset and called me. I came down to help out if I could."

"I understand Mitzi Whalen was upstairs in intensive care. If she died and Harry had turned up positive, he could have been arrested for manslaughter. Right? Which means, you were obstructing justice, Doc."

"Are you going to read me my rights before you call for backup?" I am talking tough for someone who sweats when a cop pulls him over for going through a stop sign. But somehow this entire conversation has taken on a sense of the surreal. What is true is not necessarily rational.

"Okay, Doc, this isn't a witch hunt. Just trying to find out who killed your brother. Maybe he was into drugs more heavily than you imagined. He might even have been dealing to cover the costs of his own addiction, playing around with some tough guys." He narrows his eyes, almost a squint, *the inscrutable, Oriental look*, my nasty, racist mind tells me. "Let's move on. What was your brother's financial condition?"

"He was always broke."

"Really." Wan peps up. He has found a new tail

to grab. "Did he ever ask to borrow money from you?"

"Sometimes I'd lend him a few dollars. He always paid me back."

"How much is a few dollars?"

"Never more than a couple of thousand."

"That's more than a few dollars."

"A down payment on a car. A new violin for Alan."

"A violin?"

"Alan plays like Heifitz. An eight thousand dollar violin was selling for four. I helped him out."

"He had a good job, didn't he? What about those books he wrote?"

"You spend five years writing a book. If you're lucky you make ten or twenty-thousand. Professors earn *bubkes*."

"What's that mean?"

"Not very much."

"Not like doctors, huh?"

"More in the range of detectives, I would imagine."

He smiles again, this one better natured. "What about his wife? Doesn't she work?"

"She's a school teacher."

"What does she teach?"

"Does it matter?"

"Just curious."

"Biology, I think."

"You don't know?"

"She teaches Biology. Birds and bees, caterpillars, ants, conjugating paramecium."

"Two major incomes. And always broke." Wan appears unsettled by Harry and Sandy's inability to save money.

"There are people who earn millions and are

always broke," I point out.

"That's true. Personally I'm a saver. It's hard for me to understand people who live beyond their means. They begin to borrow, get themselves into all sorts of trouble. Do you think that's what might have happened to your brother?"

"I think this is wild speculation without any basis of fact."

"Be patient with me, Doc. It's a tough case and we don't have much to go on. I'm just poking a-round for an angle. Just a few more questions, if you don't mind."

"I'd like to help, but I don't see what else I can tell you."

"Did your brother have any enemies?"

"Enemies?"

"You know, someone who might want to kill him."

"Harry was beloved by all."

"Except John Whalen."

Wan stands up and puts on his jacket, then tosses his most recently used pencil into a side pocket along with his notebook. "You've been really helpful, Doc. I want to thank you." He grabs a bit of leftover pizza crust and nibbles. "Let's get out of here. I know you want to get back to your office."

While we are waiting to pay the bill, he asks me, "By the way, just for the record, where were you on the night your brother was found dead?"

"At the Holiday Inn in Kenilworth," I say. "I had a late dinner, than went back to my room and watched TV for a while, before going to bed."

Wan insists on picking up the whole tab. At the exit door he asks me, "You live at the Holiday Inn?" New concern has crossed his round, suspicious, detective's face.

"My wife and I had a bit of a tiff. I decided to move into the motel for a few days and let her cool off."

"Excuse me for wondering, Doc, but isn't moving into a motel a bit much, after 'a bit of a tiff'?"

"We didn't throw plates or anything, if that's what you're getting at. Anyway, I'm back home again."

"Sorry to get so nosy. It's a bad habit."

"Anything else?"

"Not really. Only I was wondering--while you were at the motel that night did you see anyone, talk to anyone?"

"No."

We are outside into the parking lot. Once again he stops and questions me: "Maybe you talked with the desk clerk, or some other guest?"

"You park your car in front of your room. It's only a few feet from the entrance."

"You don't happen to remember what you watched on TV, do you?"

"The news and then a movie," I say after a moment's reflection, a bit of play-acting. I am ready for him.

"Just for the record, do you recall the name of the movie?"

"*This Gun for Hire.* It was on one of the late shows."

"Can't say I ever saw that one."

"An old Alan Ladd, Veronica Lake flic. It's about a killer, a cop, and his girl friend. She's been kidnapped by the killer and gets involved with him. You know, the victim's identifying with the bad guy sort of thing. I think it's based on a Graham Green novel. Quite good. Watch it if they show it again. It's right up your alley."

"Sounds interesting. I'll look for it."

"Is that it?"

"Go save a few lives, Doc. Once again thanks a lot for your time."

"I'd be interested in the autopsy report."

"I'll call you first off as soon as I get it. You're probably my best medical expert on this case. I wouldn't be surprised if you turned out to be a big help in figuring out who killed your brother," he says, then gives me a crummy smile, which makes my poor, spastic gut ache all the way on the drive back to my office.

CHAPTER NINETEEN

Burying Harry

Wan calls me the next day at home to inform me that the Medical Examiner has finished with Harry, and I should arrange to pick up his body.

"What's the verdict?" I ask.

"Two bullets in the head. The first one killed him. The second was for fun. Powder burns. No powder on his hand, which means that if he shot himself he was wearing a glove and someone removed it. I'll keep you informed if anything new turns up."

At a funeral home in Millburn I meet with the director, a middle-aged man with a carefully trimmed jet black beard and pencil thin mustache. He guides me through a back room like an English tour guide showing off the splendors of his castle. There are eight different types of caskets. "The cost of the funeral depends upon the type of casket one chooses to bury their beloved for their eternal rest," he says with a straight face.

Prices range from eighteen-hundred dollars for simple pine to sixty-two hundred for a casket constructed of rich walnut, with brass handles and gold plated corners. Imbedded in the wood on one side of the expensive casket is a little ivory statuette of Abraham holding Isaac's hand with one hand and pointing a finger with the other toward the Heavens.

"Harry and Alan," I say. The director hands me a tissue before the first tears have cleared my sockets.

I buy the best, telling the director that Harry would have appreciated the fancy sendoff. The director guarantees me that Harry's final departure will be accomplished with grace and dignity. He will arrange everything, including the pickup of the body, and the burial at the cemetery. The man's tone of voice, sincere and compassionate, is a work of art.

I take my Dad out to lunch. Unshaven, and with eyes sunken and red, he nibbles on his salad and keeps asking in the same monotone, over and over, "Why?"

"Maybe God blessed him by taking him out of his misery," I say. Dad has never been much into God, but since Mom died, he has joined a synagogue and has been going regularly to Friday night services, and I hoped a little God might ease his pain.

"Who could have done such a terrible thing to him?"

"Maybe Harry arranged to take his own life." A Horowitz family tradition, I judiciously do not add.

Either he doesn't understand what I am talking about, or the thought of Harry killing himself is too painful a subject to pursue, for he immediately alters the course of the conversation. "Why didn't you tell me about Harry's son?" he asks.

"I didn't want to upset you. You've been through a lot this year."

He views me skeptically. "Don't try to protect me, Roger. I resent being treated like a child. Are you still angry because I never told you about your real father?"

"You're my real father."

"Remember, none of this is anybody's fault. By not telling you about him, we thought we were doing the right thing. I can see now that it may have been a mistake."

"And my own family? When do I tell them?"

"That's the sixty-four dollar question. Only remember that it doesn't do a person any good worrying that a train may run him over tomorrow."

My father looks so worn, so defeated. I don't know how to comfort him. "Another thing," I say. "I told the police that Harry had MS."

"Your secret is safe with me."

"Thanks, Dad."

"I pray every day for you, Roger."

"Pray for Alan and Herschel."

"Sometimes out of the worst can come the most marvelous blessings. Herschel's got his father's name. May God grant him his father's intelligence and spirit."

I buy a large plot of land in a cemetery in Woodbridge directly across the street from a giant mall. After spending time at a gravesite, a mourner would be able to walk across the street and get lost in a dream world of cookies, Swiss knives, tennis balls, music tapes, books, ski equipment, stereo amplifiers, jeans, earrings, light bulbs, lawn mowers, yogurt, fluoridated tooth pastes, a phantasmagoria of American tastes, *something for everyone.* Harry would have had a good laugh knowing that within walking distance of his grave was the *Great American Dream.*

The plot is large enough to accommodate my parents, my own family, including any future spouses, Harry's family, and even Mitzi and Herschel. There may be enough space for two or three yet unborn children. However, I have decided that if Sandy becomes an Applebaum, I will blackball her from a permanent residence alongside of Harry. Such are the vagaries of the heart when it has been cruelly rejected.

The purchase of so large a parcel of land requires no insignificant amount of paper pushing, but I am assured that Harry will be properly buried according to Jewish law, even before the contract has been signed.

You're dead, you're dead. Still I must admit I experience a sense of ancestral solidarity once the deal has been concluded. With my father's permission, one day I will exhume Mom from her gravesite in Florida, and ship her to New Jersey for reburial. Mom and Dad will occupy the two graves directly in the center of the plot. To their left will be my family, to their right, Harry's, with or without Sandy.

Twenty minutes before the funeral is to begin, I dictate to the rabbi a few sentiments, which I feel he ought to make paramount in his funeral oration. The rabbi listens politely, nodding periodically almost as if he is *davening*.

"This is a joyous occasion--" I say.

The rabbi, a nice old gent with a ragged gray beard and large blue eyes, whom I had found by calling the Jewish Federation of Central Jersey, immediately interrupts me. "Are you crazy? Your brother was only forty-four. He died in his prime."

"Harry lived a terrific life. Exactly the way he wanted to, which is a helluva lot more than you can say for most of us. There are plenty who will live to ninety and never experience a fraction of the good life that Harry packed into those forty-four years."

"My job is to comfort his family, not deliver your opinion on the meaning of life. Death is always sad, even when the person who died lived well. When a man dies unnaturally, it only enhances the tragedy."

"Stand up and shout 'Hallelujah' for Harry Stone.

That's the way you can best comfort my family."

"Why don't you do it yourself?" the rabbi says to me, as if he were a father scolding a disobedient child. "It's not uncommon for someone in the family, a brother, or a son, sometimes a close friend, to deliver the eulogy. I'd have no objection."

I consider his suggestion for a moment. "I'd like to," I say, "but I'm too emotionally involved." I had considered such an option, but decided I would probably wind up blubbering something that would make sense only to Harry and me.

"Then you've got to let me do things my way." He has called my bluff and triumphed. He strides away confidently, not caring what other dumb ideas I might wish to offer.

During the funeral, I recognize many faces, some childhood friends of ours, several of Harry's colleagues from the University, family friends, Sandy's and Doris's parents and cousins, old friends of my parents, my partner and the nurses and receptionists from my office. In the rear of the hall, as inconspicuous as he can make himself, sits Detective David Wan. The majority of the mourners I have never seen before. There are quite a few young people present. It would appear that Harry had touched the lives of a lot more people than I had imagined--students, literary admirers, fellow authors. I'd bet that there are even some old girl friends present. Since Harry is now a minor celebrity, his murder case is still on page two of the local news-papers, I wouldn't doubt that there are more than a few curious onlookers as well.

The turnout is *standing room only,* which especi-ally pleases my father, who is always impressed when a funeral hall is packed to the gills. I remember a few years back when Doris's Uncle Benny, the famous bagel king of South Orange, had died and bagel devotees had turned out in the hundreds for the funeral. Dad had whispered to me on entering the inner sanctum, "You can see what a wonderful man Benny must have been. God bless him."

Our rabbi emotes like a Shakespearean actor: "Harry Stone stretched his hand out to the needy. He was cloaked in strength and dignity. His life was guided by kindness, fear of God, and love of family--" Sandy, Mitzi, Doris, and Mary Lou weep alternately, while my father maintains a stoic face. In token deference to my pre-funeral counsel, the rabbi manages: "--and he lived his life in such a way that we are left only with good memories--" But I notice that even Sandy winces when the rabbi says: "--and he never made a critical remark about anyone--" We all become a little dewy-eyed at, "--how he loved little Herschel--" before his final words, "--the Almighty has embraced Harry Stone. His soul has found eternal peace. Let us say *Amen.*"

I stand close to my father and finally get my chance to recite The Mourner's Kaddish: *"Yisgadal v'yiskadash shmey rabbah, b'alma div ra chirusay . . . "*

Later at the gravesite, while Harry's grave is being lowered into the earth, I find myself day dreaming. remembering an incident that occurred in Newark some thirty years ago.

I was teasing Harry and he began to rough me up. I kicked him and scratched one of his arms with my fingernails. He threw me to the ground and cocked a big fist. But instead of hitting me, he messed up my hair and slapped me affectionately on the cheek.

"Give up?" he asked.

"Never, you bastard!"

I tried to punch him, but he quickly pinned me. Then, without warning, he kissed me on the check.

"I'll kiss you again if you don't give up," he said.

He puckered up like a guppy and I jerked my head from side to side to avoid being kissed. "I give up, I give up," I shouted.

He kissed me anyway, then let me up. I could feel his repulsive, damp lips on my skin, and ran into the house to wash my face.

Mom asked me why I was washing my face in the middle of the day, and I told her that Harry had spit on me. She went outside to scold Harry, but Harry was nowhere to be found. "I hate it when you boys fight this way," she said, after coming back into the house.

"He started it."

"It's disgusting that he would spit on you."

"Wash out his mouth with soap, Ma. He deserves it."

"I can't imagine Harry being so mean. Are you sure you didn't provoke him, Roger? Sometimes you're a terrible tease."

"I didn't do anything." I was ready to burst into tears, and Mom put an arm around me. "Harry loves you, Roger. You know that."

"I hate his lousy guts."

"You don't hate him, Roger. Right now you're just a little mad at him."

"I wish he'd die."

"Tomorrow you'll forget all about it."

"Never," I said.

Harry becomes the first member of our family to be buried in the newly acquired Stone family plot. Alan holds Mitzi's hand during the final ceremony at the gravesite. Sandy and Mary Lou, both in black, stand side by side like marble pillars. Mary Lou weeps quietly, while Sandy stares vacantly at the coffin, until the gravediggers are finished lowering it into the hole, then she blows her nose and wipes her eyes. Doris and the girls place themselves off to one side, Naomi holding Herschel, giving him a bottle. Doris and Debbie cry the hardest. My father appears to be in a trance. I think how within the last six months he has buried his wife and eldest son. He glances at me and I refuse to guess what he might be thinking.

The rabbi strikes the usual final words: "--Death claimed thee too soon, and removed thee too early from those who loved thee. Father of all, grant that the soul of Harry Stone, loving father, devoted son, faithful husband, be bound up in the bond of eternal life, together with the souls of all the righteous that are in Thy keeping. Then shall the dust return to the earth whence it came, and the spirit shall return unto God who gave it. *Amen.*"

And it is over.

Standing next to a tree, well beyond the gravesite, John Whalen wavers like a sapling caught up in a stiff breeze. I leave my family as they slowly make their way back toward the cars and walk over to him.

A rancid alcohol odor radiates from him as if he had just finished bathing in a brewery vat. "What are you doing here?" I ask him curtly.

Whalen smiles broadly. "Helluva funeral," he says. "I love funerals. Everybody all dressed up like it was a big holiday. I guess now all you *sheenies* are goin' someplace and stuff your faces with a lot of good drink and food." His speech is noticeably slurred.

"You don't belong here. Go home."

"Hey, I'm family, ain't I. Look at it this way. Your brother was my grandchild's father, which makes him my son, right? Which makes you--my nephew." He almost doubles up in laughter.

"Just don't make any trouble."

"Why would I do that? This is the happiest day of

my life. Now that your bastard brother got what was coming to him, I'm liable to get back my wife and daughter."

Everybody has stopped walking and is staring at us. I search the area for David Wan. "Get out of here before I call the police," I say.

"Not before I piss on your brother's grave."

I throw a wild, roundhouse right that glances off the side of his head and sends him sprawling. Then I jump on him, and we go rolling around on the grass clawing at each other, each trying to find a way to free up a fist and get in a punch.

The gravediggers, two brawny young men, have no problem separating us. Finally Detective Wan appears, and with the gravediggers assistance, drags Whalen off to the side of the road, where he is cuffed and pushed into the back seat of Wan's police car.

I dust the grass and dirt off my pants and look for my glasses, which turn up broken beyond repair. My pulse is running wild, and my chest is heaving as if I had just been rescued from a drowning, but otherwise I am intact. Dad is the first of the mourners to reach me. "My God, are you okay?" he asks. "Who is that?"

"An enemy of Harry's."

"An enemy?"

"He said he wanted to piss on Harry's grave, and I lost my temper."

Dad is outraged. "What kind of a person says such a thing at a funeral? You should have socked him harder."

By now my entire family surrounds me. "I'm okay, I'm okay," I announce to all. Doris looks at me as if I am the one who has committed a crime.

Dad rescues me. "Go back to the cars," he orders everyone. Then he finishes dusting me off and, as we stroll down the hill toward the road, he intertwines an arm through mine. He smiles and says, "A very lively funeral. I didn't know you could fight so good, Roger. When you were a boy, you never liked to fight."

"I always had Harry to protect me."

"You don't need Harry anymore, Roger."

At the limo he opens the door and shoves me into the back seat. "Ladies and Gents," he says to my confused family, "I give you Gentleman Roger Stone, the new heavyweight champion of the world."

CHAPTER TWENTY

God's Justice

A week later a front page headline in the *Star Ledger* reads: **"HUSBAND ARRESTED FOR KILLING WIFE'S LOVER, AUTHOR HARRY STONE."**

At an early morning press conference, Union County Prosecutor Lawrence Ramsey told reporters that John Whalen had repeatedly threatened Stone after Stone had begun to live with his estranged wife, Mary Lou Whalen.

"We've got the weapon, a glove with powder burns, matching blood types and a motive. There's sufficient evidence to conclude that on the night of the murder Whalen had gone to Stone's apartment, and at gunpoint, kidnapped him, then drove him to the Watchung Reservation, where he shot him twice in the head."

The article goes on to state that the police found blood stains on the suspect's steering wheel and driver's seat. The gun was hidden under the spare tire in the trunk, the glove in the garbage.

Whalen's court appointed lawyer, J. Roland Bernstein, claimed that his client was innocent and would enter a not guilty plea. Bail was set at half a million dollars, a figure Bernstein considered excessive since his client had no prior criminal record. He said he would immediately file an application to the court to have it reduced.

The rest of the article detailed Harry Stone's career as a novelist and professor of English and Creative Writing at the State University. Several colleagues were quoted as saying that Stone was an extraordinary talent and a fine teacher. He had apparently resigned his position at the University last year to travel and write.

There was a brief reference to Sandy and Alan, but thankfully, no mention was made of myself and my family.

Several days later an Assistant Prosecutor calls. He introduces himself as Howard Webster, then pauses, waiting I think for me to express some recognition of his name. Unless he is a distant relative of Alex Webster, an ex-running back for the N.Y. Giants, I come up with a blank. Though I am not happy with his demand that I meet him at his office, I reschedule my morning's patients. At nine a.m. the next day I drive down to the County Courthouse in Elizabeth.

Webster turns out to be a huge, middle-aged man with a great mop of wavy, orange hair. He greets me with an ebullient, phony grin and a powerful handshake. In medicine we are often forced to make snap judgements of our patients. I find myself being struck by Webster's sense of self-importance, which, rightly or wrongly, I ascribe to his position of power as an assistant prosecuting attorney.

After poking around with a few general questions about Harry and myself, Webster asks me what I knew about the fight between Harry and John Whalen in Newark last year. Is it true that Whalen had threatened Harry? He listens without comment, which is hardly surprising, since I pretty much relate to him what I had already told Wan, whom I assume had passed on this information to the Prosecutor's office.

After he has finished interviewing me, he says, "I doubt that we'll be calling you as a witness, but thanks anyway for coming down." He sits back in his chair, crosses his arms, waiting, I think, for me to excuse myself and leave.

"Why not?" I feel compelled to ask, not budging an inch. "Don't you think a jury would want to know that Whalen made death threats against Harry? And what about his behavior after the burial. He said he wanted to piss on Harry's grave." I am hardly able to repress my annoyance. For this inconsequential interview, I have cancelled my morning' patients. Of course, if I were thinking sensibly, I should have been delighted with being excluded from the prosecution's case against Whalen and exited the courthouse with all due haste.

"You're the victim's brother," he reminds me. "Your testimony would be considered prejudicial. We've got a pretty tight case without it."

"You've got no case at all. Harry planned the whole thing. He killed himself, and framed Whalen." I sit back and await his reaction, feeling a bit like a tennis player who has just missed an easy overhead.

It is only Webster's huge bulk wedged into his chair that prevents him from sliding off his seat. "Your brother killed himself? Suicide? Not possible," he exclaims.

"It's possible."

"How could you know this?"

"He wanted me to give him pills. When I refused, he said he would get a gun and shoot himself."

"How could he shoot himself and frame Whalen?"

"He must have had an accomplice."

"A few seconds ago you were ready to testify against Whalen." With surprising agility Webster jumps to his feet and scoots around his desk. With a firm grip on my arm, he escorts me to the door in a hurry. "Thanks for your cooperation, Dr. Stone. We'll be in touch, if we need you." He's a powerful man and I suppose I should be grateful he doesn't bounce me rudely into the hallway. The office door slams in my face before I have a chance to tell him what an *asshole* he is.

You can bet a million bucks that our conversation will go unrecorded, and he will never call me to the witness stand. *The hell with it.* I have committed no crime, and I have told the truth about Harry's scheme to frame Whalen. I could, of course, take my story to Whalen's attorney, who would be obliged to call me as a witness for the defense. After telling what I knew, I would undoubtedly be subjected to a vigorous cross-examination by the prosecution. Through practice I have become a first-rate liar, but under oath, in a courtroom of law, I could easily wind up confessing all, which would include telling the truth about Harry's medical condition, and even my affair with Sandy. Harry would agree that I have reasonably "*expurgated*" my soul with the avenging arm of the law, that my conscience is clear. *Thank you, Harry.* What will be, will be, I say to myself, and hurry back to the sanctity of my office.

Four months after his indictment by a Grand Jury for the murder of my brother, John Whalen comes to trial in the Superior Court in Elizabeth.

The Prosecutor's Office was apparently willing to plea bargain the charges from murder one to manslaughter one, the state conceding that it is possible to become insanely homicidal toward a man who had first run off with your daughter and later with your wife. One columnist, who had been following the case, wrote that in some countries the accused would have been celebrated as a hero. But John Whalen refused all plea bargains, persisting in his innocence, demanding a trial, just as Harry knew he would. "All my life I've believed in God's justice, and God isn't going to let me be convicted for a crime I never committed," he was quoted as saying.

During the trial I am given a reserved seat in the second row, next to my father, Doris, and Sandy. Alan and my daughters decline to sit in on the trial after the first day. They are bored, I think, by the endless legal talk, most of which makes little sense to them. Mitzi and Mary Lou are not allowed to watch since they are witnesses for the prosecution.

The case has stirred up considerable interest and the courtroom is packed daily. My father seems, in a curious way, to enjoy the notoriety of being the victim's father, another demonstration to him, per-haps, of the importance and popularity of his murdered son, while Doris and Sandy remain silently grim.

The Prosecutor's case is based on the accused's motive, his lack of an alibi, his violent nature, and finally and ultimately, the overwhelming physical evidence: the gun, the glove, and the blood stains. A ballistic expert verifies that the bullets found at the murder scene had been fired from the same gun that had been discovered in Whalen's car. The Medical Examiner confirms that the blood on the floor of the accused's car was the same blood type as the victim's. An unemployed barber, who had been out drinking with Whalen on the night of the murder, states that both men had left the tavern together around eight-thirty, and drove away in separate cars. A young couple, who had been walking on the other side of the lake, testify that they had heard the sounds of gunshots a little before eleven. In the darkness they could barely make out a shadowy figure running from the lake up a gravel road toward the parking lot at the top of the hill. Moments later they heard the sound of a car speeding away. The Medical Examiner's report confirms that the time of death was close to eleven, which would have allowed Whalen more than enough time to kidnap Harry from his Rahway apartment, drive him out to the Watchung reservation where he then shot him. Mary Lou talks about her husband's uncontrollable temper, especially when he is drinking, and how over the years he had repeatedly beaten her. Then she goes on to describe his homicidal assault against Harry in Newark. Finally, in a tremulous voice, she drives the fatal spike into John Whalen's heart, by accusing him of molesting Mitzi when she was twelve. At which point, the jury *en masse* rolls to the edge of their seats and murderously glares at the defendant.

Whalen's attorney, J. Arthur Bernstein, does his best. On cross-examination, he asks her why, if the defendant was such a wife beater, she had continued to live with him for over twenty years, and why there are no records of her ever having been treated at a hospital for injuries, or why she had never called the police and had him arrested. Regarding Whalen's alleged sexual abuse of his daughter, since there were no witnesses, and Mitzi refuses to testify against her father, Mary Lou's accusations are considered here-say, and as such, inadmissible, and the judge orders the jury to disregard that part of her testimony. But none of it matters. You could see that the jury has already made up their minds as to what kind of a man John Whalen is.

In his closing statement, Bernstein reminds the jury that according to Whalen's drinking partner, he was so drunk that he couldn't remember where he had parked his car. Given the intoxicated state of the accused, it would hardly seem possible that he'd have the physical or mental capacity to drive all the way to Rahway from Union, force the victim into his car, drive him back to the Watchung Reservation, then return to Union, and have the presence of mind to hide the gun and glove. He goes on to suggest that while Whalen was sleeping off his drunk, the real murderer could easily have planted the blood stains in his car and hid the gun and the glove, knowing that the police would easily be able to find them.

In less than three hours, the jury finds John Whalen guilty of murder two. My father and Sandy loudly applaud the verdict and hug each other. Mitzi, Mary Lou, and I are more subdued. Mitzi, I believe, in spite of everything, still loves her father. Mary Lou puzzles me. Does she still have some remnants of love for her husband, or is she suffering from a guilty conscience?

John Whalen is sentenced to twenty-five years in prison, not eligible for parole before fifteen. As he is led out of the courtroom, he shouts that *God alone is his Judge.*

In the newspaper account the next day, several members of the jury stated that Mary Lou's testimony against her husband had damaged him the most. One juror called him a *"Monster,"* another referred to him as *"--the lowest form of creature."* The head juror summed up the feelings of the majority stating that any man who could beat his wife and sexually abuse his daughter was certainly capable of murdering another human being. My sentiments exactly.

The day after the trial, Uncle Joseph calls me from Long Island. He has picked up the story of the trial in the *Daily News*, and wants to confirm that the Harry

Stone they are writing about is his nephew.

"Then it's true?" he asks.

"Yes," I say.

The phone goes dead and I think for a moment that we have been cut off. Finally he resumes speaking: "Why didn't you call me?" He sounds offended, and I feel a pang of regret for not having notified him.

Actually, I haven't spoken a word to Joseph since the day I had met with him in Bayshore almost two years ago. Many times I had thought of phoning him, but I could not quite bring myself to do it. I think this had something to do with my desire to bury a past that I wished had never existed.

"I'm sorry, Uncle," I say. Calling Joseph "Uncle" feels strange, though not inappropriate.

"Do you think it would be all right for me to express my sympathy to your father?"

"I don't see why not."

"I don't wish to offend him. I know he has never liked me very much."

"That was forty years ago. I don't think he harbors any ill feelings toward you today."

"We are a cursed family. I pray every day for you and your children, and for Harry's son." He coughs into the phone, then asks me, "Where did you bury him?"

I tell him about the cemetery in Woodbridge.

"Oh," he responds rather off-handed. Does he believe that we should have buried Harry in Long Island, side by side with his father and grandfather and cousins, another casualty of our little *family problem*?

"You might be wise to phone me occasionally, Roger," he says. "There's no one who knows better than I what you are going through. After Israel died, I often thought it would be better to kill myself than go through the agony of waiting for my turn."

"I don't feel that way. I plan to live to ninety."

"Good for you, Roger. I wish I had possessed your optimism. I wouldn't be alone today, brooding over what might have been. God bless you and your family."

Joseph Horowitz is someone that I have met only once, yet as I hang up, I experience this odd sense of loss. I have this inexplicable feeling that I will never see or talk to him again. It is a bit like losing something you've always wanted, but would never be able to have.

CHAPTER TWENTY-ONE

More Pizza

Three months have passed since the trial. I am once again living with Doris and my daughters as a dutiful husband and father. Doris, secure in the knowledge that I am *in the bag,* seems bent on a course of *unconditional surrender,* max punishment, before she will consider forgiveness. In a recent AMA journal I read that rural areas in states like North Dakota and Alaska desperately need doctors. How nice to be appreciated by communities where the nearest medical assistance may be more than an hour's drive. Running off and starting a new life has become my latest fantasy.

Since the trial, I have not seen or spoken to Sandy. From Doris I learn that she has made arrangements to move to San Francisco with Mitzi and Herschel. Alan applied and was accepted at the University of California at Berkeley. I wonder if Stanley Applebaum, the great, smiling detective from Westfield, will be going with them, but I'm afraid to ask. I ache when I think of Sandy living in San Francisco, but physical separation between us is the best medicine for someone as obsessed as I am.

I receive a telephone call at my office from Detective David Wan. Though the case against John Whalen has been officially closed by the department, Wan wishes to get together with me *off the record to clear up a few loose ends.* I press him to be more specific, but he refuses to discuss it over the phone, and finally I agree to meet him once again at the Pizza

Hut on Route 22.

Wan leads me to a secluded corner in the restaurant, and, as expected, he orders a large pizza. This
time, however, I refuse the meatballs and onions on
my half, opting for plain. My digestive system, while
improved, requires constant dietary vigilance, a rule I
am breaking for the sake of Wan's craze for pizza.

"Thanks for coming," Wan says, while we await
our food. "You didn't have to, you know. As far as the
state is concerned, this case is over. Any time you
want, feel free to get up and walk out."

"You're not taping me, are you?" I ask, not entirely in jest. You couldn't be alive in 1982 without
having seen your share of movies in which cops tape
conversations with unsuspecting witnesses.

He laughs. "Are you afraid you might say
something incriminating? Okay. Let's go into the
men's room and you can search me."

"Are you serious? We could be reported for
lewd behavior. So what's the big mystery, Detective?"

Wan settles back in his chair, makes a conscious effort to relax with several deep breathes, then
says, "A few of the jokers at the station call me Charlie
Chan. Since they've never seen any of the old Charlie
Chan movies, they don't understand that Charlie was
this clever cop who made his reputation by tracking
down the real culprits on cases that were supposedly
open and shut. So you see, when they call me Charlie
Chan, I don't take offense. I like thinking I'm a cop
who wants to do more than wrap up a case for a
Prosecutor and pick up my weekly pay check."

The waiter brings over two Cokes, though I
had asked for water. Wan sips his drink, "Having explained who I am," he says, "I will now come to the
point, which is--I was never satisfied with our case
against Whalen. It was too neat, too perfect. Motive,

the gun, the glove, the victim's blood in the car, his lack of an alibi, no other suspect--" Abruptly, he cuts himself off, scrutinizing me before continuing, waiting, perhaps, for me to react unexpectedly. I remain steadfast, however, offer him nothing less than a Buster Keaton deadpan. Finally he goes on: "All this circumstantial evidence against him, yet Whalen refuses to admit his guilt, clinging to his innocence like a drowning man holding on to a life preserver."

"From what I understand the *perps* seldom admit their guilt."

"True. And Whalen's opinions, with his continual ranting on how God will set him free one day,does not exactly instill confidence. But you know, Doc, I believe him anyway. He's too crazy to lie. Wan pauses, then says very politely, "Let me share with you some of my thoughts."

"I can't hardly wait."

He ignores my jibe and proceeds: "The barber, the one who had been out drinking with Whalen, told me that Whalen had been so drunk and disoriented the night of the murder, that he not only had to help him find his car in the parking lot, but point him in the right direction towards his home. Doesn't exactly sound like a man about to drive around the county and commit a well-planned murder."

"Maybe he was being smart. He knew the police would suspect him, and he was trying to set up an alibi for himself by pretending to be drunk."

"If he were so smart, why didn't he throw the gun and the glove down a sewer, or into the reservoir? It took us exactly five minutes to find them. I mean who's so dumb that he casually tosses a murder weapon in his trunk, and a glove with gunpowder all over it into his garbage can. And the blood stains in the car? Give me a break? How come there was nothing on his clothes, nothing on his shoes? It was drizzling that night. You'd expect to observe at least a little mud on his shoes."

"He might have cleaned them off."

"He might have. But I examined his shoes. They hadn't been polished in months, the heels were worn, the soles were all scuffed up, the shoelaces were broken and tied. If you had just committed a murder and there was mud on your shoes, you'd scrub them clean, you might even bring them to the shoemaker the next day, or just throw them away. You see what I'm getting at?"

"A jury listened to all the evidence and convicted him. Don't you believe in the jury system?"

"Juries make mistakes," he says emphatically. On my own time, I went down to your brother's apartment house to ask tenants if they might have seen anything unusual that night. There's twelve apartments in that building and we failed to interview everyone."

"I thought you had."

"Ten out of the twelve. Before we got to the last two, the Prosecutor came up with all this physical evidence and told us to stop wasting our time. But I thought we should have at least make every effort to find an eyewitness, so last week I went back and knocked on those other two doors."

When he pauses, I am, perhaps, too quick to ask, "What did you discover?"

He raises his eyebrows ever so slightly, then says, "In apartment eleven, the couple was away visiting relatives that evening, but in twelve, I was a little luckier. An old man had been out walking his dog. On his return to his apartment he noticed in the hallway your brother about to walk down the stairs with another person. The hallway was dark and he's got bad vision. He admitted he didn't see their faces, only their backs. He said he recognized Harry by his funny way of walking. But here's the thing--he thought the other person was shorter than Harry." Wan stops for a moment, actually seems to measure me, then presses on like a man on a mission. "Someone around your height, I guess." Once again he pauses, scrutinizing me with a dark look I do not care for. "If I'm not mistaken John Whalen is an inch or two taller than Harry."

"Whalen could have been on a lower step," I cleverly point out to him.

"True, though the old man remembers seeing both of them on the landing. And here's another curious thing. He said that Harry was behind the other person."

"So what?"

"Don't you find that a little peculiar? Wouldn't you imagine that the kidnapper, the guy with the gun, would be standing behind his victim?"

"Yeah, that is a little strange," I am forced to concede. "Of course, Harry wasn't in such great shape that he would have been able to run away from someone with a gun."

"True. And like I said, the old man admitted to having bad vision, so I'm not making too big a deal out of his testimony, except that it makes another little hole in the case, and the holes are starting to add up."

"Why are you telling me all this?" I am getting edgy. 'The someone around *your* height' crack caught me off guard.

"You may be my link to the real killer," Wan explains. "You may not even realize it yourself. Be patient with me a little longer." The pizza arrives, but we both ignore it. Wan is warming up to his job. "I traced the gun," he says triumphantly. "It took all this time, but the A.T.P. finally tracked it down to a gun store in Virginia. I called up the manager and after a week of sorting through piles of papers, he came up with the sale. They sent me a Xeroxed copy of the form that the purchaser filled out. It was carefully hand printed and the signature was an indecipherable scribble. As you'd expect, the name and address was a phony. I checked the printing against a sample that Whalen gave me and you didn't have to be a handwriting expert to realize that he couldn't possibly have been the one who filled out that form. Just for the hell of it, I sent the gun shop a picture of Whalen, and a picture of Harry and you."

"Me!"

"It was a picture your sister-in-law gave me. You and Harry are standing together, big dumb smiles on your faces."

"I remember it. We were picnicking in the park with our families. Better times, I would say."

"I didn't want to ruin the picture by cutting it in half. Funny thing, the clerk who sold the gun couldn't recognize either face as the one who had bought the gun, but he did seem to recall that the man had a peculiar gait."

"Sounds like Harry."

"Or someone who was pretending to be him," Wan is quick to point out. I am relieved when he finally starts on his half of the pizza. He drinks some Coke, wipes his mouth delicately with a napkin, and clears his throat. "By the way, did you know that your brother had a life insurance policy? A one-hundred-thousand-dollar payoff on his death."

"Never knew." I am in fact flabbergasted. Why had Sandy never mentioned it to me?

"For the past two years your sister-in-law has been paying the premiums herself. She also happens to be the beneficiary."

"Are you suggesting that my sister-in-law murdered my brother for insurance money?"

"Nope. She's got an alibi. On the night of the murder, she had dinner with a detective from Westfield--" He glances at his notes. "--Stanley Applebaum. After dinner they went to a party. Applebaum said he brought her home around ten-thirty, though he was not a hundred percent certain of the time. The people at the party were all policemen and their wives, and said they remembered your sister-in-law. I wasn't happy with the vagueness of the time factor and just for the hell of it, I did a little checking on her."

"What for? You just told me she couldn't have done it." His *just for the hell of its* were starting to get on my nerves, though I do my best to remain cool and collected.

"Yes, but the man she's been having an affair with for over a year may not."

My *cool and collected* drains out of my head right into my gut.

"Are you okay, Doc?" Wan asks.

"I haven't eaten all day." I force myself to nibble on my half of the pizza. The dough sticks to my palate like hot glue and I wash it down with a Coke, which is almost as poisonous as the pizza. Tonight, I will suffer hellish abdominal pain, and I will blame it on Wan. "What other man?" I ask.

"The telephone operator at the school where she teaches told me that for the past year she had been receiving calls from a 'mystery caller'."

"They were probably from Applebaum."

"Whenever Applebaum called, he always identified himself. This guy never left his name, and Mrs. Stone never told anyone who he was."

"So somebody's been calling her. I get calls every day from people trying to sell you tax-free bonds, aluminum sidings, windows, credit cards, lawn mowers, acreage in Central Florida, vacations to Hawaii. You name it, they're selling it over the phone. And they never leave their names."

"At a public high school?" Wan says with a boyish smirk that I do not appreciate. "A couple of weeks ago, I had nothing to do one night, and just for the hell of it drove up and down Route 22, showing your sister-in-law's picture and asking questions at all the motels from Plainfield to Newark. A couple of days later I drove down Route 1 to Woodbridge doing the same thing. Not much luck at the sleaze places, so the next week I tried the better motels off the Garden State and the Turnpike."

"You think Sandy was going to motels with *The Mystery Caller*?" I wonder if my voice expresses just the right amount of righteous indignation in defense of Sandy.

"Just a hunch. Cops are full of reckless ideas. We just naturally think the worst of people. I admit it's a bad trait as a human being."

"Where did you get her picture?"

"The newspaper printed a picture of Harry and her."

"It looks like you're making a nice family collection. Are you going to buy an album and include the children?"

Wan actually seems amused by my little funny and cracks a faint smile. "The interesting thing is that one motel clerk finally did recognize her," he says. "It was quite a coincidence, Doc, because it turned out to be the same motel where you were staying--the Holiday Inn. Don't misunderstand me, I'm not making any inferences since the clerk couldn't remember the date, or the man she came with. The only reason he remembered her was that he considered your sister-in-law to be an exceptionally good-looking woman, and the only baggage she had was a toothbrush that she waved at him, which he thought was pretty cute."

"Maybe the man with her was Applebaum," I say in quiet desperation.

"I considered that. But neither of them are married and there's no reason for them to go running off to motels. Call it a cop's intuition, but I have this gut feeling that your sister-in-law was seeing a man whom she couldn't bring home, a married man, for example. Now who was he, Doc?"

"How would I know?"

"Well, that's the thing. I thought you might have some idea since I understand that you spend quite a bit of time at her house. Everybody, it would appear, depends on you to take care of things. In fact, if I'm not mistaken, you've even helped pay a few of the bills."

"Should I let my brother's family live in a flop-house on Market Street?" The son of a bitch must have checked with my bank. Could they go into your bank account that way?

"Of course. Hey, I'd do the same thing if I had a brother who had walked out on his wife and kid. It's just that I was thinking that you might be the one person that your sister-in-law would have confided to about this other man?"

"I'm sorry, but I can't help you. She never talks to me about her personal life."

"Can't win them all, I guess." Then to my surprise he pulls out of his pocket several typed sheets of paper and hands them to me. "It's the autopsy report," he says. "Why don't you give it a once over?"

"I've already read it," I tell him. "Is there something new?"

"Not really. Bear with me, Doc. I'm going a little out of my realm of expertise, so to speak. You said that your brother had MS. Do you think you might have been mistaken?"

"No."

"You're positive?"

"All of his symptoms pointed to MS."

"Hey, I don't want you to think I'm contradicting you or anything. You're the expert. Like I said, I'm a little out of my league here, but just for the hell of it, I got a hold of one of those little medical manuals that tell you about diseases." He pulls out several indexed cards and begins to read from one. "In MS there's a demyelination in the white matter disseminated throughout the CNS, especially in the cervical and dorsal regions." He looks up from the page. "I'd appreciate it if you'd explain to me exactly what that means."

The bastard knows exactly what it means, nevertheless, with as professional a demeanor as I can muster, I say, "Nerves in the Central Nervous System have this fat-like substance around it. In MS it can degenerate."

"And some of these nerves are in the backbone."

"Yes, the spinal nerve."

"That's what I figured. Just for the hell of it, I asked the medical examiner if this demyelination was something he might have overlooked since it wasn't mentioned in his report. To tell you the truth he became a little insulted. He said he always checks the spinal cord. In your brother's case, he found nothing abnormal."

"Too bad he couldn't have autopsied Harry

while he was still alive. Could be he had a brain tumor after all."

"Unfortunately, as we both know, your brother's brain was pretty well wiped out by the gunshot wounds."

"So I guess we'll never find out exactly what was wrong with Harry."

"I think you know already, Doc. I think he was a lot sicker than you told us. Maybe you've got your reasons, good ones, for not telling us the truth, and maybe it has nothing to do with this case, so I'm not going to make too big a deal of it. If you want to share a little bit with me here, I give you my word it's strictly confidential."

"It would appear that you know more about Harry's condition than I do."

Wan puts away his notes, then collects from me the autopsy report. "I have a couple theories about the murder. Interested?" He clears his throat, sips a little more of his Coke. If there was a podium to mount, he'd be climbing all over it.

"Very much so," I say politely.

"I thought you might be . . . The first one is that this mystery man murdered your brother and pretty soon we'll be seeing your sister-in-law moving to another part of the country. A couple months later, she'll remarry, but who will know or care."

Like a good preacher, he pauses to allow his congregation a chance to absorb and consider his words. "What's the second theory?" I ask dispassionately.

"It's my main one. But before I give away all my secrets do you mind my asking you a few personal questions?"

"How personal?"

"Very personal," Wan says. "Like when you

left home and moved into the Holiday Inn you must have had a pretty good fight with your wife. Right? You think you could tell me exactly what you were fighting about?"

"It was all a big misunderstanding."

"I have to confess that I did a little snooping in your neighborhood. I asked a few of your neighbors about your family. They all said the same thing. Solid family, terrific relationships. I understand you've been married twenty years. When you moved out, your neighbors were all shocked. I guess that sort of news gets around fast."

"*You talked to my neighbors?*"

"Believe me, I was very discreet."

"My family has to live with these people. They send you hate mail, if you don't cut your lawn. As far as they're concerned, I could have been away on a vacation, or at a convention."

"Sorry about that," he says rather off-handed.

"I was only gone for two weeks, for chris-sake."

"Which I'm happy for. Still, to live in a motel for even just a couple weeks after all those years of love and mutual respect seems a little odd."

"Why don't you ask my wife about it? It was her idea."

"I would never think to do a thing like that. You can't ask a woman to talk about such personal matters."

"Only one's friends, is that it?" I am laying it on. I really don't give a damn what my neighbors, who are not really my friends, believe. "Listen, I can't tell you what we were arguing about, but I assure you it had nothing to do with Harry."

"I understand perfectly. Anyway, the less said the better, don't you think? I mean there's the kids, your professional reputation. People have a way of blowing out of proportion the importance of minor improprieties."

"So what's your other theory?"

"It's a long shot, but to tell you the truth I like it a lot." Wan has finished his half of the pizza. He ogles my leftovers. "You see," he continues, "I believe that an essentially decent human being is capable of committing a crime when the crime he's committing serves a basically humane purpose. Now you take a man, who say has a dying brother, a brother who's in a lot of pain, and the brother tells the man that he wants to end his life and needs his help. The fact that the man is in love with the brother's wife, and there's a big insurance payoff might have nothing to do with him wanting to end his brother's suffering."

"He might not even have known about the insurance policy." Curiously, I think I'm actually beginning to enjoy this conversation.

"Very possible. Let's take this hypothetical situation a step further. Let's say that the brother wanted his suicide to look like a murder for a specific reason, one that had nothing to do with any life insurance payoff. Suppose there was this drunk who likes to beat women and sexually abuse children, and he's threatened the brother's family. They would need protection, wouldn't you agree? But the law can do nothing to protect them until a crime has been committed. What can he do about it?"

"Run him over, or put him in jail."

"Exactly what I was thinking. I was also thinking that if my theory is correct, we have a hopeless dilemma."

"How's that?"

"You don't want to prosecute a man for a crime that some might argue should not even be considered a crime, if the big winner turns out to be this bastard who ought to be shoveling cowshit in hell for the rest of his life. On the other hand, *the law is the law*. If you begin to bend it, it will break, and what will become of a world without rules and regulations."

"Chaos and anarchy."

"You couldn't have expressed my sentiments better." Wan picks up a fork and points it toward the tip of my nose. "Do you have any solutions to this problem, Doc?"

"None."

"Here's what I was thinking. If our Good Samaritan could somehow find a way to present to the court evidence that would acquit our innocent man, as rotten as he is, this story might yet have a happy ending."

"Except the bad guy would be on the loose again."

"We'd read him the riot act, make sure he behaves himself in the future. We'd remind him of life in a place where picking up a piece of soap in the shower can become a memorable experience. But it might be wise for the woman and child to relocate to another part of the country anyway. At least for a while. They've got the insurance money, and even if they have to pay it back, I'm sure our Good Samaritan could give them a hand if they needed it."

"Suppose our Good Samaritan is unable to change things without implicating himself?"

"That would be too bad. But I have a feeling that he'd be able to find a way. It could, perhaps, make things easier if the evidence the law needed for a reversal were to somehow fall into the hands of a *clever detective*." He actually winks. "So what do you think of my theories?" he asks.

"I think you've got a great imagination."

262

"That's what I was afraid you'd say. By the way, are you going to eat the crust?" I push my plastic plate toward him. "Thanks, Doc. You're a sport. "

"I hope you find your man," I say.

"Or woman," he quickly adds as he begins to nibble on my leftovers.

CHAPTER TWENTY-TWO

Alphonse O'Neill

The sun is dropping behind the tall maples that line up like sentinels guarding the lake's shoreline. Rays of light zigzag across the water between shadows cast from the overhanging branches. Sandy and I walk on the curved gravel path along the lake, our hands touching ever so lightly. There is an un-natural silence between us.

We find a small alcove surrounded by bushes and trees about fifty feet from the water, and sit on moss and pines, leaning back against a large oak. Through the bushes I observe in the fading twilight another couple strolling down the road about a hundred yards away. We are pretty much alone.

I put an arm around her shoulder. Her muscles tense, but after a moment she butts up against me. "Thanks for meeting me," I say. "I wasn't sure you would."

"You shouldn't have been concerned," she says. "I was beginning to panic that I would never see you again."

She had grown older this past year. Streaks of gray run through her soft, brown hair. Creases beneath her eyes flaw a perfect complexion. She looks drawn, weary. My brother Harry has finally taken his toll on her.

"What did you tell Doris about tonight?" she asks.

"A medical meeting." One more lie. Positively the last, I vow to myself.

She is dressed in a pale yellow blouse and loose fitting cotton slacks, which flatten her backside and hide the shape of her long, slender legs. No matter.

She could drape herself in a burlap bag and she'd still look good to me.

"I've missed you," she says.

"There's always Stanley," I remind her in spite of admonitions to myself before I picked her up to keep Stanley Applebaum out of the conversation.

"I'm not going to marry him," she says flatly.

"But I thought--"

She interrupts me, unwilling to let me read her mind. "Six months ago when he first asked me, I put him off, hoping I would come to love him in time--." She pauses, nervously twirls a tress of hair with a forefinger, then continues, "--the way I loved Harry . . and you." She places a hand on my thigh, possibly a reflex, or maybe she is affirming an old right of proprietorship. "Last month I told Stanley about my decision to move to San Francisco. He said he didn't think I was being very fair, that if I didn't love him enough to marry him, I shouldn't have let him fall in love with me in the first place."

"We all take chances." I will always be jealous of any man she has known or will know, except for Harry, who loved her before I did.

"I want to start a new life." She removes the hand from my thigh, which has the immediate effect of depressing me. "Harry haunts me like a ghost. Do you know that I still sleep on my own side of the bed? During the night I'll fling an arm out and my hand will touch the unused pillow, and I'll let it lie there out of habit for hours." Ghosts, especially Harry's, are not what I wish to hear about, and I quickly change the subject. "Why San Francisco?" I ask.

"A college roommate asked me to share her house with her. They say it's a good place to work and live. In the old days Harry and I always loved it there."

The old days. The sixties. The Kennedys, Johnson and Dean Rusk, Ho Chi Minh and General Giap, Martin Luther King and Malcom X, Kent State and Selma, Alabama, The Chicago Seven, Richard Daley, William Kuntsler, communes, pot, LSD. While Sandy and Harry were riding freedom trains and burning draft cards, I was trying to get through medical school and hospital residencies. Whenever we'd receive a postcard from them, Doris would remind me that we weren't doing enough to fight against the *war* and *racial injustice*.

"How soon will you be going?" I ask.

"I don't know. First I have to sell the house."

"That could take months." In spite of all my resolutions to the contrary, I hope she will never leave, especially now that I know she isn't going to marry Stanley.

"There's something else." She hesitates, and I become anxious. "Harry had a life insurance policy. I'm supposed to receive a hundred thousand dollars within the next few weeks. I'd like to return the money you've given me, and I'm going to need your advice on how to invest the rest of it."

"Inspector Wan told me about the life insurance," I say.

"Wan? He knew about the money?"

"You may have to give it back."

"Why?"

"Some policies don't pay off on suicides. I had lunch with Wan yesterday. He believes that Harry killed himself. He also believes that I assisted him."

She pushes forward, looks toward the lake where a flock of geese in formation are skimming the surface of the water on take-off. "I don't care about the money," she says bluntly. "If they want it back, I'll manage." She leans back again. "Wan is crazy. We both know that you had nothing to do with it. I'll talk to him."

"Don't worry. He can't prove anything. Keep your nose out of this."

"But you don't understand." She reaches into her purse and hands me a letter. "I was going to give this to you before I left for San Francisco."

"I don't want to read it."

"You must," she says dramatically.

There is no mistaking Harry's wild scrawl. Slowly I read aloud: *place rahway new jersey date october 27 1981 to the union county prosecutor i harry stone of sound mind and questionable morality hereby do swear that the events i am about to relate to you are the truth the whole truth and nothing but the truth so help me mother the murder of harry stone me the aforementioned was perpetrated by one alfonse oneill at the time of this writing alfonso oneill's age is around thirtyfive he stands five-nine has a fighting weight of one hundred and sixty color of hair dark brown color of eyes dark brown distinguishing features a small scar on his right cheek a tatoo of a black widow spider on his right arm a tatoo of a giant beetle on his left arm he prefers vodka to gin ale to beer speaks with a western drawl look for him in some pool hall or beach or whore house or museum or zoo studying class insecta his intellectual passion to mention a few of the possibilities i gave alfonse ten thousand dollars to shoot me and frame john whalen by smearing my blood in*

*his car the gun was purchased in old virginia
i cashed in a ten thousand dollar tax free
bond new york port of authority seven point
six percent due in twenty twentytwo to pay
alfonse there is a record of the sale at the
rahway city bank on irving avenue in rahway
I gave him two thousand dollars just before he
shot me the other eight thousand was to be
mailed to him by a friend after john whalen
was arrested i have also instructed this same
friend to mail to you this letter five years
after johnny boy was sentenced for the crime
of murdering me i harry stone am sentencing
johnny boy whalen to the agony of being
convicted for a crime he didn't commit and
to prison where I pray he will be beaten and
sodomized no less than he beat and sodomized
his wife and daughter my life has been slowly
eroding away i prefer to die on my own terms
hence alfonse oneill*

I tuck the letter into an inside jacket pocket.
Alphonse O'Neill is the unexpected, even with Harry
writing the book.

What are you going to do with that letter?" Sandy
asks.

"Give it to Wan. He'll ask questions and I'll make
up answers. He'll figure out a way for Whalen to be
released from jail."

"You may get yourself in trouble with the Prosecutor. Let me give the letter to Wan. I can tell him
the truth. They won't prosecute me."

"What makes you so sure? You could be accused
of planning the whole thing to get the insurance

money, that it was you who hired Alphonse O'Neill and tricked Harry into writing the letter."

"But you don't understand. *I'm Alphonse O'Neill.*"

She kneels and clasps her hands together. With her head bowed, she looks as if she is about to pray. Instead she begins to cry. She cries like a child who's scrapped her knees falling off her bike. She's letting it all out. For Harry? For herself? Certainly not for me. Nevertheless, I can't stand to see her so miserable. I bend down, and kiss one of her wet cheeks, and beg her to give it a rest.

It seems as if she is sobbing for an eternity before she looks up at me. I wipe her face with my handkerchief. She takes a deep breath, blows her noise loudly into my soiled piece of cloth, then seems to regain her composure. We are back talking.

"I tried to think of what I was doing as a final act of love," she says, "but I tell you, Rog, there's nothing in life that can prepare you to blow apart a man's head."

"You shouldn't have done it," I say angrily. "Why didn't you tell me what was happening?"

"At first I refused him."

"What made you change your mind?"

"Huntington's."

"You knew?"

She removes her hands from my shoulders and steps back so she can view me better. "I'm not a fool, Rog. I spoke to a several doctor friends, and they were bewildered by Harry's symptoms. They all agreed that it definitely wasn't Multiple Sclerosis. One of them suggested Huntington's Disease, and advised me to investigate the medical history on Harry's side of the family. I did a little reading, then called your father. He's a lousy liar. Finally he said he would tell me the truth if I promised not to tell you."

A father's betrayal. I immediately forgive him. No basically truthful person can keep such a secret when confronted by a determined inquisitor. "So you found out about Israel Horowitz?"

"Yes." Her arms dangling by her side, she looks as if she is fighting back the next deluge of tears. "I drove down to Rahway and confronted him when he was alone. He told me that I should mind my own business. I pleaded with him to let me help him. I wanted him to come back home. Alan and I would take care of him for the rest of his life. After a while he stopped being so difficult. I actually thought he was going to cry. *'Huntington's wasn't anyone's fault,'* he said. I shouldn't have to feel guilty about anything. He could never come home because he couldn't stand the thought of Alan and I watching him slowly turn into a vegetable. The idea of not being able to read or even understand the simplest concepts terrified him. If I truly cared about him, I would help him kill himself while he still had the will and mental capacity to want it to happen. After that he called me constantly, begging me to help him. I finally caved in."

"But how could you have agreed to frame Whalen?"

"Harry told me that, according to Mary Lou, Whalen had raped Mitzi more than once. After some serious prodding, Mitzi confessed that it was true."

"Then why did she refuse to testify against him in court? Isn't it possible that she lied to you? Kids can to do that when it serves their best interests."

"Who makes up such stories? I think she was too ashamed to testify against him. Whalen deserves what he got and I'm glad I put him there."

"I'd like to know what happened at the end."

"You mean with Harry?"

"Yes."

"I don't think I can tell you." She gives me an anguished look, but I don't withdraw the question. I have this absolute need to know.

"Please," I beg her.

She sits back on her haunches, gazes at the treetops. "*The devil is an angel, too,*' he said, before I released the safety catch and handed him the gun. He gave me that terrible, unnatural smile of his and told me that he had been waiting all his life for this moment. I walked away and looked out across the lake and waited. My heart was pounding so hard I thought I'd faint. Just before he shot himself he shouted, *'Doomsday is near: die all, die merrily.'* The shot echoed across the lake like a giant firecracker. I held my breath and watched the ducks and geese take to the air in droves as if they were afraid someone was shooting at them. And then I was all alone with Harry."

"And you shot the second bullet into his head to make it look like murder?"

"Harry was face down, his head so shattered that I couldn't tell into which part of his brain he had fired the bullet. I thought I was going to throw up. I kept telling myself that if I didn't go through with the plan it would be as if Harry died for nothing, and I became someone I never thought I could be--a conspirator, a person of action. All that practicing with a gun gave me an odd sense of confidence that I was going to be all right, that I was going to be able to go through with the plan."

"What happened next?"

"First, I pulled off the glove he was wearing and stuffed it into my coat pocket, then I took out a clean handkerchief and saturated it with his blood, then put it in a small plastic bag, which I sealed and put into the other pocket. Finally, I picked up the gun and shot him at the base of his skull."

"Just like that?"

"Not just like that. But I did it. *I had to.* Then I began to run up the hill as fast as I could, reminding myself that if the police caught me with a smoking gun, Alan would always believe that I had murdered his father."

"How did you know that Whalen would be home?"

"Harry and I had been following him for days. Every night after working, he'd go to the same bar in Union, drink for a couple of hours, then return to his house. After about an hour, he'd shut off the lights and go to bed. He never locked his car, always left it in the driveway. He was quite predictable."

"Wan said that you couldn't have done it because you were with Stanley at the time."

"He didn't calculate the time correctly. Stanley was a perfect alibi. After the party, I called Harry. Please, he begged me. He couldn't take it any longer. Mary Lou was working. It was a dark, rainy night, not the sort of evening people would be inclined to stroll around the reservation. I told Alan and Mitzi that I was going out to pick up milk for breakfast. Then I drove to Rahway for Harry."

"And the gun?"

"A week before Harry bought a fake ID in New York. We went down to Virginia where we found a gun shop outside of Norfolk. Harry seemed to know exactly what to do, like he had been planning this for years." She forces a smile. "My life with Harry was always an adventure. Right to the end."

"Wan traced the gun to the dealer. The dealer

remembered that the man who bought the gun had a funny walk. The handwriting on the application didn't match Whalen's."

"Once he gets this letter, he won't care." Sandy stands up and walks to the edge of the clearing. "I can't tell you how relieved I am to have told you all this. How come you never suspected me?"

"Actually I did. Harry had also asked me to help him. Since I refused, I figured that it must have been either you or Mary Lou. I double checked Mary Lou's alibi. She worked from four to twelve, never left the diner for a minute. You're right about Wan not calculating the time correctly. You could have come home from the party nearer to ten than ten-thirty, and had plenty of time to drive to Rahway then back to the Reservation before eleven. I figured Alan and Mitzi were probably upstairs and didn't even realize you were out, or maybe they figured you were still at the party. Kids have no sense of time."

"Do you hate me for what I did?"

"I blame myself. I should have given him some pills and none of this would have happened. . . Where in God's name did you ever find the nerve?"

"I discovered inside myself a stranger who is more me than I could ever have imagined. I think maybe that stranger is inside all of us, though we can live our whole lives and never realize it."

We walk back along the perimeter of the lake. She points out the spot where Harry shot himself. There are footprints in the mud, a pile of twigs at the shore's edge. No human blood, no human remains. I listen for the sounds of gunshot, but there is only silence, only memory, mostly hers, I suspect, which she will have to deal with for the rest of her life.

The last lingering rays of sunlight have descended behind the Watchung Hills, and twilight will soon give way to night. A full moon is just beginning to climb over the horizon. There'll be a fine, cloudless sky this evening, with light from a billion stars illuminating the Universe, unlike that ghostly, dreary night when my brother Harry blew out his brains. I experience this profound sadness, an irreversible sense of loss, which somehow the splendor of this night seems to accentuate.

"Don't worry," she says. She reaches down and takes my hand. "You're not going to get Huntington's Disease. Fifty-fifty. I like the odds. One dead brother in our family is enough." She does not mention Alan and Herschel. To contemplate their risk is, perhaps, more than she is willing to do.

"Maybe I've got it already."

She stops walking and looks fiercely at me. "No!"

"Haven't you noticed how crazy I've become? Two years ago would good old dependable Rog have made love to you?"

"You've got it mixed up. I'm the one who seduced you, remember."

A sudden breeze shakes the small branches above us, orange and brown leaves floating like feathers to settle on the gravel path. One falls on my shoulder and she sweeps it away with the back of her hand as if she is a mother cleaning up her child before she sends him off to school.

"But suppose I really have got it," I say.

She brushes her lips against mine and whispers, "We're not supposing anymore today." She runs a palm over my cheek. "Lets go to a motel," she says.

Less than twenty feet from us a young couple sits on a large rock holding hands. Silently, they stare up at the moon, which has turned into a giant orange disc. Loud music blares forth from a transistor radio by their side.

"Heavy metal." I am not the father of teenagers for nothing. I smile at her. "Now?" I ask.

"It may be our last chance."

"Like a sort of goodbye present?"

"Sort of. Partners in crime. Our last secret."

"I can't do it"

"Why?"

"I don't know why. I just can't."

"I love you, Rog. I'll always love you."

"That's good enough for me." It is, of course, not good enough, but I have this feeling that by turning down something I want very much, I might turn out to be a halfway decent human being after all.

I wrap my arms around Sandy and kiss her, an exquisite, final exchange of oral fluids. We break apart, smile coyly at each other, and begin the walk back toward the car. I am going to drive her home, then return to my wife and children, slightly tarnished, but still intact.

Before we drive off I look back toward the lake. I can almost hear the shots and the geese honking crazily in the aftermath. I want to talk to Harry one more time. I want to tell him that Dr. Dependable will be okay. *Rest in peace, big brother, rest in peace.*

CHAPTER TWENTY-THREE

EPILOGUE

To Thine Own Self Be True

1984

Harry has been dead now for almost two years. Today would have been his forty-sixth birthday. I cancel my late afternoon patients and drive to the cemetery in Woodbridge, taking back roads to avoid passing the motels that Sandy and I had slept in.

This is my first visit to his grave since the unveiling, over a year and a half ago. I don't think Harry would have cared very much. At Sandy's grandmother's gravesite funeral, about ten years ago, I recall Harry quoting one of his English poets, "*The grave's a fine and private place,/But none, I think, do there embrace./*" Which are exactly my sentiments. Hanging around cemeteries makes about as much sense to me as bird watching.

On the day of my wedding, I had asked Harry if he thought I was doing the right thing in marrying Doris. Although, I don't think he was particularly fond of Doris, I believe he thought that she was probably the right person for me. He gave me his best enigmatic look and said, *'This above all: to thine own self be true.''* Which is what I had engraved on his tombstone.

'To thine own self be true.' But who is smart enough to ever really know one's own self. And aren't we really *many selves*? So where are you, Harry, to help me figure out who I am and what I'm supposed to do with my life. Rise, big brother, from

your coffin (which is the best money could buy) and give me a final parting shot. I could use it.

Last year geneticists came up with a test that could possibly determine if one is carrying the defective gene for Huntington's. Since then I have been asking myself why I would want to know that one day I would become ill with a terminal disease where there's no cure.

Harry would probably have advised me to take the test, if I have nothing better to do. What about Alan and Herschel?

I'll be meeting Sandy in Chicago next month at a medical conference. Whether Alan should be told that he ought to take the test is one of the things we have agreed to discuss. Of course, Alan will want to make his own decision on that score at the appropriate time. As far as I know Sandy still hasn't told him that Harry had Huntington's. For that matter I haven't told Doris or my children either. One day I will find the courage to tell them, and Doris will insist that I take the test. If I refuse, she will penalize me half the distance to the goal line.

This will be the third time that Sandy and I will have met since she moved to San Francisco. When we are together, I am insanely happy and wish we could be together always. When we are apart, I find reasons, often trivial, to be angry with her, preferring the pain of anger to the pain of loving her and not being able to be with her all the time.

Alan is now a second year English student at Berkeley. Last year he switched his major from premed to English. In a letter he wrote me about six months ago, he said that while he still wanted to be a doctor, he didn't think he had the right temperament for the profession, or the stamina to spend four years in medical school, one year as an intern, three years in residencies, before you can begin to practice. The English major was less demanding, and it allowed him time to play his violin again. He enclosed an article, he had written, which had been published by the school magazine entitled: "*Playing Mozart while under the influence.*"

"Alan wants to be you, not me," I tell Harry. Fair is fair.

And my own children? Naomi is a freshman at Old Dominion in Norfolk, Virginia, majoring in what the colleges now call "Recreation and Leisure." She recently took a silver medal in the backstroke at a conference swim meet. Last month I asked her what her long term ambitions are. She replied simply, "To be good enough to swim at the NCAA championships." On the hand, Debbie, now a junior in high school, is talking about becoming a psychiatrist, which worries me, since most psychiatrists I know are unhappy, disturbed people.

These days Doris is concentrating on her body. She has lost fifteen pounds through diet and aerobic exercise and shows off her new figure with tight pants and skirts. Our sexual life has improved, though I sometimes find it necessary to fantasize about Sandy in order to do my conjugal duty.

If Doris discovers that I am meeting with Sandy twice a year, she will crazy-glue my testicles to my penis while I sleep. It goes without saying that I am the epitome of discretion when I go off to these medical conventions. All this will end when Sandy meets another man and no longer chooses to see me anymore. How I will deal with that inevitability is problematical. I can still remember that when Sandy first began to sleep with Stanley Applebaum, I became seriously deranged.

So Harry, what should I do? Should I just say *fuck*

it and go off to San Francisco. And if I should develop Huntington's? Maybe Sandy is thinking the same thoughts that my mother did when Joseph Horowitz proposed to her forty years ago. *To bury one brother is enough.* Though she says she loves me, she has never expressed any interest in my leaving Doris to go west and be with her.

I look at the grave and hear Harry's voice. *"Whatever happens in your life, you must face it like a man, not like some whining pussy."* Harry always was a sweetheart whenever you asked him for a little advice.

Mary Lou Whalen is living with a zookeeper from Staten Island. She quit her job in Rahway at the diner and is working near the Staten Island Zoo at a Burger King. I haven't spoken to her in almost a year, but according to Mitzi, she's very happy with her new boy friend, whom she says reminds her of Harry. It occurs to me that Sandy sleeps with me mostly because I am Harry's brother, which makes the zookeeper and I *'birds of a feather'*, so to speak.

While in prison, John Whalen became a *Born Again Christian.* Within two weeks after being released, he joined a religious sect in Texas, and no one has heard from him since. All charges were dismissed against him, after a handwriting expert confirmed that the letter I sent to David Wan was written by Harry, and the tax free bonds, which he alludes to in the letter, were in fact cashed by him shortly before his death.

The F.B.I. circulated a "Most Wanted" poster of Alphonse O'Neill in post office and banks around the country. A drifter, who had tattoos of spiders on his arms, was picked up in Glendale, California several months ago, and was given room and board at the local precinct for two days before being sent back into the streets.

Wan informed me of the prosecutor's decision while we were eating at a Chinese restaurant near my office. It turned out that Wan prefers Chinese to Italian and thought that Pizza Hut was my idea. How Wan managed to reopen the case and keep Sandy and I out of it, rates him as a better detective than Charlie Chan. As always he was very polite, but after we said goodbye in the parking lot, he thought it might be a good idea if we never saw each other again, *officially* or *unofficially*.

Don't fret, Harry, a year at Rahway State Prison for Whalen wasn't bad. Not quite the ten or twenty you had hoped for, but on the positive side, it doesn't appear as if he will ever cause Mitzi and Herschel any problems in the foreseeable future.

Six months ago for no special reason I called Joseph Horowitz. His home phone had been disconnected but 411 listed an office number in his name, also in Bayshore. I spoke to one of the secretaries in the firm that still bears his name, who informed me that Mr. Horowitz had had a stroke last year and died in his sleep. "It was quite unexpected," she said. "He was in perfect health. I guess you never know when your number is up." She seemed genuinely sad, and I let it go at that.

Three months ago, my right eyelid began to twitch. It continued to bother me for about two weeks, then the twitch disappeared. During those two weeks, day and night I waited for new symptoms to appear. Not one of the best times in my life.

Maybe one day, *when I've got nothing better to do,* I'll just go ahead and take that damn test. If it's negative, I'll come back and dance on your grave, old brother. And if it's positive--what the hell, there's always Alphonse O'Neill. What was good enough for

280

you, Harry, is more than good enough for me.

I drop a few small stones on the grave and head back to my car. On my way home I think I'll stop at the Woodbridge Mall and pick up a nice present for Herschel, which I'll give to Sandy when I see her in Chicago. Sandy tells me that everything about that little sucker reminds her of Harry.

What else is new?

PUBLICATION ORDERS

Profits from the sale of this book will be equally shared with the *Huntington's Disease Society of America*.

To purchase additional copies of **DEVIL'S DANCE** write:

Ironbound Press
55 Highlander Drive
Scotch Plains, New Jersey, 07076

Include your name, mailing address, telephone number, and the number of books you wish to purchase. Please enclose a check or money order for $15.00/ per book, plus $1.50 for shipping and handling of the first book. Add $.50 for each additional book in the same order. Make check or money order payable to Ironbound Press.

If you wish to make a direct contribution to the Huntington's Disease Society of America, send your check or money order to:

Huntington's Disease Society of America
158 West 29th Street, 7th Floor
New York, New York 10001-5300